**PRAISE FOR
THE *NEW YORK TIMES* BESTSELLING
SECOND CHANCE CAT MYSTERIES**

"A surefire winner."
—Miranda James, *New York Times* bestselling author

"An affirmation of friendship as well as a tantalizing who-dunit, *The Whole Cat and Caboodle* marks a promising start to a series sure to appeal to anyone who loves a combination of felonies and felines." —*Richmond Times-Dispatch*

"Ryan kicks off the new Second Chance Cat Mystery series with a lot of excitement. Her small Maine town is filled with unique characters . . . This tale is enjoyable from beginning to end; readers will look forward to more."
—RT Book Reviews

"If you enjoy a cozy mystery featuring a lovable protagonist with a bevy of staunch friends, a shop you'd love to explore, plenty of suspects, and a super smart cat, you'll love *The Whole Cat and Caboodle*." —MyShelf.com

"I am absolutely crazy about this series . . . The cast of characters is phenomenal . . . I loved every minute of this book."
—Melissa's Mochas, Mysteries & Meows

"This is an enjoyable series, in part for the lessons in refinishing, reimagining of old items but also for the friendships between the characters and the murders they solve."
—Kings River Life Magazine

"If you are looking for a charming cozy mystery with a smart main character and an adorable cat, then you should check out *The Fast and the Furriest*." —The Avid Reader

W9-BVS-165

Titles by Sofie Ryan

No EsCaPe ClawS

A SECOND CHANCE CAT MYSTERY

Sofie Ryan

BERKLEY PRIME CRIME
New York

BERKLEY PRIME CRIME
Published by Berkley
An imprint of Penguin Random House LLC
1745 Broadway, New York, New York 10019

Copyright © 2019 by Darlene Ryan
Excerpt from *Curiosity Thrilled the Cat* by Sofie Kelly copyright © 2011 by
Penguin Random House LLC
Penguin Random House supports copyright. Copyright fuels creativity, encourages
diverse voices, promotes free speech, and creates a vibrant culture. Thank you for buying
an authorized edition of this book and for complying with copyright laws by not
reproducing, scanning, or distributing any part of it in any form without permission.
You are supporting writers and allowing Penguin Random House to continue to
publish books for every reader.

BERKLEY and the BERKLEY & B colophon are registered trademarks and BERKLEY
PRIME CRIME is a trademark of Penguin Random House LLC.

ISBN: 9781101991244

First Edition: January 2019

Printed in the United States of America
1 3 5 7 9 10 8 6 4 2

Cover art by Mary Ann Lasher / Bernstein & Andriulli
Cover design by Katie Anderson

This is a work of fiction. Names, characters, places, and incidents either are the product
of the author's imagination or are used fictitiously, and any resemblance to actual persons,
living or dead, business establishments, events, or locales is entirely coincidental.

If you purchased this book without a cover, you should be aware that this book is stolen
property. It was reported as "unsold and destroyed" to the publisher, and neither the author
nor the publisher has received any payment for this "stripped book."

Acknowledgments

Special thanks go to my editor, Jessica Wade, and her assistant, Miranda Hill. Many times I'm the one who gets credit for their efforts. My agent, Kim Lionetti, is both advocate and cheerleader and I'm deeply grateful. I don't know what I'd do without her.

A big thank-you to all the readers who share their stories and photos of their cats with me. I love hearing from you!

And as always, love and thanks to Patrick and Lauren. I wouldn't want to do this without you.

Chapter 1

The first thing I saw when I made it to the back wall of the storage unit was Elvis, sitting on top of a wooden casket. He looked at me, cocking his head to one side, and his expression seemed to say, *Look what I found!*

"Good grief, what's that doing in here?" I said.

He didn't answer. Not that I expected him to, seeing as he was a small, black cat and not the swivel-hipped King of Rock and Roll.

I reached up and ran my hand over the smooth surface of the long wooden box. When I'd bought the contents of the storage space—and a second one three doors down—I'd given things a cursory check, just enough to feel comfortable about making an offer. The fact that the owner of the building had taken that offer without haggling had made me wish I'd offered a little less. At the time, I hadn't spotted the coffin—that's definitely what it was—sitting on several wooden packing crates by the end wall.

"Hey, Sarah, you all right?" my brother Liam called. He'd come along as muscle to help me load my SUV and the trailer it was pulling. He'd been in town for several days, consulting on the harbor front development project.

"I'm fine," I said, raising my voice a little so he could hear me. "You won't believe what Elvis found."

"Let me guess. The real Elvis in one of those white jumpsuits?"

The cat Elvis, who as far as he was concerned *was* the real Elvis, wrinkled his nose as though he'd understood Liam's words.

"Ha-ha. Very funny," I said. "No, he found a coffin." I looked around for Charlotte but couldn't see her. Charlotte Elliot worked for me part-time. She was also one of my grandmother's closest friends, which was how she'd ended up with a job at my shop.

"Ha-ha. Very funny back at you," Liam retorted. I could hear him moving boxes and furniture out of the way as he made his way to me.

"I'm not joking. It has to be at least six feet long. I think someone made it."

"It's probably just some big wooden box." He gave a grunt of effort and I saw a stack of boxes behind me shift sideways.

"There's a cross carved on the top and there are four handles on the side. It's a casket."

Liam poked his head above a six-foot-long metal toboggan that was blocking his way and grinned at me. He was a shade over six feet himself, with blond hair and blue-gray eyes. "You better hope the person who rented this space wasn't trying to save money in other ways besides not paying for the last six months." He craned his neck and studied the wooden box. "Assuming that's *not* the person who rented the space in the first place."

There was an orange foam football sitting on an upside-down wooden chair that looked like it had been wrapped in zebra-print duct tape. I threw the football at his head. It bounced off his left shoulder and landed near his feet.

"Your elbow's too high," he said. "Your arm should be making a right angle."

I stuck out my tongue at him.

Elvis's curiosity seemed to be getting the better of him. He scratched at the edge of the wooden box then looked at me.

"You're right," I said. "We should take a look inside, but you'll have to move." I picked him up and put him on the seat of the flipped-over chair. My hair was coming loose from the ponytail I'd pulled it into when we'd arrived at the warehouse. I yanked the elastic loose, raked my fingers through my hair and refastened it.

"You're not really going to look inside that thing, are you?" Liam asked.

"It's pretty much the only way we're going to find out what's in there." I looked over my shoulder at him. "And by the way, if that box actually does have an occupant they'll hear me scream over at the shop."

Liam snatched the foam football from the floor. "I'm ready to protect you," he said, a grin pulling at the corners of his mouth.

"Good to know that if there's a zombie inside you'll bean him with a perfect spiral," I said dryly.

He traced a finger down the outside of his left arm. "Note the perfect right angle, which is what will enable

me to throw that perfect spiral, should it become necessary, baby sister." Liam—who was technically my
stepbrother—was a month older and never let me forget it.

I laughed and shook my head. He was such a
smartass.

Then I hooked my fingers under the thin edge of the
lid, blew out a breath and lifted. Elvis craned his neck
to see. We exchanged a look.

"So?" Liam couldn't see the inside of the casket from
where he was standing.

"Well, I wasn't expecting this," I said. The cat murped
his agreement, whiskers twitching.

"Expecting what?" Liam asked impatiently.

I glanced over my shoulder at him again.

He looked at me with one raised eyebrow. "I was only
kidding before about someone actually being—" He
stopped for a moment. "There isn't, is there?"

"It's full of tea," I said.

"Tea?" His eyes darted from side to side and a frown
knotted his forehead.

"Uh-huh," I said. "Boxes of tea, lots of them. And
two, maybe three, Pendleton blankets." I ran my hand
over the soft, cream-colored wool with the traditional
green, red, yellow and black stripes at the border. "We
shouldn't have any problem selling these in the shop."

My business, Second Chance, was a cross between a
vintage store and a secondhand shop. We sold everything from furniture to dishes to guitars—mostly things
from the fifties through the seventies. Some of our stock
had been repurposed from its original use: a side table
made from an old library card catalog cabinet or a law-

yer's bookcase turned nightstand. But much of it just needed someone to appreciate its beauty.

The store was located in an old red brick house from the late 1800s, at the edge of downtown North Harbor, Maine. We were maybe a fifteen- to twenty-minute walk from the harbor front and not far from the off-ramp for the highway, which meant we were easy for tourists to get to.

As a kid I'd spent my summers in North Harbor with my grandmother, my dad's mom. It was where my father had grown up. Eventually I'd bought a house that I'd renovated and rented. For several years I was the host of a late-night syndicated radio show that featured classic rock music. When the media company that owned my station and seven others changed hands, I was replaced by a music feed from California and a nineteen-year-old with a tan and ombre hair who gave the temperature every hour. I'd landed on Gram's doorstep, at the urging of my mom, to try to figure out what I wanted to do next. I'd ended up staying in North Harbor and opening Second Chance.

I picked up one of the boxes of tea and checked the label for the best-before date. "Hey, this is good for another six months."

"You're not really going to drink that stuff, are you?" Liam asked.

"Sarah, what brand of tea is it?" Charlotte called.

"Red Rose," I said.

"Proper tea bags?" Charlotte took her tea very seriously.

"As far as I can tell."

"And how many tea bags are there in the box?"

I turned it over in my hands. "Seventy-two." I looked at the other boxes packed carefully in the wooden casket. "There must be a dozen boxes here at least."

Charlotte appeared then behind Liam. She was wearing a chambray shirt with the sleeves rolled up. She reminded me of actress Helen Mirren. She was tall with lovely posture and white hair cut in a sleek, chin-length bob.

"And a red box," she said, beaming at me. "Splendid!"

"Why does the color of the box matter?" Liam asked, a look of puzzlement on his face.

"Because it tells me that it's Canadian Red Rose tea," Charlotte said.

I nodded because I knew what she meant. Liam didn't. He frowned. "And the nationality of the tea is important because?"

"Because it's orange pekoe, which is Rose's favorite," I said.

Rose Jackson was another of my grandmother's long-time friends, a tiny dynamo in sensible shoes. She also worked for me part-time. She swore the Canadian version of Red Rose tea made a very different cup from the tea the company sold here. Any time we went "across the lines," as she called a trip over the US/Canadian border, our first stop was always a grocery store so Rose could replenish her stash. I knew she'd be tickled with this find.

Rose was also like a second grandmother to me and to Liam. She doted on him and he in turn would do anything for her, including, it turned out, carry a six-foot coffin outside and strap it to the trailer attached to the back of my SUV.

"I have a feeling I'd like whoever rented this storage unit," Charlotte said, putting her arm around my shoulders. "He or she was clearly a very practical person." She patted the top of the casket. "Short-term storage for now and long-term storage for later. Very sensible."

Liam rolled his eyes and Charlotte winked at me.

"You're not going to actually sell that thing in the store, are you?" he asked.

"I'm not sure," I said. "We've sold some pretty odd things." I nudged Charlotte with my hip. "Do you remember that suit of armor?"

"I most certainly do," she said with a smile. "I'm the one who cleaned and polished it. And don't forget about those department-store mannequins."

I nodded in agreement. The life-sized figures had come from a department store that had gone out of business. To my amazement it turned out there were people who collected old department store mannequins. After a short stint in our front window as members of the band KISS—part of our Halloween window display— the four figures had been disassembled, packed and shipped to a man in northern Michigan.

I studied the long wooden box. "This may be pushing it, though," I said. "But I'm pretty sure Avery will be able to come up with a way to use this in the front-window display for Halloween."

"Whatever she does it will be creative," Charlotte said. "You know she's been painting pumpkins black, don't you?"

I nodded. "She asked me for black paint, cheesecloth and twinkle lights. I don't have any doubt that window will be creative."

Avery wasn't one of my grandmother's friends. She was, however, the granddaughter of one of them, Elizabeth Emmerson Kiley French, aka Liz. The teen had come to live with her grandmother after some issues at home. Avery went to a progressive private school that only had classes in the morning. In the afternoon she worked for me, a setup that had turned out well for everyone.

Liam had wrapped the long wooden box in a couple of padded moving blankets. He checked the tension on the bungee cords holding it in place on the trailer and then straightened up, brushing off his hands. "You know Christmas is coming and Dad does like practical presents," he began with a teasing smile.

I shook my head emphatically. "No. We are not giving Dad a casket for Christmas."

He cocked his head to one side. "I'm serious. You know how hard it is to figure out what to get for him." The gleam in his blue-gray eyes told me he wasn't really that serious.

"No," I said once more. "We're not giving our father a gift that says *Merry Christmas, Peace on Earth, Is your will up to date?*" I held up one hand before he could say anything else. "However, as you like to remind me, you are older than I am, so if you want it, consider it yours."

I'd seen Liam set the foam football on top of a cardboard carton in the trailer before he grabbed the bungee cords, so I was ready when he launched it in my direction. I snagged the ball out of the air and did my endzone victory dance, which I admit looks a lot like the Bird Dance. Then I handed the ball to Charlotte and went back inside.

I cast a critical eye around the storage unit, trying to

decide what would fit in the space we had left in the trailer and the SUV. Charlotte had discovered several boxes of books. They should fit into the back of the SUV, I decided. The books all seemed to be hardcover and would probably bring a few dollars each.

"I'll check out all of them," Charlotte said as we carried the cartons out. "Maybe we'll get lucky and find a first edition or two."

It wasn't that far-fetched. We'd found treasures before in odder places, including a Les Paul guitar in a barn and a Marklin model train in a pack rat's home. Our stock came from a variety of places: yard sales, flea markets, people looking to downsize. I'd once rescued a table from a ditch by the side of the road. I was also a regular customer of a couple of trash pickers. I'd already let one of those pickers—Teresa Reynard—go through the leftovers from the first storage unit we'd cleared out and I'd promised her the chance to go through the remains of this unit as well.

We strapped the toboggan Liam had discovered and a vintage wooden sled next to the casket in the trailer and filled the SUV with boxes. By the time we were ready to leave, the unit looked a lot emptier. By my estimate the contents of the first storage space would recoup more than what I paid for both, which meant the second one would be all profit.

Charlotte and I—along with Elvis—headed back to Second Chance in the SUV. Liam followed in his truck, which we'd also filled with a snow blower, a wheelbarrow and a collection of wire racks and rods that I was fairly certain was a closet organizing system, and several boxes of vintage canning jars.

I was very glad to have Liam's help. Normally Mac, my second in command, would have been with us. Mac Mackenzie was the proverbial jack-of-all-trades. There wasn't anything he couldn't fix or reconfigure as far as I'd seen. He was all lean, strong muscle with light brown skin, dark eyes and close-cropped black hair.

Mac had given up his life as a financial adviser in Boston to come to Maine and sail every chance he got. Eventually he wanted to build his own wooden boat. He'd come to work with me when the shop first opened because, he'd said, he liked working with his hands. Second Chance was my store, but Mac was more partner than employee. Most important, he was my friend. Beyond that, I wasn't sure.

I missed him like crazy. Mac had been back in Boston for the last month, spending time with his former wife who was in a rehabilitation center after a carbon monoxide leak had left her in a permanent coma. Two weeks after he'd left, his wife, Leila, had died. Liz, Rose, Rose's gentleman friend, Alfred Peterson, and I had driven down for the memorial service. We hadn't seen Mac since. He had stayed in Boston to wrap up Leila's affairs. He and I often talked on the phone late at night, and more and more I found myself looking forward to those conversations and to the texts we'd sometimes exchange during the day. He'd texted me that morning.

Having a healthy breakfast?

I'd laughed at the words. Mac knew that what I most needed first thing in the morning was coffee and lots of it.

A bacon sandwich and coffee, I'd texted back.

His response made me laugh. Elvis craned his head

toward my phone on the counter almost as though he were trying to see what was so funny. *The four main food groups: sugar, salt, fat, caffeine.*

There's tomato in the sandwich. That's a vegetable.

Elvis fixed his green eyes on my face and tipped his head to one side. It was the same pose he used on customers in the shop. I should have been immune, but he was cute, especially with the scar that cut across his nose. I fished a bit of bacon out of my sandwich and held it out to him.

The phone signaled another message.

Tomatoes are technically a fruit.

I smiled at the phone, wishing we were having the conversation in person. *So I'm having a fruit and a vegetable.*

That got me a single right bracket—Mac's version of a smile emoji.

"Do you mind if I put my window down a little?" Charlotte asked as we headed back to the shop.

"Go ahead," I said. It was a gorgeous September day, sunny and warm, and the slight breeze brought a hint of the ocean in through the SUV's window.

North Harbor is located on the mid-coast of Maine. "Where the hills touch the sea" is the way the town has been described for more than two hundred and fifty years. It stretches from the Swift Hills in the north to the Atlantic Ocean in the south and is located north of Camden and Rockport, closer to Canada, which means we see lots of tourists from there. The full-time population is just over thirteen thousand, but that number triples in the summertime with summer residents and tourists.

North Harbor is a lovely small town, full of beautiful old buildings, award-winning restaurants and quirky little shops. I'd never been sorry I'd decided to stay.

It didn't take us long to unload everything once we got back to Second Chance. The boxes all went into the workroom behind the store and everything else went into the old garage at the end of the parking lot that Mac and Liam had converted to work space.

My brother was a building contractor who spent most of his time these days refurbishing older houses and sharing his expertise on other restoration projects. His specialty was passive solar technology and he was working on a plan to add solar panels to the garage work space in the spring. Liam had been back and forth to North Harbor several times since he'd started consulting on the harbor front project. He was staying with Charlotte's son Nick.

"Where do you want the tea box?" Liam asked after everything else had been unloaded.

"Garage," I said.

"Workroom," Rose countered. She'd come out to see what we'd brought back. She was a good six inches shorter than me, with soft white hair and a warm smile. She fixed her gray eyes on me. "Sarah, dear, we need to unload all the tea and the blankets." Charlotte had told her about our find. "It'll be a lot easier to do that inside." She ran a hand along the smooth wood of the top. "I think this is yellow birch," she said approvingly. "An excellent choice." She tipped her head to one side and looked at me. "Did you know shipbuilders in colonial times used yellow birch because the resin in the wood makes it more resistant to rot?"

"I didn't," I said, shaking my head. Rose was a former middle school teacher. She knew more about the history of the state than most of the texts in the library.

"I knew that," Liam said, trying and failing not to look smug.

"Of course you did," Rose said approvingly. "You were always good at history." She reached over and patted his cheek. "You must be as dry as a covered bridge. I'll get you a cup of coffee."

She started for the shop and Liam gave up on trying to restrain his cat-that-swallowed-the-canary grin. "And no one likes a smartass, Liam," she added without breaking stride or turning around.

I bit my tongue so I wouldn't laugh until Rose was inside. Then I grinned at Liam. "She's got your number," I said.

He grinned back. "I swear Rose has eyes in the back of her head or maybe some kind of ESP." He studied the wooden casket. "Do you think the two of us can get this thing inside?"

"We got it on the trailer," I said. "Let me prop the door open and we'll give it a try."

I wedged the back door open while Liam undid the bungee cords and unwrapped the moving quilts. With a little grunting and more than a little swearing—not all of it on his part—we managed to get the tea-filled casket into the workroom.

Avery poked her head around the doors to the shop. "That is so awesome," she exclaimed. Her dark hair was cut in shaggy layers and she was dressed all in black; the collection of bracelets on her left arm were the only color she wore. "When Charlotte said you found a coffin I thought she was gooning me." She studied the long wooden box. "You think anyone's actually used it?"

Like her grandmother, Avery wasn't one to beat around the bush.

"Other than to store tea, no, I don't think so," I said.

She shrugged. "Cool," she said and then disappeared around the door again.

Liam and I followed her into the shop. There were no customers—not surprising because Monday afternoons were usually quiet, especially in late September. The summer tourists were gone and it was too early for the leaf peepers. There was no sign of Elvis. He'd probably followed Rose upstairs for a treat. Avery was busy replenishing our covered bucket display.

In what could have turned out to be a moment of insanity I'd bought three dozen small galvanized buckets for what amounted to pennies each, from a flower shop that had gone out of business. Avery had come up with the idea to decorate the buckets with strips cut from area maps. We had a box full of them. The map-covered pails had been a big hit with tourists looking for a souvenir of their time in Maine with some practical appeal—the buckets were great for holding craft supplies or kitchen utensils.

Rose came down the stairs from the second floor then, carrying a cup of coffee for Liam and another for me.

"Thank you," I said, taking the stoneware mug from her.

Charlotte was behind her, knotting her apron at the waist. "I thought I'd start unpacking the tea," she said.

"You're certain it's Canadian tea?" Rose asked.

Charlotte looked at her friend over the top of her glasses before pushing them up her nose. "Of course I'm certain, Rose."

Rose turned her attention to me. "And you think there could be a dozen boxes?"

"Maybe more," I said.

She clasped her hands together and beamed at me. "Wonderful!"

I continued to look at her without saying anything.

Her cheeks turned pink, which just made her look like a naughty and adorable little girl. "I know I wasn't exactly enthusiastic about you buying what was in those storage units."

I nodded but still didn't speak. "Did your cheese slide off your cracker, dear?" she'd asked when I came back from my meeting with the new owners of the storage warehouse to say I'd bought the contents of two units, close to sight unseen.

Now she reached over and patted my arm. "And I think we can all agree that this time I wasn't as right as I usually am."

I didn't dare look at Liam because I knew if I did, I'd start to laugh.

Rose turned her attention back to Charlotte. "Before you get started, there was someone here looking for you."

Charlotte frowned at her. "For me?"

"A young woman, not that much older than Avery. She said she'd be back." Rose glanced at her watch. "Any time now."

"Did she give you her name?" Charlotte asked.

"Mallory Pearson. I got the feeling she's a former student."

Charlotte nodded. "She is. She'd be close to twenty now. I wonder what she wants."

Rose glanced out the front window at the street. "I think we're about to find out," she said.

Mallory Pearson came through the front door. She was tiny, as Charlotte had said, maybe twenty years old with blond hair in a thick braid over one shoulder, dressed in gray leggings and a blue hoodie. And she looked like the weight of the world was on her shoulders. She smiled when she saw Charlotte and her whole body seemed to sag with relief.

Rose shot me a look and I felt certain we were thinking the same thing. This wasn't a social call.

Liam put a hand on my shoulder. "I'm going to get the last few boxes," he said in a low voice.

I nodded. "I'll be out in a minute."

Charlotte had walked over to greet Mallory, wrapping her in a warm hug. Now she was listening intently as the young woman talked, her expression somber. Rose watched them for a moment then she leaned over to me. "I'm going to go start unpacking that tea," she whispered.

As she turned to go Charlotte called to her. "Rose, could you wait a minute, please?"

Rose stopped, turning back around. Charlotte looked at me. "You, too, please," she said. She put an arm around Mallory Pearson's shoulder and they walked over to join Rose and me. "This is my friend Sarah Grayson," she said. "She owns Second Chance."

The young woman gave me a shy smile. "It's nice to meet you," she said. "I like your store."

"Thank you," I said.

She shifted her attention to Rose. "Hello again, Mrs. Jackson."

Rose gave her a warm smile. "I'm glad you came back," she said.

Charlotte gave Mallory's shoulders a squeeze. "Tell them," she urged.

Mallory took a breath and let it out. "I want to hire you," she said, the words coming out in a rush. "I want you to get my father out of jail."

I don't know what I'd been expecting her to say but not this. Along with working for me part-time, Rose and Charlotte also ran a detective agency, Charlotte's Angels. The team included Avery's grandmother, Liz, and Rose's gentleman friend, Mr. P. The name was a play on Charlie's Angels, although for the most part they just went by the Angels. Mr. P. had met all the state's requirements and received his private investigator's license. The four of them were actually pretty good at solving mysteries, although they tended to pull everyone around them into their crime solving efforts—especially me.

"Who's your father?" Rose asked.

"Mike Pearson," Mallory said.

There was something familiar about the name but I couldn't put it into context.

"He's six months into a five-year sentence for criminal negligence in the death of my stepmother, Gina." She stopped for a moment and swallowed hard before continuing. "He was beaten in jail. He has broken ribs, a concussion and bruises all over his body. He won't make it through another four and a half years in that place." She squared her shoulders, seeming to pull from some inner reserve of resolve. "And he doesn't belong there anyway. He isn't guilty of anything."

"I remember Michael," a voice said behind us. Liz had come in while Mallory was talking. I wasn't sure how much of the conversation she'd heard but it seemed she'd heard enough. "He worked for the Emmerson Foundation one summer years ago."

Mallory nodded. "I know. I've seen a photo of Dad with you, Mrs. French."

Liz joined us, her heels tapping a sharp staccato on the wooden floor. She was always elegantly dressed, blond hair curled around her face. I'd never seen her in yoga pants or a sweatshirt. "Keep going," she said to Mallory.

The young woman gave an almost imperceptible nod. "My stepmother was an alcoholic. She had been waiting for a bed in rehab. They told Dad to make sure she didn't have access to lighters or matches. She'd started a fire once before when she was drinking. Our garage almost burned down. But that day Dad had found out that there was going to be a bed available for her in a place called Haven House."

Now I could put the name into context. I remembered coverage of the story in the news: Gina Pearson had died in the fire that had gutted her home the previous December, just two weeks before Christmas. A barbecue lighter and a bottle of vodka had been found by her body.

"But wasn't your stepmother's death ruled an accident?" Rose asked, a frown creasing her forehead. "Why was your father charged with anything?"

NO ESCAPE CLAWS   19

Mallory played with the end of her long braid. "There was a witness. Our next-door neighbor who's a retired judge, saw my dad at our house after the fire had started. He saw Dad walk away and . . . and he didn't call 911. The police said he knew there was a chance that Gina was still inside . . ." She didn't finish the sentence but she didn't need to. The implication was that Mike Pearson had left his wife to die in that fire.

Mallory cleared her throat. "My father pled guilty. There was no trial. I know he only did that to spare my brothers and me. It was bad enough as it was."

"What did your father say?" Charlotte asked. She kept her arm around the young woman's shoulders. "How did he explain what happened?"

Mallory was already shaking her head. "That's the thing. He didn't. He's never said anything about what happened." Her chin came up and her gaze swept over us. "I know my dad. I know the kind of person he is. He wouldn't have left Gina in that house if he'd known she was there. He wouldn't have done that to anyone but especially not to her. She didn't deserve him but that didn't matter. He still loved her."

Her mouth moved as though she were testing out what she wanted to say next. "Gina was fun before she started drinking. She was happy. She'd put on music and dance with us with that sparkly sort of look in her eyes and her hair swirling all around. Dad promised that he wouldn't give up until she was that person again. He's never made a promise he didn't keep. You can ask anyone who knows him."

"Mallory, where are you living right now?" Liz asked.

"Here, with our grandmother," she said. "She used

to live outside Washington—the city, not the state. She just came here to be with us. But she wants to move back there to give Greg and Austin, my brothers, a chance at a new start."

She shifted to look at Charlotte. "Please, Mrs. Elliot. I won't even be able to see Dad if we're in Washington. He'll die in that place and he shouldn't even be there. Please."

It was impossible not to feel for Mallory. Her family had been pulled apart. Why wouldn't she want to save whatever she had left? I thought about my own dad. Technically, Peter Kennelly was my stepfather, but to me he was just Dad. And I was his child just as much as Liam was. If Dad were in prison, I would move heaven and earth to get him out.

Charlotte turned to face Mallory. "I can see how much you love your father," she said. "I remember him when you were my student. He came to every parent-teacher night."

"So you'll help me?" Mallory asked. The hope etched on her face made my chest hurt.

"I have to talk to everyone else," Charlotte said, her voice gentle. "I'm going to need a little time before I can give you an answer."

Mallory's face fell, but all she did was nod. She shifted her gaze to Rose and me. "Thank you for listening," she said in a soft voice.

Charlotte walked her over to the front door. She gave Mallory a hug and the young woman left. Charlotte came back over to the three of us. I wasn't sure what she was thinking. Her brown eyes were serious, but I couldn't tell which way she was leaning. "So? What do you think?" she asked. "Should we take the case?"

"Yes," Rose said, nodding her head.

Liz spoke at the same time. "No," she said, shaking her head for emphasis.

I waited to see what Charlotte was going to say. Then I realized they were all looking at me.

Chapter 2

I held up both hands and shook my head. "Oh no," I said. "I'm not getting in the middle of any debate between you and Liz because no matter what I say someone is going to be mad at me."

Rose reached up and patted my cheek. "I could never be mad at you, sweet girl," she said.

"Sucking up is not going to work," I told her firmly.

She smoothed the front of her flowered apron, seemingly unperturbed that her attempt to win me over hadn't worked. "Cookies would have worked," she said.

"Well, you don't have any cookies unless you've hidden a couple in your pocket," Liz retorted. "And Sarah is far too smart to fall for any of your flattery."

I looked at Charlotte, who was fighting a losing battle not to grin at the two of them. "Roll up your pant legs," I said to her. "It's too late to save your shoes."

"Save her shoes from what?" Rose asked, looking at the floor.

"From all the bull you two are spreading around," I said.

I saw the corners of Charlotte's mouth twitch but she managed to keep her grin in check.

Rose caught one of my hands with her own two. "Sarah, we have to help that child after all she and her brothers have been through. The fact that Mike Pearson isn't talking about what happened means he's protecting his children. He shouldn't be punished for that."

"Or it means he's guilty as charged," Liz interjected.

"Why are you such a Negative Nelly," Rose said, hands on her hips.

"And why do you have to be Rebecca of Sunnybrook Farm?" Liz flicked a bit of lint off the sleeve of her yellow sweater.

It wasn't the first time Rose and Liz disagreed about something and I was certain it was far from the last time. Somehow the fact that they didn't always see eye to eye hadn't hurt their friendship at all.

"Seeing the glass as half-full isn't a bad thing, you know." Rose was getting wound up now, color rising in her cheeks.

"There *is* no glass in this case," Liz said firmly. "Just a man who got tired of being married to a drunk."

Charlotte leaned her head against mine. "I didn't really think it through when I asked you all to stay, did I?" she asked, keeping her voice low.

"Nope," I said.

"And you're going to remind me of this later, aren't you?"

"Absolutely."

Liz and Rose were still arguing, although the conversation seemed to have taken a detour onto the subject of breakfast smoothies, of all things. Liz loathed smoothies unless they were made with ice cream and chocolate sauce, which as Rose liked to point out, were actually the ingredients for a chocolate milk shake. Whenever Rose and Liz got into a debate over something, the discussion tended to swerve off into the conversational ditch.

Rose was just about to say something else when Liz's phone rang. She pulled it out of her purse, frowned at the screen and then held up one perfectly manicured hand. "I have to take this," she said. She looked at all of us. "Don't go anywhere."

"You agree with me, don't you, Sarah?" Rose asked after Liz had stepped away.

I shook my head. "I love you, but I'm not getting sucked into the middle of this."

Rose turned to Charlotte. "I know *you* agree with me."

"I'm not sure how I feel," Charlotte said. "And more important, I'm not sure what we can do. How can we get Mallory's father out of prison?"

"We can prove he's not guilty," Rose immediately said. "Do I need to remind either one of you about how unreliable the testimony of eyewitnesses can be?" She had strong opinions on the subject. And a list of references on her phone that backed them up.

Charlotte shook her head. "No, you don't. It's just that I remember the fire that killed Gina Pearson and I remember Mike Pearson being charged." She exhaled slowly. "The witness who saw Mike is Neill Halloran. *Judge* Neill Halloran. Do you really think we can discredit him?"

Halloran was a distinguished name in North Harbor. The town had been settled in the late 1760s by Alexander Swift. The Hallorans had been in North Harbor almost as long as the Swifts. Charlotte was right. The police had an unimpeachable witness in Judge Halloran.

Liz rejoined us then. I couldn't get a sense of what she was thinking. The teasing glint in her eyes that she'd had when she and Rose had been arguing was gone. There was no indication anymore that she was close to giving a bemused snort of exasperation at something Rose said.

"Is everything all right?" I asked.

"That call was from Michael Pearson's lawyer," she said. "He had a message from his client."

Rose and I exchanged a look. She seemed as confused as I was.

"He knows what Mallory is trying to do," Charlotte said.

Liz tucked the phone back in her bag. "I don't think there's any doubt about that. The message was that he deserves to be in prison and he's specifically asking us not to take the case."

"I know it was a long time ago," I said. "But what do you remember about him from that summer he worked for the foundation?"

Liz straightened one sleeve of her sweater, a way to buy a little time, I was guessing, as she thought about my question. "It *was* a long time ago," she said. "Michael actually worked mostly on camp business."

The Emmerson Foundation ran a summer camp for kids who wouldn't otherwise get to go. The Sunshine Camp had been one of the foundation's first projects and I knew Liz was very proud of it.

"Not with Michelle's father?" Growing up, Michelle

Andrews—who was now a detective with the North Harbor police department—had been my summertime best friend. Each June we'd just resumed our friendship where we'd left off at the end of the previous summer like all the months between hadn't happened.

When we were fifteen, Michelle's father, Rob Andrews, had been arrested for embezzling funds from the Sunshine Camp and my thoughtless, childish comments about him had destroyed our relationship. We'd only recently reconnected in the last year.

"As a matter of fact, yes," Liz said in answer to my question. "Michael wasn't a counselor. He worked here in town, in the office."

Liz shrugged. "Mostly what I remember is a young man who worked hard. Everyone liked him. Elspeth could tell you a lot more than I can. They got to be friends that summer."

Elspeth was Liz's niece. She ran Phantasy, a very successful salon and spa here in town.

"Just friends?" I asked.

"As far as I know," she said, "but Elspeth has always been very closemouthed about that kind of thing, so who knows. One thing I can tell you is that she's always refused to believe that Michael left his wife to die in that fire."

"This just proves we have to take the case," Rose said. She focused all her attention on Liz. "You know that Mallory's father sending you this message doesn't make sense. If he's really guilty, what does he have to worry about? We won't be able to get him released from prison. And if he isn't guilty, why doesn't he want our help, anyone's help?"

Liz looked thoughtful, lines pulling at the corners of her mouth.

"What if that child is right?" Rose continued. "What if Mike Pearson pled guilty because he *feels* guilty over not being able to stop his wife from drinking, over not being able to save her?" She held up both hands. "It's so obvious." She looked at all three of us and then she stretched out her arm in front of her, palm down.

"I'm not doing this," Liz said. "This is not the Patriots' locker room." I knew that stubborn set to her shoulders.

I also knew the equally stubborn stance Rose had taken up. She continued to look at Liz, but she didn't say anything more.

The silence stretched between them, probably not nearly as long as it seemed. Then Liz made an exasperated motion with her hand like she was shooing away a bug. "Oh for heaven's sake," she muttered. She reached out and put her hand on top of Rose's hand.

Rose smiled and then looked at Charlotte.

"I don't want to get Mallory's hopes up over nothing," Charlotte said. She sighed softly and added her hand to the pile.

I knew what was coming.

"We can't do this without you, dear," Rose nudged.

I glanced across at the cash desk and imagined Mac leaning against it smiling at me. He would have told me to have faith in the Angels' rather unorthodox way of doing things. Then he would have laughed when I insisted I wouldn't get sucked into this case.

I extended my arm and put my hand on top of the

others. "I'm not going to jump up and yell 'go team,'" I warned. "We're not the Patriots' offensive line."

"Well, of course we're not," Rose said as though even the thought was ridiculous. "Although that Rob Gronkowski is a lovely, exuberant boy." She smiled. "We're not a football team. We're the Angels."

Heaven help us, I thought.

Chapter 3

"The first thing I need to do is bring Alfred up to date," Rose said.

"Where is Mr. P.?" I asked. He could usually be found out in the Angels' sunporch office working on his laptop.

"He's at the library," Rose said, patting her pocket in search of her phone. "He's doing a workshop on online security for seniors."

I knew she meant teaching the workshop, not taking it. Alfred Peterson was a little bald man with wire-framed glasses and pants that were generally hiked up to his armpits. He also possessed a keen mind and the computer skills of someone typically a fraction of his age. It was his computer skills and his rather eclectic resume of volunteer activities that had helped him meet all the requirements to be licensed as a private investigator by the state of Maine. For the past several months he'd been mentoring Rose as she worked toward getting her license.

Rose checked her watch. "Alfred should be here in a little more than an hour. Once he gets up to speed we'll see what we can find out about the fire and about Gina Pearson's death. Right now, I think we could all use a nice cup of tea." She smiled at me. "And I'll get you a fresh cup of coffee," she said, taking my mug of coffee, which had gone cold. She headed for the stairs.

Charlotte touched my arm. "Speaking of tea, I'm going to go start unpacking it all. And I'll call Mallory and let her know we're going to look into her father's case." She started for the workroom.

I turned to face Liz. Folding my arms over my midsection, I smiled. "And what are you going to do?" I asked.

She smiled back at me. "I'm going to do what I do best." She held out one hand in a gesture I'd seen before, and studied her manicured nails, painted a pale lavender. "I really need to get my nails done."

Her nails looked perfect. They always looked perfect. That wasn't the point. Not only would Liz be able to pick her niece Elspeth's brain at Phantasy, she'd also be able to glean whatever gossip was still floating around town about Mike Pearson and his late wife. The salon was better than Google for information gathering.

Liz leaned over and kissed my cheek. "Nice job not picking sides, kiddo," she said, a knowing gleam in her eyes.

I realized that no matter what Liz had said, in the end she would have gone along with the Angels taking Mike Pearson's case even if his attorney hadn't called and made her second-guess her initial no. Family mattered to Liz and as she liked to teasingly remind me, we were all family, whether we liked it or not.

"Love you," I called to her back as she reached the door, waiting for the reply I knew I'd get and did.

"Yeah, yeah, everybody does," she said with a wave of her hand and then she was gone.

I turned back around and for the first time remembered that Avery was in the room. She was dusting the shelves of a squat bookshelf I'd painted a delicate shade of blush pink before she restocked it with more of the map-embellished pails. They surrounded her as she knelt on the floor. In one she'd piled children's wooden ABC blocks. Another of the small buckets held facecloths that had been rolled and tied with ribbon. A third was filled with fizzy lavender-scented bath bombs that Avery herself had made. I realized she had heard everything that had been said from the moment Mallory Peterson walked in the door.

"Well?" I asked.

Avery set down the microfiber cloth she'd been using on the shelf and the stack of bracelets she was wearing slid along her arm. "Well, first of all I agree with Rose," she said.

That didn't surprise me. While Avery loved her grandmother, she and Rose were kindred souls in many ways—both up for trying new things like green smoothies and Japanese art movies—and they were very close. Avery's mother's last name was also Jackson, which the teen insisted meant she and Rose had some kind of family connection. Avery had even briefly used Jackson as her last name when she'd been fighting with her father.

"It's just weird that someone in jail would turn down help to get out." Something on the shelf right in front of her caught her eye. She grabbed the cloth and rubbed vigorously at a spot before she turned her attention back to me. "But before that lawyer guy called Nonna I pretty much was on her side." She glanced at the stairs. "Don't tell Rose that."

"My lips are sealed," I said.

Avery set the bucket full of blocks on the middle shelf, considered it for a moment and then moved it to the top one. "I might be able to find some stuff out," she said.

As a general and unspoken rule we tried to keep Avery out of the Angels' investigations. That didn't always work.

"What kind of stuff?" I asked warily.

She set two other little pails on the middle shelf of the low bookcase. "Just stuff about that family," she said with an offhand shrug. A little too offhand for me. "I kinda know her brother."

"Mallory's brother?"

She glanced over at me. "Yeah. His name's Greg."

"What does 'kinda know' mean?" I asked, trying not to sound like an adult giving her the third-degree even though that's exactly what I was doing.

"He goes to my school," she said. "And he's in two of my classes. So I know him, but we don't exactly hang out."

She seemed to be using a lot of qualifiers.

"Maybe I could talk to him."

I reached over and straightened the edge of a quilt. "Maybe you could," I said. "And if you do find out anything—"

"—tell Rose or Mr. P. and don't do anything stupid," she finished.

"Exactly," I said.

Rose came down the stairs then with a fresh cup of coffee for me.

"Thank you," I said. I looked over at Avery. "I'm just going to make sure everything from the storage unit has been unloaded. Rose and Charlotte will be in the workroom. Yell if you need help."

"Okay," she said. Most of her attention was once again focused on the collection of little pails.

Rose followed me out to the workroom. Charlotte had set a cardboard carton on a Mission-style wooden chair that had come from the first storage unit, and was packing it with the boxes of tea. Rose joined her and peeked inside. Then she looked at me, her eyes sparkling. "This is a splendid find, dear," she said, clasping her hands together. "Although I can't imagine why anyone would have left all this lovely tea in a storage unit."

"Do you think it's possible someone was smuggling tea in from Canada?" Charlotte asked, a twinkle in her dark eyes.

"Maybe," I said. "The thought had crossed my mind."

Rose shook her head. "If they did, it's very disrespectful behavior."

"So does that mean you don't want to keep all this tea?" I asked, gesturing at the carton, which was already half full of Red Rose boxes.

"Of course it doesn't," she said. "That would be even more disrespectful."

Charlotte gave her a nudge with one elbow. "Did you see those?" she said, indicating the blankets. "I think they're the real thing."

Rose reached over and ran one hand across the

cream-colored wool. "I think you're right." She looked at me. "These blankets might do very well on the store Web site."

"All right," I said. I glanced over at the door. I needed to see how Liam was doing. I hadn't meant for him to get stuck with all the unloading. "Could you go over them and see what condition they're in? They'll need to be cleaned and then Avery can take pictures."

Since I'd discovered Avery's artistic side I'd been letting her take more of the photos for items on the Web site. I was convinced it had helped sales, which is one of the reasons I had given her more hours and a small raise.

Rose nodded. "I'll take care of it."

"Thanks," I said. "By the way, the tea is all yours."

She beamed at me and leaned over to kiss me on the cheek. "You are a darling girl. Thank you," she said.

I stepped outside to discover that Mr. P. had arrived earlier than expected. He was standing by the now-empty trailer behind my SUV talking to Liam. He smiled as I joined them. "Hello, Sarah," he said. "Liam and I were just talking about the plans to winterize the sunporch."

The Angels had been using my sunporch as a base of operations since they took on their first case a year ago. The problem was that the uninsulated space with its old, drafty windows was too cold to work in during the winter months. Rose had raised the idea of finding office space somewhere else, which had struck me as a very, *very* bad idea.

I figured that doing some work in the space would actually kill two birds with one stone. It would add to

the overall value of the building—not that I was planning on selling it—and I'd still be able to keep an eye
on whatever investigation the Angels had going on.
When I'd explained my reasoning to Liam he'd immediately agreed to do the work and to see what deals he
could find for me on supplies.

The Angels already paid me a monthly rent. I'd ob-
jected to the stipend and been firmly informed that if I
wouldn't take the money the Angels would be setting
up shop somewhere else. So each month half the money
I received went to the Friends of the North Harbor Library and the other half to the Mid-coast Animal Shel-
ter. I felt better about taking the money and I reasoned
that since Rose didn't know what I was doing, she
couldn't argue with me over it.

Instead of paying me more rent for the space once it
was essentially winterized, I'd suggested a trade. Mr. P.,
with his superior computer skills, could do background
checks on some of the vintage guitars and the owners
of those instruments, which seemed to be showing up
at the shop on a semiregular basis. I'd said no to two
possible sales because the backstories of the guitars
seemed a little sketchy. One of them was a 1966 Martin
D-18 with mahogany back and sides and a spruce top.
I still regretted letting that one go. So the Angels and I
had made a deal and since Liam was in town he'd offered to get started on the sunporch work.

"I was just telling Alfred about the windows," Liam
said.

Mr. P. shook his head. "I can't imagine someone
changing windows just because they didn't like the look
of the mullions."

Liam rolled his eyes the way he'd done when he'd originally told me the story of a former client who had decided to replace the windows in two rooms on the back of his house because he didn't like the way the small panes of glass "chopped up the view." The client had told Liam to do whatever he wanted with the almost-new windows that had been replaced. There were just enough of them for the sunporch space and since they were otherwise destined for the landfill I felt good about giving them a second life.

"The guy gets his view and we get windows that don't let the wind blow through in January," I said.

"A win-win," Mr. P. said, nodding approvingly.

Liam gestured in my direction. "I forgot to tell you that since Mac is still in Boston, Nick offered to give me a hand."

Nick was one of Liam's closest friends, although technically I'd known Nick longer. I still wasn't sure exactly what we were to each other. Rose had done everything but lock the two of us in a closet together to try and generate something romantic between the two of us but it hadn't taken. "That's nice of him," I said.

"Yeah, Nick's a nice guy," Liam agreed. The gleam in his eyes told me he was trying to get a rise out of me. More than once he'd suggested I "lay a big wet one" on Nick and see where it led.

I turned to Mr. P. deciding my best play here was a change of subject. "Rose said you were doing a workshop at the library. How did it go?"

"Very well," he said, nudging his glasses up his nose. "They were a surprisingly savvy group. Most seniors are not as gullible as people your age seem to think."

I smiled. "I'm glad to hear it."

"Rosie sent me a text," he continued. "It seems we have a new case."

Liam looked at me, one eyebrow raised. He didn't say anything.

"We do," I said.

"Then I should get inside and get briefed," Mr. P. said. He turned his attention back to Liam. "I'm available to help you and Nicolas with the sunporch. After all, it is going to be our office."

Liam pulled a hand over the back of his neck. "I'll let you know what the plan is as soon as I talk to Nick."

Mr. P. nodded, hiked his pants that were almost at his armpits a little higher, and headed for the back door.

I leaned against the side of the trailer. Liam bumped me with his shoulder. "You have a case?"

"No," I said. "The Angels have a case."

"Same thing, Sarah," he said, sizing me up with an amused expression.

I was already shaking my head. "No it's not. I'm not in the private investigating business. I mostly just drive them places."

He laughed at the face I was making. "Okay. We'll go with that. So what's the case? Is it the girl who came to see Charlotte?"

I nodded. "Uh-huh. One of her students. Her father is in prison. It's possible he shouldn't be."

Liam was still grinning. "You know how Nick is going to take this, don't you?"

"He's trying to be more flexible about Rose and his mother and . . . everything."

He laughed again. "I hope you're right." He pulled

out his phone and checked the time. "I need to go get cleaned up. I have a meeting later."

I raised an inquiring eyebrow. "Work or personal?"

"None of your business," he retorted.

"So personal," I said.

He made a face.

I laid my head on his shoulder. "Thank you for all your help today."

"No problem," he said, "but you know that if Mac doesn't come back soon you're going to have to hire someone. I'll help you anytime I can but I'm not going to be here forever."

"Mac's coming back." It was what I said to everyone who broached the idea of me hiring a replacement.

Liam planted a kiss on the top of my head but said nothing.

I pushed away from the side of the trailer and straightened up. "Hey, do me a favor," I said. "Don't say anything to Nick about this new case."

He gave a snort of laughter. "Don't worry. There's not a chance I'm going to be the bearer of *that* news!"

"I'll see you tomorrow?" I asked.

He nodded.

He started for his truck and I headed for the garage.

That evening Elvis and I had supper with Gram and her husband, John. It was the fifth time I'd been invited since they'd gotten home a month earlier. I wasn't sure if the invitations were coming because Gram had missed me or if she was worried about what I'd come up with for supper if I were left to my own devices.

Cooking had been a difficult skill for me to master. I

hadn't managed to learn anything in the Family Living classes at school, although in my defense after the second fire I was sent to study hall instead. My mom and Gram hadn't had any success, either. In the end it had been Rose, with some assistance from Charlotte, who had taught me basic cooking skills and was helping to expand my repertoire. I wasn't sure if it was just because of her skill as a teacher that Rose had succeeded where everyone else had failed. Or if it was because of her patience—or maybe stubbornness was a better word.

The second-floor apartment smelled like garlic, spices and tomatoes. I knew what that meant. "My favorite, beef stew!" I exclaimed, throwing my arms around Gram when she opened the door. Elvis slipped past her legs.

"I thought you'd like it," she said with a smile.

"You spoil me," I said.

She tucked a stray strand of hair behind my ear. "What's the point of having grandchildren if you don't spoil them a little?"

Isabel Grayson Scott was maybe an inch or so taller than my five foot six inches, depending on whether she was wearing heels or flats. Strong and solid, she had piercing blue eyes behind red-framed glasses. She wore her wavy white hair cropped short, which showed off her gorgeous high cheekbones. My father had been her only child, which meant that technically I was her only grandchild, but when Mom and Dad had gotten married Gram had welcomed both Peter and Liam. "There's no such thing as too many people to love," she'd told me once.

Gram made her way back to the stove and I turned to get a hug from John. John Scott could have been actor Gary Oldman's older brother. He had the same brown hair, streaked with gray waving back from his face, and the same intriguing gleam in his eyes. There were thirteen years between him and Gram, which had raised some eyebrows when they began seeing each other, but Gram didn't seem anywhere near her seventy-four years and she didn't care what other people thought.

The two of them had gone on an extended road trip slash honeymoon, living in a small camper van and working on low-income housing projects up and down the East Coast, including a little time in eastern Canada. I was so glad to have them home.

"How did you make out at the storage unit?" John asked.

I took a seat at the table. The layout of the apartment was similar to the layout of Rose's at the back. There was plenty of room for a large table in the kitchen.

"You're not going to believe what we found," I said.

Gram smiled at me over her shoulder. "Well, since you're here at my table I'm guessing it wasn't a map to the Lost Dutchman's gold mine."

"Not even close." Elvis had come back from his prowl around the apartment and now he settled himself at my feet. "We found a casket."

"Unoccupied, I hope," John said with a smile.

"Thankfully," I said. "It was full of boxes of tea, for the most part."

"Tea?" Gram frowned. "Was it any good?"

"The expiry date on the boxes is months away. Rose made a pot this afternoon. It seemed good to me and she was happy." Rose had made an actual sigh of contentment after her first sip.

I reached down and settled Elvis on my lap. He craned his neck in the direction of the kitchen so he could watch Gram. Elvis liked her beef stew as well. "It was Red Rose tea. *Canadian* Red Rose," I said.

"I'm guessing you gave it all to Rose," John said. He and Gram had brought Rose two boxes back from their time in Nova Scotia.

I nodded. "I did. We also found several Pendleton blankets—the cream ones with the stripes—that are in excellent shape. Those should sell pretty quickly either in the shop or on the Web site."

"Charlotte said you discovered some books as well." Gram lifted the lid of the stew pot and peered inside.

"There's a copy of *A Bear Called Paddington* she thinks may be worth something."

"Depending on the condition of the book and whether it's a first edition it may be worth quite a lot," she said. "What year is it?"

"Umm, 1958, I think."

She nodded. That seemed to have been the right answer.

"Hardcover?" she asked. "With the dust jacket?"

I pictured the book Charlotte had set on my desk. "Yes and yes."

Gram smiled. "Then you have something that may be worth several thousand dollars."

"I didn't know you knew about old books," I said.

She glanced over her shoulder at me and smiled. "I've spent lots of time with your mother over the years. I've picked up a few things."

"Why would someone leave a valuable book in a storage unit?"

John set a plate of rolls on the table. "Why would someone leave a coffin in a storage unit?"

I nodded. "Good point."

Gram reached for a large spoon on the counter. "The Angels have picked up a new case." It wasn't a question.

"You were talking to Charlotte."

Gram gave the stew a stir, set the lid on the pot again and came back over to the table. She smiled at Elvis before turning her attention back to me. "Gina Pearson's last name was Knox before she married Michael Pearson. There have been Knoxes in this area almost as far back as there have been Swifts—although in the case of the Knoxes they've always been working *for* the Swifts, not *with* them. Charlotte wondered if I knew anything about the family."

"Do you?"

Gram sighed softly. "Just that there have been alcoholics in that family all the way back through the family tree."

I stroked Elvis's fur. He continued to watch Gram as though he were following the conversation. And who's to say he wasn't?

"I don't like to speak ill of the dead," she continued, "but Gina's mother was what they used to call a mean drunk—angry and hostile when she was drinking, unhappy when she wasn't and an overwhelmed mother of six pretty much all the time."

"Gina had genetics and more working against her," I said. I felt a twinge of guilt. I'd been judging the woman without knowing much about her.

Gram nodded. John caught her hand and gave it a squeeze and she smiled at him. "Moira—that was Gina's mother—lost her own mother when she was twelve and she didn't really have any role models on how to parent. I'm not making excuses for Gina, mind you. She had more than one chance at rehab, but I do think she deserved some understanding and compassion. And that seemed to be pretty scarce when she was alive."

Gram shared a little more about Gina Pearson's family history as we ate. I found myself feeling a lot more compassionate toward the woman. I'd never found North Harbor to be judgmental, but I had a feeling Gina had had a different experience. I couldn't help thinking how lucky I'd always been to have my mom and Gram as well as Liz, Rose and Charlotte to support me and to be good role models.

Before I headed back downstairs with a container of stew and another of chocolate thumbprint cookies I hugged both John and my grandmother. "I'm so glad you're home," I said.

John and Gram exchanged a smile. "We are, too," she said.

Mr. P. drove in with Rose and me the next morning. He seemed just a little distracted. Elvis settled himself on the backseat, where he eyed Mr. P. with some curiosity as though the cat, like me, wanted to know if he'd found out anything new. Elvis was up to date on everything related to the case. I talked to him about things. Maybe it was a little weird, but it was way less strange than walking around the apartment talking to myself, I reasoned.

I was fairly certain Mr. P. didn't have anything to share. If he had, he would have been quick to tell me what he knew. And it turned out I was right.

We were about halfway to the shop when Rose asked about my evening. I told her about having dinner with Gram and John and shared what I'd learned about Gina's family.

"I wish Rosie and I had something to tell you," Mr. P. said behind me. "So far I've found very little to add to what we already know about the fire and Gina Pearson's death. She was home alone. She'd gone on a binge and Mallory's father had taken all three kids to a friend's home. Michael Pearson told the police he hadn't gone back to the house."

"Do you know where he claimed he was?" I asked.

Beside me on the passenger side Rose was already nodding. "He said he just drove around trying to decide what to do. The situation wasn't working for the children. He discovered his phone was dead and by the time he realized and plugged it in the house was on fire."

I flipped on my turn signal. "Obviously the police thought he was lying."

"Judge Neill Halloran had been the Pearsons' neighbor for the five years they'd lived in the house," Mr. P. said. "The judge saw Michael Pearson at the house the night of the fire, and he saw him walking away. He was certain he'd seen Mike turn and look back at the burning house."

"Not an easy witness to discredit," I said.

Rose nodded. "There was no question about his integrity. Neill Halloran was known for his fair and ethical behavior on the bench. He's the last person who would lie or misrepresent the facts."

Were we wrong, I wondered. Was Liz's initial reaction about this case the right one?

I slowed down to let the car in front of me make a left turn and glanced at Rose.

"Oh we're not giving up," she said, as though she'd just read my thoughts. "There's something we're not seeing." She put a hand on her chest. "I can feel it."

I turned my attention back to the road.

"Do you think I'm silly?"

I shook my head. "No, I don't." Rose had great instincts. I'd learned to trust them.

"There has to be something we're missing."

"How are we going to find it?" I asked. I looked over at Rose again as I pulled into the store's parking lot.

Her expression turned thoughtful. "Desperate times call for desperate measures," she said.

Chapter 4

It was a busy morning at the shop. There was a customer waiting when we opened, a tourist heading back to New Hampshire looking for a rocking chair she'd seen the day before. It took some maneuvering, but Mr. P. and I managed to get it securely into the back of her SUV, wedged between two suitcases, several shopping bags and an oversized inflatable—and fully inflated—lobster.

"You have very good spatial acuity, my dear," Mr. P. said, as the woman pulled out of the parking lot.

"I guess I do," I agreed, brushing off the front of my jeans. They had sand and bits of dried grass stuck to the denim from when I'd crawled into the back of the customer's car. "I think it comes from all the forts I used to make with Josh when we were kids." Josh was Josh Evans, another summer friend from my childhood and more recently the Angels' lawyer on a couple of occasions.

Mid-morning, Jess dropped in with some pillows she'd made from fabric I'd found in the first storage unit. She was probably my closest friend. Jess had grown up in North Harbor, but we hadn't really known each other, probably because I was a summer kid. We'd gotten close when I put an ad on the music department bulletin board at the University of Maine looking for a roommate. Jess was studying art history and was rarely in the buildings that made up the School of Performing Arts so she insisted it was fate that had brought us together. I think it was the fact that Jess had a crush on a tall, bearded music major that was responsible for her seeing my ad that day. She had been the only person to call because it turned out she'd taken the ad down after she saw it to stop anyone from getting in touch with me before she could.

Jess had a great sense of funky style, and with a sewing machine and a pair of scissors she could make over just about any piece of clothing. Everything she restyled ended up in the clothing shop on the waterfront in which she was part owner. Jess has been making her own clothes since she was a teenager because she's curvy and could never find anything that fit her right.

"These are great," I said, pulling two of the cushions out of the canvas carryall she'd handed me. Jess had cut the fabric into fat triangles and seamed those together to make the cushion covers. They were all a mix of bold colors—red, tangerine, lemon yellow, blue, sea green.

"I did some smaller ones that I was going to keep but I may end up bringing them here instead," she said, pushing her long, dark hair behind one ear.

"Whatever works best for you," I said. "Once we get into fall, people start nesting. These should sell pretty quickly." I stacked the cushions on the cash desk.

Charlotte had gone out back to get two large, ornate picture frames that Avery and I had refinished and turned into bulletin boards. I'd finally decided where I wanted to hang them.

"The Angels have a new case," I said.

"Anyone I know?" Jess asked, picking a stray strand of thread off one of the pillows.

I shook my head. "I don't think so. Their client is a former student of Charlotte's."

"You do realize that Nick is going to have a cow."

"Uh-huh. Liam already pointed that out."

"Oh yeah, I invited him to join us for the jam," she said. Jess and I were pretty much regulars at Thursday Night Jam, aka the jam, at The Black Bear Pub. The house band played old rock and roll and anyone was welcome to sit in for a song or a set.

"Liam or Nick?" I asked.

"Liam. You know Nick will be there unless he's working."

"Is there something going on between you and my brother?"

She laughed. "No." Then she raised one eyebrow, smiled slyly and said," At least not yet."

Her expression went from amused to serious. "Has Mac said when he's coming home?"

I raked a hand back through my hair. "There are things he needs to take care of in Boston. The house hasn't closed yet and there's still a lot of paperwork."

Jess studied me for a long moment and I couldn't really read the expression in her blue eyes. "He'll be back," she finally said. She gave me a hug and left.

Charlotte came in from the workroom then. "Are those the cushions made from the fabric we found in the first storage unit?" she asked, picking one up and turning it over in her hands.

I nodded.

"Jess does lovely work," she said. "I like the pattern. Would you like me to price them and put them out?"

"Yes, to both," I said. "The tags are by the cash register." I pointed to the second floor. "I'll be in my office if you need me."

I headed upstairs but instead of going to my office I went into the tiny staff room for a cup of coffee. I'd sounded defensive when Jess had brought up Mac. That was probably because I hadn't talked to him since Sunday evening. I'd gotten the breakfast text on Monday but nothing more since then. I missed Mac and not just for the dozens of things he handled around the shop. I missed the way he'd help me keep my perspective whenever the Angels had a case. I was fairly certain I was going to need that, especially when Nick found out what was going on.

That afternoon Charlotte, Avery and I went back to the storage unit. I'd just parked the SUV when my phone signaled a text.

It was from Mac. *On my way to the airport. Call you later.*

Airport? I wondered where he was going. If he were coming back to Maine he would have been driving. I read the words again. Mac had said he'd call me later. I'd just have to wait to find out what was going on.

With the storage unit partly empty, it was easier to look at what else was inside. Along a side wall we discovered a dressmaker's dummy, a treadle sewing machine and another box of fabric including some beautiful embroidered pale yellow tulle. Charlotte held up the buttery yellow material. "I'm sure Jess will create something wonderful with this," she said.

As we loaded the large cardboard box into the SUV

it dipped sideway and an old wooden cigar box fell out. Avery picked it up and looked inside. The box was full of beads. "Look at these, Sarah," she exclaimed. "They're beautiful. Some of them have to be really old."

I peered at the contents of the box. Avery was turning beads over in her fingers, making excited little exclamations of surprise. "Would you like to have them?" I said.

She stared at me. "Seriously?"

"Yes."

The teen's eyes lit up and she flung one arm around me in an exuberant hug. "I'd love them! Thank you." She put the box on the front seat, gave the top a little pat and then bounded back inside.

Charlotte smiled. "I'd love to have that child's energy and enthusiasm."

"Maybe you should start having a green smoothie every morning," I said with a teasing grin as I righted the tipped-over carton of fabric.

Charlotte put her hands on her hips. "I will when you do," she said with an equally teasing gleam in her eye.

I laughed. I loved my coffee and everyone knew that.

It was late afternoon before we returned to the shop. The SUV was packed full and so was the trailer. We'd been able to get both the sewing machine and the dressmaker's dummy onto the trailer through a combination of effort and luck. I was certain both would sell in the shop. Those sort of older items were always popular.

Mr. P. came out to help us unload everything else. "How was your afternoon?" I asked as we pulled another box of mason jars out of the back of the car.

"Nothing we couldn't handle," he said. "We kept the ship on course."

"I wouldn't expect anything less," I said.

With the four of us working together it didn't take long to unload everything except the sewing machine and the dressmaker's form. Mr. P. stood next to the trailer. I could tell by the way he was squinting at the last two items he was calculating whether the four of us could lift them out. I had a feeling that would be harder than loading them had been.

"There are a couple of pieces of plywood we can use as a ramp," he said. "And we have the wheeled dolly. We can definitely move the sewing form. Maybe the sewing machine as well."

I hesitated.

"Without anyone dislocating anything, my dear."

Avery and I hauled out the plywood and the dolly, and to my surprise we managed to get everything into the garage with less exertion than I'd expected.

"I'm glad you were here," I said to Mr. P. "I wouldn't have thought to use the plywood and the dolly. Thank you."

He smiled. "It's just physics, my dear, but you're welcome."

I sent the others inside, locked the old garage, unhitched the trailer, and pulled the SUV into its usual spot. I headed in hoping I'd find that there was one of Rose's molasses oatmeal cookies left in the staff room. Instead I stepped into the shop and learned exactly what Rose had meant when she'd said desperate times called for desperate measures.

Nick was standing in the middle of the room. Rose was with him.

I walked over to them. "Hi," I said. Rose was looking

very pleased with herself. Nick, on the other hand, didn't look like the top of his head was about to blow off the way he usually did when the Angels had a case. I wondered what the heck was going on.

"Hello, dear," Rose said. "How did you make out? Did you find anything interesting in the storage unit?" She gave me a guileless look that might have fooled some people but didn't fool me for a second.

"A couple of things," I said. "I found a box of old beads that I let Avery have. Charlotte discovered another box of those canning jars. Anything interesting happen here while we were gone?"

"As you can see, Nicolas dropped in," she said, patting his arm with one hand. He towered over Rose but there was no question which one of them was in control of the situation. "And he had some information to share about Gina Pearson's death." She gave him her sweet, little old lady smile. "But I'll let him tell you. I need to get Alf a cup of tea. He must be parched." She hurried away

I looked at Nick. "I didn't expect to see you here," I said.

"I didn't expect to be here," he said with a smile.

Nick Elliot was tall, well over six feet, built like a big teddy bear only with muscles instead of padding. He had sandy hair and the same brown eyes and warm smile as his mother. When I looked at him I could sometimes still see the shaggy-haired, wannabe musician I'd had a crush on when we were teenagers. I couldn't remember a time when Nick hadn't been in my life and he and Liam had been friends since they were seven.

Nick worked as an investigator for the state medical examiner. He had a PhD in criminal psychology. He had worked as an EMT to put himself through school and Charlotte had harbored a not-so-secret hope that he'd go to med school.

"So what exactly is this information Rose is talking about?" I asked, walking him over to the front window, where there was a bit more privacy.

"I talked to the current medical examiner. She pulled up the file on Gina Pearson's autopsy—it was done by her predecessor—and Claire concedes it might—*might*—be possible that the injuries on Pearson's neck, which the old medical examiner had attributed to an earlier suicide attempt, were in fact made in some other fashion."

I held up a hand as the meaning of his words sank in. "Wait a minute. Are you saying Gina Pearson was strangled?" I stared at him, flabbergasted.

He swiped a hand over his mouth. "No one is saying for certain that's what happened. Claire isn't willing to alter the cause of death at this point. And the body was cremated."

"But it could have happened."

"Yes."

I studied his face. "And you think it did," I said. I didn't phrase the words in the form of a question.

He was silent so long I didn't think he was going to answer, but finally he nodded.

I looked down at my feet to hide a smile but Nick noticed. "Yes, I am on the same side as Rose Jackson. Go ahead and laugh."

"I'm not laughing at you," I said.

"Yes. You are."

"Rose called in that favor you owed her, didn't she?"

Several weeks before, Rose had conspired to set me

up so Nick and I could talk after we'd had an argument. I remembered him showing up in the shop's parking lot, wearing a suit because he'd been in court, pulling off his sunglasses with a tentative smile.

"I conspired with Rose, Sarah," he'd said. "That should tell you how much I want to fix this thing between us."

Nick had looked so earnest standing there that I couldn't help laughing. "Now you owe her," I'd told him.

"Which shows just how important this is to me. Please, tell me what I can do to fix things."

And in the end, we had fixed things.

I sidled up to Nick now, bumping his hip with mine. "So was it worth it now that you have to pay up?"

He smiled at me. "Absolutely."

Nick and I had a volatile relationship at times, but things were good between us right now and I was glad. I'd known Nick all my life and I loved him like a brother.

There wasn't really anything more to say. Nick said he'd do a little more digging around and left. Liz came to pick up Avery, and Rose and Mr. P. headed out with them as well. I dropped Charlotte off and Elvis and I headed home.

My house was an 1860s Victorian that had been divided into three apartments somewhere around thirty years ago. It hadn't been in very good shape, at least cosmetically, when I bought it, but it had good bones. Dad, Liam and I had done most of the work on my main-floor apartment and Gram and John's second-floor one. Mom had helped decorate with yard sale chic. She had a great eye for color. For a long time the third small apartment at the back of the house had stayed empty. It was where my parents or Liam stayed when they came to visit. Then, when the lease on Rose's apartment at Legacy Place hadn't been renewed, Avery had suggested Rose move in. Rose had turned down Mr. P.'s offer to move in with him. Originally she was going to stay only until she found somewhere else to live, but having her close by had worked out a lot better than I'd expected. We respected each other's privacy and I liked having a constant source of cookies close by.

I glanced up at the second floor as I pulled into the driveway. There were no lights on in Gram's apartment, which meant I was on my own for supper. Luckily I'd made shepherd's pie over the weekend—following Rose's instructions to the letter. I stuck it in the oven to heat while I changed my clothes and put a load of laundry in the washer.

My kitchen, living room and dining room were one big, open space with tons of light from the double bay windows at the front of the house. My bedroom overlooked the backyard, which would have been nothing but grass if it hadn't been for Gram and Rose. Instead there was a raised flowerbed full of perennials and two hanging baskets by the back door.

I wandered around the apartment, straightening a cushion on the couch, picking up a clump of cat fur from the floor, lining up my shoes. I couldn't stop thinking about what I learned from Nick. Had someone actually murdered Gina Pearson and then set the Pearson house on fire? Could Mike Pearson have done that? Was *that* why he didn't want us digging into things?

I wished Gram and John were home. Or Rose. I'd tried Liam earlier but I hadn't heard back from him.

Probably in another "meeting." And I knew Jess had a date.

Elvis was at the top of his cat tower. I stroked the top of his head. "Liam is right," I said. "Everyone does have a more exciting life than I do."

The cat rolled over on his back and began to move his paws in the air as though he were doing some kind of feline aerobics routine. The message seemed to be, *Speak for yourself.*

The shepherd's pie was good. Against all the evidence, Rose was actually teaching me how to cook. I gave Elvis a tiny taste of the meat and vegetables in their tomato sauce and he licked his whiskers.

"You're welcome," I said.

It was about quarter to nine when I settled on the sofa with the remote and the cat beside me. I was about to turn on the TV when there was a knock at the door. Elvis immediately looked at me. "Oh, you want me to get that," I said.

He wrinkled his nose at me and made a low murp as I got up. Sometimes I thought sarcasm was wasted on that cat. Other times I wasn't so sure.

I was hoping it was Gram at the door, maybe with cookies? Or Rose with cookies. It turned out to be Nick with a box of microwave popcorn and two bottles of Maine root beer. Not cookies but close enough.

"Hi," he said. "Are you doing anything?"

Elvis meowed loudly from the couch.

"As you just heard, no, we're not." I opened the door wider. "C'mon in."

Nick made popcorn while I opened the root beer. "Do

you have any real butter?" he asked, opening my refrigerator door and peering inside.

"As a matter of fact, I do. Rose insists on it for making
cookies." I pointed. "Second shelf."

He grabbed the butter, straightened up and closed
the door. "You made cookies?"

"Sort of," I said, suddenly feeling a little defensive
about my culinary efforts. "I mean I did all the work,
but Rose was at my elbow the entire time."

"And?"

I held out both hands. "And as you can see my apartment is still standing and the cookies were pretty darn
good, if I say so myself."

Nick smiled. "Good for you. Next time save me one."

"I will," I promised. I actually had saved him a cookie.
I'd saved him six. I'd put them in the freezer so I wouldn't
eat them and then discovered that frozen cookies can be
defrosted pretty quickly in the microwave.

Nick and I settled on the sofa with the popcorn on
his lap and Elvis on mine.

"Have you come up with anything else on the Pearson case?" I asked.

The smile faded from his face. "I spoke to an old
friend who's an arson investigator down in Portland
and got him to take a quick look at the original arson
investigator's report on the fire." There was a moment
of silence filled only by the ticking of my kitchen clock.

"And?" I prompted.

"It's possible that Gina Pearson started the fire, but
given the amount of alcohol that would have been in
her system at the time he said he found it hard to believe
she did."

I sighed. "Nick, she was an alcoholic who had been in rehab more than once. She would have had a higher tolerance for alcohol than a lot of people."

Nick nodded. "I told him that. He wouldn't commit to anything on the record—and I can't blame him when it wasn't his case or even his jurisdiction—but he told me that it was possible that she was just too drunk to have started that fire."

"Could the fire have been an accident?" I seemed to have fallen into the role of devil's advocate, which was something Nick usually took on.

He made a face, his mouth pulling to one side. "No," he said. "There's evidence that the fire was set."

I pushed my hair back off my face, tucking it behind one ear. "So if someone else started that fire that's more evidence Gina Pearson was murdered."

Nick nodded. "Yes."

I stared at the ceiling, feeling a little numb. "So now what?" I asked.

"I was thinking about talking to Michelle when she gets back to see if she knows anything, but I'd have to tell her why I was asking."

Like Nick, Michelle wasn't exactly enthusiastic about the Angels getting involved in police business.

"She's going to find out at some point," I said, reaching for the popcorn. Elvis shifted on my lap. He seemed to like the smell of the popcorn more than anything. It was probably all the butter Nick had drenched it with.

"I know," he said. "I just don't know how she'll take finding out that for once I agree with Rose."

I pressed my lips together so I wouldn't laugh, but it didn't work. "I'm sorry," I said. "I shouldn't be laughing but who would have thought that you using Rose to apologize to me would lead to this."

"I do see the irony of me being on the same side as Rose and my mother when in the past I was butting heads with them."

"I guess you can teach an old dog new tricks," I said. Elvis lifted his head and looked around. "Figure of speech," I told him, stroking his fur.

"Rose is very observant and Mom has very good instincts about people," Nick said. "And if you tell either of them I said that I will never buy you another plate of chips and salsa as long as I live."

I made a show of pretending to zipper my lips together. Nick grinned and threw a piece of popcorn at me. I grabbed it midair and ate it.

"So what happens now?" I asked, settling back against the couch again. I was surprised by how much information Nick had gotten in a few hours although I really shouldn't have been. If Rose was like a pit bull in sensible shoes when she set her mind to something, the same could be said for Nick, except he was larger and had a little stubble.

"I can't just ignore what I've learned," he said. "I'm going to talk to Claire again and I am going to tell Michelle what's going on as soon as she gets back from seeing her mom. Maybe she'll be open to taking a second look at the case."

"You know the Angels aren't just going to sit around and do nothing."

He nodded. "I know. Between Mr. P.'s computer skills and the fact that my mother, Rose and Liz know everyone in town, maybe we'll get something else we can use."

I noticed he'd said "we" twice in that sentence. I didn't point it out.

Nick's head was on my shoulder and I thought how comfortable it was, the two of us on my couch, sharing a big bowl of popcorn as if we were a couple. Except we weren't a couple, no matter how hard Charlotte and Rose especially had all but shoved us at each other. I'd come to see that there was no heat between us—not the way there had been when we were teenagers, which may have been mostly because, hey, *back then we were teenagers*.

I remembered a conversation I'd had with Liz just a few weeks ago.

When Nicolas walks into a room after you haven't seen him for a while, do your toes curl? she'd asked. She'd gone on to explain. *Sarah, a lot of people say passion is overrated but I disagree. That kind of heat between two people can keep you warm when life gets cold. And it's going to get cold.*

I took a deep breath and let it out. *Ask him*, a little voice in my head said. "Nick do your toes curl when you see me?" It was a bit easier to get the words out when I couldn't see his face.

"What do you mean, do my toes curl?" He shifted his head so he was looking up at me.

I noticed he hadn't said yes. I leaned down and kissed him. "How did that feel?" I asked. His mouth was warm and the stubble on his face scraped my chin.

He smiled. "Good."

"You had more enthusiasm for the root beer," I said.

He sat up. "Sarah, what's going on?"

"Nothing," I said. "That's the thing. We've both been back in town more than a year and absolutely nothing has happened, despite the best efforts of Flora, Fauna and Merryweather."

He smiled at my comparing his mother, Rose and Liz to the good fairies in *Sleeping Beauty*. "I've known you all my life, Nick, and I can't imagine it without you in it, but—"

"—but you want the birds to fly over the heather."

I couldn't believe he'd remembered. He was talking about the movie *Wuthering Heights*, the old black-and-white version with Merle Oberon and Laurence Olivier. We'd watched it at a library film festival the same infamous summer that I'd boldly French-kissed him. Nick had joked at the way the filmmaker had cut to birds rising up from the windswept moors—the birds flying over the heather—when the two main characters, Cathy and Heathcliff, were intimate. He'd thought it was silly. I'd thought it was so wildly romantic

He studied my face for a long moment. "You want passion."

"Yes, I do," I admitted. "And I want it for you, too." I couldn't help feeling a little sad. Nick and I together would have made so many people so happy.

Nick continued to look at me and I had the feeling he knew what I was thinking. He put his arm around me and I leaned against him. "Do you really think that kind of thing is out there?" he asked, his voice a bit husky all of a sudden.

I thought about Mac. I'd had no idea I'd miss him so much.

"I hope so," I said.

Chapter 5

Nick stayed for another half hour. We talked about the shop, about his job, about what it was like to share living space with Liam. We both agreed my brother used his abnormally long monkey arms to stick things in out-of-the-way places just to be annoying.

Finally Nick stretched and said, "I should get going."

"Thanks for the popcorn," I said.

He grinned. "Thanks for the half a pound of butter I put on it."

I followed him to the door. "Will I see you at the jam Thursday night?" I asked.

"Of course," he said. "We're friends, Sarah. We're family and we always will be." He gave me a hug, kissed the top of my head and left.

I straightened the sofa cushions, rinsed the two root beer bottles and put them in the recycling, and dumped the few unpopped kernels of popcorn into the trash. I thought about my neighbor, Tom, once telling Rose and me that when he was a boy those leftover kernels were called "old maids."

"Such a terrible way to have referred to anyone," he'd said. Then he'd smiled. "My dear mother once chastised my very stern and formidable grandfather for using the term when referring to his sister—who, for the record, had no interest in any husband or any man, for that matter. 'Then what would you call a woman of a certain age who had no husband?' he'd asked. 'Lucky,' my mother retorted."

"I think I would have liked your mother," Rose had said.

Tom had smiled at her. "I suspect the two of you would have been as thick as thieves," he'd said in his warm Scottish burr.

"Is that what I am?" I asked Elvis. "An old maid?"

The cat seemed to actually think about my words and then to my amusement vigorously shook his head. I leaned down and picked him up. "Thanks for the vote of confidence," I said, kissing the top of his furry black head. Somewhere in his previous life Elvis had learned the art of listening, cocking his head to one side, focusing his green eyes on the speaker's face and making encouraging little murping sounds to keep the conversation going. Maybe that was why I tended to talk to him like he was a person.

He leaned over now and licked my chin and I set him on the floor again.

By the time I'd gotten the coffeemaker ready for the morning and turned off the light, Elvis had disappeared. That probably meant he was in the bedroom starting his nighttime routine, which mostly involved an elaborate face-washing followed by the two of us pretending he wasn't going to sleep on the chair by the window.

Twenty minutes later Elvis was settled in his chair watching some kind of car chase on TV while I searched for the mate to the one slipper I'd found by the bed. "Did you take my slipper?" I asked the cat.

He gave me a blank look. That didn't mean he hadn't had anything to do with my missing slipper. Just that he was really good at not looking guilty.

The phone rang. I looked at the caller ID and smiled. It was Mac. "Hi," I said, dropping onto the bed and tucking my feet underneath me so I was sitting cross-legged. "It's good to hear your voice."

"Yours, too," he said. "I'm sorry I didn't call earlier. I was stuck in a meeting."

"Where are you? Is everything okay?"

"Everything is good. I'm in Montana. I had an unex-pected offer on a small piece of property that Leila and I own—owned. We bought it on impulse on our hon-eymoon. It's really the last big thing I need to take care of as far as the estate goes. The agent thought it would take a while to sell so the offer was a surprise."

Montana. I pictured snowcapped mountains and endless blue sky. "Did you think about keeping it?" I glanced over at the closet and noticed the toe of my missing slipper sticking out under the edge of the door.

"No. It was past time to sell. I have different dreams now." He cleared his throat. "I probably could have handled all the paperwork from Boston but it just seemed faster to fly out and deal with it all in person."

The sleeve of my flannel pajamas had fallen down

over my hand and I pushed it back up my arm. "When are you coming back?" I asked. "I mean back to Boston."

"In the morning." He yawned. "Sorry. Changing time zones has gotten to me."

Elvis glanced over at me and yawned as well. Was I putting people—and cats—to sleep?

"Tell me about the Angels' new case," Mac said.

"How did you know they have a case?"

"I had a text from Alfred."

That shouldn't have surprised me. The two men had gotten to be friends, despite the fact that Mr. P. was old enough to be Mac's father. And they had a lot more in common than would seem apparent at first glance. They were both smart, resourceful, kindhearted and deeply loyal.

I gave him the short version of what was going on—including Nick's role.

"So let me get this straight: Nick and Rose are working together?"

"Yes they are," I said. "See what happens when you leave us for so long?"

There was a silence that went on a bit too long and then Mac asked, "What's next?"

I shook my head even though he couldn't see me. "I don't know. If Gina Pearson's death wasn't an accident . . ."

"You're thinking it's possible her husband could have killed her."

I sighed. "I'm just afraid we might end up making things a lot worse for Mallory and her brothers."

"You'll figure it out," Mac said. "You always do and if you need to talk you can call me. Even if it's the middle of the night."

I stifled a yawn of my own. "You might regret saying that."

"I won't," he said. "Get some sleep. I'll talk to you soon."

We said good-bye and it wasn't until after I'd set my phone on the night table that I realized once again he hadn't said anything about when he was coming back to North Harbor.

I got up early and went for a run. Elvis watched me, one eye open, the other half closed as I pulled on a hoodie and tied my running shoes. There were dark clouds overhead and I hoped that wasn't some kind of omen for the day.

Elvis was sitting on a stool at the counter when I got back. He gave me an expectant look that I knew meant he was looking for breakfast—his own and a taste of mine if he could manage to mooch it.

I showered and got dressed. Then I made breakfast, Greek yogurt, berries and one of Rose's apple raisin muffins for me, Tasty Tenders for Elvis.

I decided to leave early for the shop. Rose wasn't working until after lunch so I could head out whenever Elvis was ready and he'd been very pointedly sitting by the door for a good five minutes. When I stepped outside my door I discovered Rose and Mr. P. waiting in the hall. Rose had one of her massive tote bags, which I hoped held cookies or a coffee cake, and Mr. P.'s messenger bag was over his shoulder.

"Good morning, dear," she said. "May Alfred and I ride with you?"

"Merow," Elvis said as he headed for the front door. It seemed to be okay with him.

"Of course you can," I said. "Did you and Charlotte trade shifts?"

"No," she said, shaking her head. She didn't elaborate further.

"Let me take that bag for you," Mr. P. said. Along with my purse and my briefcase I was carrying a bag of vintage pot holders, which I'd brought home to wash and iron.

"Thank you," I said, handing over the brown paper shopping bag. I locked my door and we headed out to the SUV. As usual Rose took the front passenger seat and Elvis joined Mr. P. in the back without complaint. As we drove Rose told me about the film she and Alfred had gone to see at the library the night before, some kind of epic fantasy in French, with subtitles.

It was raining by the time we got to the shop. Liz's car was in the lot and I saw Charlotte in the passenger seat. I looked at Rose. "What's going on?" I asked.

She looked surprised. "It's a strategy meeting. Thanks to Nicolas now we know we have a murder to solve." She held out one hand and I dropped my keys into it. Then she opened the passenger door, popped open the very large, flowered umbrella she'd pulled from her bag and started for the back door. I saw Liz and Charlotte follow her.

Mr. P. put a hand on my shoulder. I turned in my seat to look at him. "Don't worry, Sarah," he said. "Rosie has a plan."

I didn't have the heart to tell him that's exactly what *was* making me worry.

Mr. P. shared his oversized umbrella and we dashed to the back door. I held Elvis inside my coat so he stayed

dry. Rose had already gone up to put the kettle on because this detective agency ran on tea.

We gathered around a long table that I'd been putting
off refinishing because I couldn't decide what to do with
it. It occurred to me that what I should do was give it a
couple of coats of paint and save it for the Angels' office
when it was done. We seemed to have at least one "strategy meeting" in every case they took on. Finally everyone had a cup of tea and Charlotte had sliced the coffee
cake that Rose had brought in her bag.

Rose looked around the table. "Are we all on the same
page?" she asked. Her gaze stopped at me.

"I talked to Nick last night, if that's what you mean,"
I said.

"He told you what the arson investigator told him?"

I nodded.

She broke a slice of the coffee cake in half but didn't
take a bite from either piece. "So the first thing we need
to do is figure out who might have wanted to kill Gina
Pearson."

"How about Mike Pearson?" I said.

Rose shook her head. "Mike Pearson didn't murder
his wife."

I wrapped my hands around my teacup. They were
suddenly cold. "You don't know that, unless there's
something you haven't shared with the rest of us."

Charlotte leaned toward me across the table. "Sarah,
is there something *you're* not sharing with the rest of us?
Why do you think Mike is the killer?"

"I don't necessarily think he is," I said, "but are you
ready if he turns out to be?" This time I was looking
around the table at all of them.

"You're thinking about Mallory and her brothers," Charlotte said.

I nodded. "She came to you to help get her father out of prison. Are you prepared to maybe keep him there for the rest of his life?"

"That's not going to happen," Rose said. It was impossible to miss the certainty in her voice. "If Mike Pearson wanted his wife dead, all he had to do was let her drink herself to death. He didn't need to strangle her."

"He was—he is—a good father," Charlotte added. "When Mallory was my student he didn't miss a single event—not a parent-teacher night, not an awards assembly, not a school play." She twisted the plain gold wedding ring she still wore around her ring finger. "I talked to several teachers who have had Mallory's younger brothers as students. He was the same way with both of them. Does that sound like a man who would murder his wife and set his house on fire?"

It didn't, however I knew that murder wasn't always logical. People did things in the heat of the moment. Charlotte was still looking at me. They all were. I remembered what Nick had said about his mother's insight into people. Could I go forward on the premise that Mike Pearson had not killed his wife, because I *was* part of this investigation? I could protest all I wanted, but I'd get pulled in. I always did. I wasn't as sure about Mike as Rose and Charlotte were but I did trust both their instincts. I could at least give the man the benefit of the doubt. *For now.*

"Okay," I said.

Liz leaned sideways so she was in my line of sight

and waved two fingers at me. "Wait just a minute, missy. Don't you want to know what Alfred and I think?"

"Are your opinions any different from Rose's and Charlotte's?" I asked, reaching for a slice of coffee cake. I could smell cinnamon and brown sugar.

Mr. P. shook his head. "I'm in agreement with both of them," he said.

I popped a bite of the cake in my mouth and raised one eyebrow at Liz.

"I agree with the others, but it's nice to be asked," she said.

"I'll try to remember that," I said, stifling a smile.

"I think for now we should keep what we've learned about Gina's death from Mallory," Charlotte said.

Rose nodded. So did Mr. P.

"Well, of course," Liz said, picking up her cup.

"I agree," I said.

"So do I," a voice said from the far end of the work-room. I turned around. Nick was standing there. He was wearing jeans and his hands were in the pockets of a navy windbreaker. The shoulders of the jacket were damp and so was his hair.

Rose got to her feet. "What exactly is it you think you're agreeing to, Nicolas?" she asked. She wasn't at all intimidated by Nick, and he didn't look intimidated by her, either. Although he really should have been.

"You're going to try to find out who killed Gina Pearson and set that house on fire," he said.

"Does that mean you think she was murdered?" Charlotte said.

Nick nodded. "I do, Mom. And I think I can help."

He looked at Rose and she looked back at him. I felt

like I was watching a pair of gunfighters—the grizzled veteran and the wise-guy kid with something to prove. In this case the grizzled veteran wouldn't shoot the kid's gun out of his hand if he messed up, but there was a possibility that she'd whack him with a loaded tote bag.

"All right then," Rose said. She looked across the table at Mr. P. "Alfred, would you please make coffee?"

"Of course," he said, getting to his feet.

"Nicolas, would you like a piece of coffee cake?" she asked, turning her attention back to Nick.

"I would," he said. "But is this it? Don't you do a group cheer or an all-for-one thing with your hands stacked up on one another's?"

I wasn't sure if he was teasing or partly serious.

"No, we most certainly do not," Liz said, looking at Nick over the top of her glasses to press the point home.

"We could," Rose said. "If it would make Nicolas feel included."

I had gotten up and was getting a chair for Nick. I was careful not to look in his direction, afraid that I'd start to laugh.

"We could, but since we're not a hormone-addled boys' hockey team, we're not." Liz set her cup down on the saucer with a clink as if to make the point that the discussion was settled. "Sarah's getting him a chair. Alfred is making him coffee. He's included Rose. Move on."

"Fine," Rose said, a tiny edge of petulance in her voice.

I set the chair at the table. "Having fun?" I whispered as I passed in front of Nick.

We spent the next few minutes deciding what we were going to do next. Mr. P. offered to see what he could dig up on Gina Pearson's previous trips to rehab.

"I have some connections at the hospital," Liz offered. I knew the Emmerson Foundation had been a generous donor to the Northeastern Medical Center. "I could ask a few questions." In other words, she'd use her considerable charm, and the Emmerson last name, to get answers that otherwise would be a lot harder to find.

Charlotte offered to see if she could pick up any hints about Mike and Gina's relationship from their younger children's teachers.

Nick took a second slice of coffee cake. "I'm going to talk to Claire again to see if I can get her to amend Gina Pearson's official cause of death." I knew very little about the state medical examiner, but Nick seemed to like her. Maybe he could get her to reconsider Gina Pearson's cause of death.

"That would be a big help," Rose said. "Especially if we want Detective Andrews to reopen the case." She was moving around the table gathering plates and cups.

"We want Michelle to reopen the case?" I asked as I got to my feet.

Rose turned to look at me. "Well, yes, dear. Of course we do."

I folded the chair I'd been sitting on and reached for the one Rose had vacated. "Umm, why?"

"Because we need to get Mike Pearson out of jail and the best way to do that is to get the case reopened and then find the person who actually killed his wife." She moved behind me and patted my arm. "And the police do have some resources that we don't. We need to get everyone in the boat rowing in the same direction." She smiled at Nick. He smiled back at both of us.

I knew this whole cooperation, let's-hold-hands-and-sing-Kumbaya thing wasn't going to last but it was kind of entertaining. "What would you like me to do?" I asked Rose.

"Talk to Isabel," she said. "She went to school with Neill Halloran. See what she can tell you about the judge."

I nodded. "What are you going to do?"

"Find a recipe for jam-jams."

"Jam-jams?" I said. Mr. P. had folded his chair and I took it from him, taking all three back to where they'd been hanging on the far wall of the workroom.

"Yes. Melly Halloran, the judge's mother, won a blue ribbon three years running at the state fair for those cookies." She started for the door as though her words had explained everything.

"Hang on a minute," I called after her. "I don't understand what the judge's mother's cookies have to do with us figuring out who killed Gina Pearson."

Rose gave the faintest of sighs and turned back around. "Melly Halloran made prizewinning cookies."

"I get that," I said.

Nick drained the last of his coffee and got to his feet. He grabbed his chair and the empty one beside him and looked at me. I pointed to a spot in front of where I'd hung the folding chairs. He nodded.

"So it stands to reason that Neill Halloran likes jam-jams."

I nodded. "Okay, I'll give you that."

"And since he's a widower it's probably been a while since he's had homemade cookies." She sounded a bit like she was explaining to a three-year-old why it was a bad idea to eat dirt.

"Still with you," I said, although I wasn't sure where the conversation was going.

"So if we show up with a plate of jam-jams he's far more likely to talk to us about why he says he saw Mike Pearson after the fire started when we know he couldn't have."

"Got it," I said.

Mr. P. was already on his way to the sunporch.

Charlotte gestured toward the shop. "I'll go open up," she said.

I nodded. "Thanks. I'll be there in a minute."

"Have a good day," she said to Nick.

He smiled and raised one hand. "You, too, Mom." He dipped his head as he moved past me. "You have a good day, too, Jam-Jam," he said with a grin.

Liz was still standing by the table. She walked around the end of it and came over to me. "Could you stop by this evening?" she asked. "I mean, if you don't have plans." She gave me a guileless look.

"I don't," I said, ignoring that little comment about my dating life—or lack thereof. "What's up?"

"Michelle will be back soon and there are a couple of things I need to talk to you about before that happens."

I nodded. "Okay."

Liz glanced at her phone and then tucked it back in her purse. She looked up to see that I was still looking at her. "What?" she said. "Do I have spinach from one of Avery's drink-this-and-you'll-live-forever smoothies?" She shuddered.

"No," I said, linking my arms through hers and starting for the door. "I was just thinking that you're a good person. You didn't have to help Michelle try to clear her father's name."

"Yes, I did," Liz said, her expression serious. "When I first found out what Michelle was doing I was convinced she was wrong. Now it's beginning to look like there's a good possibility that I was wrong about Rob Andrews's guilt and I need to know the truth just as much as Michelle does."

I gave her arm a squeeze before letting go. "We'll figure it out," I said.

Liz opened her umbrella and we stepped outside in time to see Nick pulling out of the lot. Liz watched him go with a bemused expression on her face. "I never thought I'd see the day when Nicolas and Rose would be working together," she said. "Talk about strange bedfellows."

"I'm kind of afraid it's not going to last," I admitted.

Liz gave a snort of derision. "Of course it's not going to last. The whole thing is going to explode like a bowl of pudding in a microwave." She shrugged. "So we take our fun where we can get it." She headed for her car. "See you tonight," she called over her shoulder.

It turned out to be a busier day than I expected. A bus full of concertgoers on the way to Boston to see James Taylor stopped in. I sold two guitars, all but one of Michelle's pillows and all of Avery's map pails. And our collection of old vinyl records was seriously decimated.

Rose had gone home to work on her cookies when Avery arrived for her shift. Mr. P. had stayed behind to do more digging into Gina Pearson so he drove home with Elvis and me.

"Any luck?" I asked.

"I'm not sure," he said, pushing his glasses up his nose. "Gina Pearson was in rehab three times in two years. Between the first and second trips she was in an accident that seriously injured a teenage girl."

I exhaled loudly. "That's bad." I shot Mr. P. a quick glance. "Did she do any jail time?"

He shook his head. "No. She received a suspended sentence, community service and a court-mandated return visit to rehab."

"Which I'm guessing didn't work." I stopped at the corner and looked both ways before turning.

"Sadly, it didn't," he said.

"What happened to the teenager she hit?" I asked.

"She's doing well now. But it hasn't been easy. Her name is Hannah Allison. She was only fifteen at the time of the accident. According to what Elizabeth learned the doctors thought they might have to amputate part of her leg."

I grimaced at the thought.

"It seems she's a big Patriots fan," Mr. P. continued. "A couple of the players went to see her when she was a patient at Boston's Children's Hospital and they stayed in touch. That kept her story in the news."

"I'm surprised Gina didn't get any jail time."

"I think it helped that a former judge spoke on her behalf."

"Not Judge Halloran?" I shot him a quick look.

He nodded. "One and the same, my dear."

"So the judge speaks up in Gina's defense and later is the same person who ties her husband to her death," I said. "That's an awfully big coincidence." I slowed down to let the car in front of me make a left turn. From the corner of my eye I saw a hint of a smile on Mr. P.'s face.

"You know how Rosie feels about coincidences," he said.

I couldn't help smiling, too. "The same way she feels about fat-free brownies. She doesn't care for either one of them."

I pulled into the driveway. "I need to talk to Gram about the judge as soon as I can," I said.

"That could be very helpful," Mr. P. said, reaching for his messenger bag, which was at his feet.

"Maybe we can figure out what really happened to Gina Pearson," I said as we headed for the door.

"I have no doubt about that," Alfred said. "You have a lovely evening." He patted my arm and started for Rose's apartment.

It wasn't until I was inside my own place that I realized I'd said "we." *Maybe we can figure out what really happened.*

I was part of the investigation no matter what I said, no matter how much I *said* I didn't want to be. Like Nick, I was part of the team.

After supper Elvis headed for the bedroom. The cat was a *Jeopardy!* junkie, another holdover, I surmised, from his previous life. Monday through Friday the cat faithfully watched the game show. Somehow he seemed to know it was just a weekday thing.

No one was certain whether Elvis had been abandoned or whether he had wandered away from his previous owner. He'd just appeared one day down along the harbor front and after spending some time mooching meals at several different restaurants and charming pretty much everyone he met, the cat had come home with me. Elvis was a very social cat. Customers who had been in the store before looked for him the moment they came through the door.

I headed for the bedroom myself, turned on the television and made sure it was set to turn off once *Jeopardy!* was over. My cat watching one game show was okay, but anything more than that would just be weird.

Liz had the kettle on when I got to her house. I'd stopped at McNamara's and managed to snag a couple of lemon tarts for us.

"I saved them for you," Glenn McNamara said as he rang them up along with a blueberry muffin for my breakfast in the morning.

I frowned at him across the counter. "How did you know—" I stopped. "Never mind," I said. "Liz called, didn't she?"

He grinned. "This morning."

"My favorite. How thoughtful," Liz said when I handed her the small cardboard box containing the tarts.

I resisted the urge to roll my eyes.

Liz made the tea and we sat at her kitchen table. "Where's Avery?" I asked.

"Working on a class project with a couple of friends." She put one of the tarts on her plate. "That reminds me. Do you still have that box of flowerpots? You didn't give it away, did you?"

I shook my head. "No. Did you want them for something?"

"Avery has an idea. She says she can make them a lot

more interesting." She cut the lemon tart in half. "All I can tell you is that it seems to involve black paint and cheesecloth."

I took a sip of my tea. "She might as well have at them," I said. "I'd be lucky to get a couple of dollars for the whole box."

"Thank you," Liz said. She took a bite of her pastry and gave me a blissful smile.

I put the other tart on my plate. "So tell me what you found out. You said you were going to talk to Wilson and a couple of people who were on the board back when Michelle's dad was running the Sunshine Camp." Liz was digging into the history of the summer camp and the Emmerson Foundation itself under the guise of putting together a book about the foundation. What she was really doing was looking for evidence that Rob Andrews hadn't embezzled money from the summer camp.

"I didn't find out a damn thing." She shook her head in annoyance. "I didn't get anywhere with Wilson. He dismissed the entire thing as self-indulgent."

Liz and her brother often clashed over the foundation. She claimed he still held a bit of a grudge because their grandfather had put Liz in charge of the charity when he stepped down instead of Wilson. Abernathy Emmerson had apparently been a very progressive man for his time.

"What about the board members you talked to?"

"Neither one of them had anything useful to offer." She picked up the knife and cut the remaining half a tart into two pieces and immediately ate one. Then she held up a finger as something occurred to her.

I waited.

"There was one thing," she said finally. "David Jacobs, who'd been a board member the longest, said he still found it hard to believe that Rob Andrews had embezzled the money."

"Did he say why?"

"Just that Rob seemed to genuinely care about the kids that came to the camp." She made a face. "For a minute I had the urge to smack him with my purse. Why in heaven's name didn't he say something at the time?"

I got up for the teapot and refilled both of our cups. "It wouldn't have made any difference," I said. "The case against Michelle's father was pretty much airtight."

Liz shook a finger at me. "That in itself should have been a red flag," she said. "There was too much evidence. It was too damn easy. Rob Andrews was a smart man. He wouldn't have been that careless."

I sighed. "I know. The same thought's occurred to me."

Just recently Liz had unearthed some of the minutes of the board meetings from the time period when Rob Andrews ran the Sunshine Camp. The only incongruity we'd found was passing mention of several projects that then seemed to disappear without any explanation. There hadn't been any money attached to those projects but the lack of information on them anywhere in the foundation records rankled Liz.

"Did you ask Wilson about those proposed projects we can't seem to track down?" I asked, taking a bite of my own tart. I could see why they were Liz's favorites. The pastry was crisp and flaky and the filling was lemony with just a hint of sweetness.

Liz looked so elegant sitting there with her tea, legs crossed, not a hair out of place, but there was nothing elegant about the snort she made in response to my question.

"He claims he doesn't remember them," she said. "And he probably doesn't. Wilson has never been a details person. No one else seemed to know what I was talking about, either."

"Do you really think these projects are connected in some way to Rob Andrews?" I asked.

She shook her head. "I don't know. What I do know is that back then there were things going on that I *didn't* know about. So maybe I didn't know everything about Rob Andrews, either."

Chapter 6

"What about Mike Pearson?" I asked.

"What about him?" Liz said.

"Is it possible he might know anything?"

Liz shrugged. "I doubt it. He was just a summer student for one year."

I shifted in my chair, pulling one leg up underneath me. "What was he like back then?"

She eyed me across the table. "Are you asking what he was like as an employee or are you asking if I saw any indication that someday he'd walk away from a burning house with his wife's body inside?" One eyebrow went up. "I know you're not one hundred percent convinced that Michael had nothing to do with his wife's death, Sarah."

"I know that you and Rose and Charlotte believe in him," I said, "and I trust your judgment." She opened her mouth to say something and I held up my hand. "I'd still feel better with some kind of evidence. There are three kids who've already lost the only mother they knew. I don't want to see them lose their dad, too."

"It won't happen," Liz said. Her expression turned thoughtful. "To answer your question, I remember Michael as being young, keen and interested in everything. It didn't matter what job he was given, he never gave anything less than his best. He always did a bit more than he was asked but it wasn't in a just-trying-to-get-ahead kind of way. If you want to know more about Michael you should talk to Elspeth. They spent a fair amount of time together that summer."

"I might do that," I said. There was one tiny bit of tart left on my plate. I ate it. "So are we going to talk about the elephant in the room?" I asked.

Liz made a show of looking around the kitchen. "And which elephant would that be?"

"John," I said.

The lines around her mouth tightened. John Scott had been the youngest member of the board of the Emmerson Foundation during Rob Andrew's tenure at the Sunshine Camp. Back then he'd also been Bill Kiley's grad student. The late William Kiley had been a very well-respected history professor and Liz's first husband.

"C'mon, Liz. John and Gram are settled and we need to tell John what's going on. You know he's trustworthy and he's way more likely to remember things from those board meetings than anyone else is."

"I have talked to him a couple of times under the pretext of working on the so-called history of the foundation, but all I've really gotten is just general reminiscences. And I hate to put him in the middle of something."

"There isn't anything to put him in the middle of," I said. Liz's expression was troubled. "Or is there something you aren't telling me?"

For a moment she didn't say anything, then she sighed softly. "I need you to give me your word you won't tell anyone, not John, not Isabel and for now, not Michelle."

I felt a sinking feeling in the pit of my stomach but I nodded. "I promise." I knew if I didn't, Liz wouldn't tell me anything.

"I think there's money missing from the foundation itself. Going back years."

"How many years?"

She rubbed the space between her eyebrows with two fingers. "Maybe as far back as Rob Andrews's time."

Now my stomach felt like it was doing somersaults. John Scott, just like his mentor, Bill Kiley, had been a history professor, but John's area of expertise was American business, specifically the private financial system and its management. His undergrad degree was in business, not history. That was why Liz had wanted him to join the board of the Emmerson Foundation in the first place.

"I've known John for a long time. He's not a thief. He's a man of integrity. In fact, I'll stake my own integrity on that. I don't want to open a can of worms and dump the mess in his lap."

It was a metaphor that sounded more like it should have come from Rose, but I knew what she meant.

"Do you think this could be connected to Michelle's father?" I asked.

"Seems like too much of a coincidence not to be," Liz said.

I thought back to my earlier conversation about coincidences with Mr. P. "More proof that Rob was framed then."

Liz nodded. "I think it's a possibility. I may as well tell you that Channing has found a good forensic accountant who is going over years of the books. It's going to take time but I hope that will get us some answers." She narrowed her gaze at me. "And don't go getting ideas, missy. This is business only."

Channing Caulfield, who on occasion Charlotte would refer to by his childhood name of Chucky, just to tease Liz, had carried a torch for Liz for a long time and he'd helped with foundation business for years. The former bank manager still did some consulting for an investment firm and had also helped out on a couple of the Angels' recent cases. Liz insisted she had no romantic interest whatsoever in the man but I suspected she liked him a little more than she was admitting. Since she'd been butting into my love life for years I got a kick out of teasing her about Channing. As I'd pointed out to her, lots of women would consider him a catch. He had lots of hair and, as far as I could tell, all of his original teeth.

"So let's just keep this possible missing money between us—you, me and Channing—for now," I said. "The whole idea of a book about the foundation is a good cover. We can do more digging."

Liz nodded. "There were five other people on the board. Talmadge Dixon is dead but the others are around and more or less in their right minds. And I should get in touch with Marie."

"Who's Marie?" I asked.

"Marie Heard. She was Wilson's assistant for years. She took notes at all the meetings and I'm pretty sure she helped Rob with camp business on occasion. Marie started at the foundation when my grandfather was still there—straight out of secretarial school, as they called it back then. She probably knew better than anyone how things worked."

"We should talk to her." I pulled out my phone to see if I could find a number for the woman.

Liz got to her feet and carried her plate and cup over to the sink. "Marie retired and moved to Arizona. I asked Wilson, but he lost touch with her. I have no idea how to track her down."

"I do," I said. "Ask Mr. P. to look for her under the guise of wanting to interview her for the book project."

"That's a good idea," she said. "And I'm going to tell people that you're helping me with this whole thing." She made a face. "I hate lying but for now I need to."

I got up and took my own dishes over to the counter. "By the time we're done we're probably going to have a lot of stories and information about the Emmerson Foundation. I think you *should* consider a book." I smiled at her. "Then, technically, none of what we've been saying actually would be a lie."

"I like the way you think," Liz said, giving me a big smile in return.

I wasn't 100 percent sure I should be flattered by her vote of confidence.

Chapter 7

I got home to find Elvis snoozing on top of his cat tower. He opened one green eye, looked at me and then closed it again. I'd noticed lights on upstairs in Gram's place. I decided to call her and see if she was busy. I needed to ask her about the judge, and if John was home I could start sounding him out about the foundation.

"Hi, Gram," I said when she answered. "Would you and John like some company?"

"John isn't here," she said. "But Rose is. She made cookies. I'm being her guinea pig. Why don't you join us?"

"I don't want to interrupt anything."

"We're debating the merits of raspberry jelly versus strawberry-rhubarb jam. We could use another opinion."

"I'm on my way," I said. I decided I could wear my slippers up to Gram's. I grabbed my keys and stopped to give Elvis a scratch. "I'm going upstairs for a while," I told him. "Are you coming?"

He lifted his head, seemed to consider the question for a moment, then yawned and rolled over onto his back.

I knocked on Gram's door and then went in. Gram and Rose were in the living room. Gram got to her feet and wrapped me in a hug. "Hello, sweetie," she said.

I was so glad she was finally home. I'd missed her hugs, her smile, the way she thought everything Liam and I did was fantastic.

"You missed your brother," she said as I took a seat on the couch. "He had supper with us."

"Did he say how the plans for the demolition work along the harbor front are going?"

"Slower than he'd like. But he did say he's going to be able to salvage more than he expected."

"I'm glad to hear that," Rose said. "I know most of those buildings that are coming down for the development can't realistically be saved and I'm not one of those old fuddy-duddies who's against any sort of change, but I am glad some things are going to be salvaged. I'd hate to see everything from North Harbor's history just wiped out."

"Me, too," I said. "I know Liam's managed to save a couple of fireplace mantels that are slated for the new hotel." I looked at the coffee table between us. It held three small plates, each with a couple of cookies on them. "So these are the cookies you made?" I asked.

Rose nodded. "There are three batches. I couldn't decide which jam to use, among other things."

"I already told you, use the raspberry jelly," Gram said. "I know there were raspberry canes in the Halloran's back garden."

"There were raspberry canes in the back garden of all the houses on that street back in the day, Isabel," Rose said. She pushed a plate at me. "Try one of these."

I picked up the small jam-filled cookie and took a bite. It was good. Better than anything I could make. "That's good," I said.

"But what's missing?" Rose asked.

I frowned at her. "I didn't say there was anything missing."

"But you're still holding half a cookie and you didn't swoon the way you do when you have one of my chocolate chip cookies."

"I don't swoon when I have chocolate chip cookies," I said a little defensively.

"Yes, you do, dear," Rose said as though there was no point in discussing her assertion. "You take a bite and then you make a little groaning sound."

"I've heard you do that," Gram agreed.

I took another bite of the cookie, trying to figure out what it was that kept me from my so-called swooning. "A little too much molasses," I said finally. I looked at Rose. "I'm not trying to criticize. It's just that the flavor of the molasses seems to be competing with the jam, if that makes any sense."

Rose nodded her approval. "It makes perfect sense." She pushed the second plate at me. "Try one of these."

I picked up one of the cookies and took a bite. The cookie had a crisp outside with a soft inside. This time the molasses flavor was more subtle and didn't overpower the slightly tart strawberry-rhubarb jam filling. "Mmmm, this is really good," I said around a mouthful of cookie.

Rose and Gram exchanged a look.

"I'm not swooning," I said, popping the other half of the cookie in my mouth.

Gram got up and went into the kitchen. She came back with a glass of water. "Here. Cleanse your palate," she said.

I took a drink of water. Then I gestured at the third plate. "Should I try one of those?"

"If you don't mind, dear," Rose said.

I took a bite of the third cookie. "This is good, too," I said after a moment.

She smiled at me. "There's a 'but' coming."

I narrowed my eyes at her in mock annoyance. "Yes. A big butt. Mine, if I keep eating cookies like this."

"A man likes to have something to hold on to," Rose said with a saucy grin.

I put my hands over my ears for a moment and shook my head. "I'm going to just pretend I didn't hear that," I said.

She laughed. "So you'd say number two is your favorite?"

"Yes. The cookie is perfect and so is the jam. Not too sweet. Not too tart."

Rose looked at Gram. "You win," she said.

I was licking jam off my thumb so it took a moment for the significance of her words to sink in. "Wait a minute," I said. "What do you mean, Gram wins? This wasn't a competition, was it?"

They exchanged another look. "Busted," Gram said, raising an eyebrow.

"I'm sorry," Rose said. "We just wanted an unbiased opinion and we didn't want to put you on the spot."

There was still half of the third cookie left. I reached for it. "So who made what?" I asked.

Gram pointed at the first plate. "Rose made those,

but she wasn't really happy with them. We found two other recipes so I tried one and she tried the other."

"So cookie number two was yours?"

She nodded. "Yes. But it wasn't really a fair competition. I was using the recipe that my mother used to make." She turned to Rose. "I still prefer the raspberry jelly for a filling, but I don't see how you could go wrong with the strawberry-rhubarb jam, either."

"I'll get the recipe from you and make a batch in the morning," Rose said.

"Take these ones I just made," Gram said.

"Are you sure?" Rose asked.

Gram nodded. "Of course."

Rose smiled. "I will, then. Thank you."

I leaned back on the sofa, kicked off my slippers and tucked my feet underneath me. "Gram, tell me about the judge. You were friends when you were in school, weren't you?"

She nodded. "We were in the same homeroom in grades 10 and 12." Her expression turned thoughtful. "He's always been a straight arrow, but not a goody two-shoes. For instance, there were parties and some drinking back then. Neill didn't drink but he wasn't judgmental about people who did. He was an A student, president of the student council and co-captain of the hockey team."

"He sounds like he was pretty much perfect," I said.

Gram smiled but there was a tinge of sadness in it. "The bar was set very high for Neill."

"What do you mean?" I asked.

Rose began to nod. "I forgot about Connor Halloran."

"Neill had an older brother, Connor, who died in

Vietnam very early in the war," Gram said. "He left big shoes behind to fill."

Something in her voice told me that Gram had a soft spot for Neill Halloran.

"Did you ever go out with the judge?" I said.

She nodded. "I did."

Rose looked at her in surprise. "I didn't know that, Isabel."

"I still have a few secrets," Gram said.

Rose smiled. "Clearly."

"It was only a couple of dates." Gram turned her attention back to me. "Then I met your grandfather."

From the corner of my eye I could see that all of a sudden Rose was struggling mightily not to laugh.

"What's so funny?" I said.

Rose pressed her lips together, but the bubble of laughter she'd been fighting to hold down got out anyway. She looked at Gram. "Don't tell me you've never told this child how you and Matthew met?"

Gram's cheeks turned pink. "I thought we were talking about Neill Halloran," she said stiffly. "And Sarah isn't interested in how Matthew and I met."

"Yes, I am," I said. "Was it romantic?"

Rose gave a snort of laughter. "Well, your grandfather always said love hit him over the head."

Gram sent her a daggers look.

"Although technically, wasn't it your math textbook?" Rose asked.

I couldn't help laughing now myself. "Gram, what is it with you hitting men over the head?"

Gram looked bewildered. "I haven't been hitting men

over the head," she said. "Other than your grandfather, and he provoked me."

I scrunched up my face at her. "That's not true. You met John when you knocked a book off a shelf at the library and hit him in the head."

"That was an accident," she said indignantly, color flooding her cheeks again. "The book wasn't shelved properly and, on top of that, the shelf was crooked."

"What about Clayton McNamara? You hit him with your book bag."

"First of all I was six. And second he should have ducked. Who doesn't duck when they see a book bag coming at their head?"

Rose was still laughing. "Your grandmother is like the Canadian Northwest Mounted police," she said.

I caught the reference and grinned at her.

"I don't get it," Gram said.

"They always get their man," Rose and I said in unison.

Gram shook her head. "Rose Jackson, you've been a bad influence on my granddaughter. I was gone too long." I knew she wasn't really annoyed. She wasn't any better at hiding a smile than Rose was.

I reached over and grabbed her hand. "Yes you were gone too long and I'm glad you're home. Now tell me more about Judge Halloran."

She gave my hand a squeeze and then let it go. "As I said"—she shot Rose a look—"I went out with Neill a couple of times but nothing came of it and yes, then I met your grandfather. I can promise you that Neill is one of the good guys. He's kind and fair and it makes perfect sense that he tried to help Gina Pearson and that he told the police about seeing her husband the night of the fire. Neill will do the right thing, always."

I gathered up the plates and went out to the kitchen to get a glass of milk. When I came back, I set my glass down and put my arms around my grandmother's shoulders. "Tell me why you hit Grandpa with your math book," I said.

"You're like a dog with a bone," she said, wrinkling her nose at me.

I cocked my head to one side. "Gee, I wonder where I learned that?"

"Sarah should know her family history," Rose said, all innocence.

I took my seat again, folded my hands in my lap and looked expectantly at Gram.

"Fine," she said. "When we were in high school we changed classrooms for different subjects. And at that time there were no lockers so we kept everything in our desks in our homeroom. Your grandfather sat at my desk for his first-period math class."

"You weren't in the same class?" I asked. I'd known my grandparents had met their senior year of high school. I'd just never asked about the details.

"No. I took what you'd call AP math, Matthew was in the regular class."

"He did something, didn't he," I said. I leaned forward. "What was it? Did he draw all over your desk or swipe your pencils?"

"He ate my lunch."

I stared at her. "He *what*?"

"He ate my lunch. It was in my desk. My mother had

made me a bacon sandwich and there were two choco-late chip cookies as well. It was first period and he ate the whole thing. When I confronted him he just shrugged and said he was hungry." Gram smiled at the memory. "I was so angry I hit him with my math text-book and stalked away."

"What happened then?" I asked.

She looked away for a moment. "According to a cou-ple of girls who were standing nearby he turned to his buddies and said, 'I'm going to marry that girl!'"

"Those chocolate chip cookies? They're the ones I make that you like so much," Rose said. "Your grand-mother gave me the recipe."

"So I guess you could say that Grandpa had good taste," I teased.

Rose smiled at my grandmother. "Yes, sweet girl, he definitely did."

Chapter 8

Rose drove in with me in the morning. "Alfred will be in later," she said as she fastened her seat belt. Then she adjusted her sweater, smiled at Elvis and finally focused her attention on me. "You look like you want to say something. What is it?"

I did up my own seat belt and started the SUV. "Did anything Gram said last night about Judge Halloran change your opinion about Mike Pearson's guilt?"

"No," she said without any hesitation. "All we know is that the judge believed he saw Mike. I'm sure he told the police the truth from his perspective. That doesn't mean he isn't wrong." She adjusted the large tote bag she'd set at her feet. "And for the record, I don't have blinders on. I'm just trying to work with the facts we have at the moment."

I pulled out of the driveway and from the corner of my eye I saw Rose pull a notebook and a pen from her bag. "What are you doing?" I asked.

"I'm making a suspect list," she said. "It was remiss

of me not to have done so sooner. And yes, I am putting Mike's name on it."

"Thank you," I said.

"Alfred told me about that car accident Gina had. I think we should add the parents of that young girl she hit."

I nodded in agreement. I didn't have children but if someone had hurt Liam or Gram or Mom or any of them I wasn't sure what I might do in anger.

"Alfred is still checking to make sure Gina didn't have any other accidents."

"Rose, do we know anyone who lives in that neighborhood?" I asked. When I said "we," what I really meant was her and Liz and Charlotte.

The car in front of me slowed down and put its turn signal on. "Mrrr," Elvis said beside me. The cat was a backseat driver no matter where he was sitting in the SUV. He looked over his shoulder when I backed up and checked traffic in both directions at every stop sign.

"I see it," I said.

"Are you looking to talk to the Pearsons' neighbors?" Rose asked.

I shot her a quick glance. "I thought we might get a better sense of what kind of marriage they had. Which might work in my favor or might work in yours."

"I'll ask around," she said.

When we got to Second Chance, Mr. P. was waiting by the back door. If Mac hadn't been in Boston I'm sure we would have found the two of them having coffee. Ever since we'd made the small apartment for Mac up on the second floor above the shop, I'd gotten used to arriving to the coffeepot being on and Mac waiting with a cup for me. It was a chance to go over the upcoming day and talk about longer-term plans for the shop. Now it was usually me who made the coffee and the conversation was with Elvis. He wasn't much for long-term planning.

"I thought you were coming in later," Rose said.

"We could have picked you up." I set Elvis down and unlocked the back door.

"It's all right," Mr. P. said, taking Rose's bag from her. "Sammy dropped me off." He held the door open for us and I gestured for Rose to go ahead of me.

"What were you doing with Sam?" Rose asked.

I'd been wondering the same thing. Sam Newman was like another father to me. He'd been my biological father's best friend. Over the years he'd told me stories and shared photos of my dad, helping to keep him alive. Sam was also the reason I had Elvis. I'd stopped in to see him and discovered him and the cat having breakfast.

"Who's your friend?" I asked.

"That's Elvis," Sam said.

"Why Elvis?"

Sam shrugged. "He doesn't seem to like the Stones, so naming him Mick was kinda out of the question."

Mr. P. was smiling. I recognized that expression. He'd learned something. "I have another possible suspect in Gina Pearson's death. A man named Gavin Pace."

"What's the connection?" I asked.

"Gavin Pace and Gina Pearson had an affair."

"Good heavens," Rose said. "When did this happen?"

"Sometime after her second trip to rehab." Mr. P. flipped on the lights. "They worked together before Gina lost her job."

"Wait a minute," I said. "How does Sam tie in to all of this?"

"It seems that Gavin Pace's wife, Molly—actually, ex-wife now—had some kind of confrontation with Gina at The Black Bear just a few days before the fire. I went to see Sam to ask him about it." Mr. P. nudged his glasses up his nose. "And if you're thinking that Gina was drunk, Sam says she wasn't. According to Sam, Gina was minding her own business and the other woman accosted *her*."

"How did you find out all of this?" I asked as we stepped into the store proper."

He smiled. "Gina Pearson's former coworkers are very talkative."

"I don't suppose anyone mentioned Molly Pace threatening to kill Gina, did they?" Rose asked.

Alfred shook his head. "No, but she did threaten to kill her husband in front of half a dozen witnesses."

"Interesting," Rose said, heading for the stairs. It was pretty clear Molly Pace would be going on her list.

It turned out to be a busy morning. I sold a 1973 Martin D-18 guitar that I'd bought from Clayton McNamara when we'd cleared out his house. The guitar needed work. There was a pick guard scratch and a small back crack, but I felt that I'd given the buyer a decent deal and made a fair profit for myself. I was just about to head upstairs for a late lunch when a woman came in the front door. She stopped and looked around.

"Hi," I said. "Could I help you with something?"

She looked to be in her early forties with dark hair

worn in a short bob and black framed, nerd chic glasses. "I'm looking for Charlotte Elliot," the woman said. "Is she here?"

Charlotte was in the workroom sorting through the box of fabric we'd found at the storage unit. She'd already come in once to show me a couple of 1960s vintage aprons, which had made Avery's eyes light up.

"She is," I said. "I'll go get her for you."

She gave me a tight smile. "Thank you," she said.

Charlotte was at the workbench. She had two tea towel calendars spread out next to the aprons. "Look at this, Sarah," she said. "They're from 1964 and 1967. I had this same one from 1967 in my kitchen when I was first married."

The linen dish towel featured a large orange, green, and yellow rooster atop the months of the year. I was guessing it had been meant more for kitchen décor than for drying dishes.

"Someone will want that," I said. Anything that triggered memories of childhood or the early years of marriage was popular with our customers. I gestured over my shoulder. "There's a woman here to see you."

"Who is it?" Charlotte asked.

I shook my head. "I'm sorry. I forgot to ask her name."

"It's all right," she said. "It's probably one of the parents. I think I told you we're having a book sale at the school next month."

I nodded as we headed for the door. "Why don't you take that box of books that we brought back from the storage place. I mean if you want them. We don't really sell that many books here." As Gram had suspected *A*

Bear Called Paddington had turned out to be a valuable first edition, but the rest of the books were only worth a few dollars each.

Charlotte smiled. "If you're sure, yes. I'd be happy to take them."

She was still smiling as she approached the woman, who had taken only a couple of steps into the store. "Hello," Charlotte said. "I'm Charlotte Elliot. You were looking for me?"

The other woman nodded. "I'm Katy Mueller." She offered her name as though it should mean something to Charlotte. From the slightly confused expression on Charlotte's face I could see it didn't.

Katy Mueller could see it, too. She cleared her throat. "Gina Pearson was my best friend."

"You're here because of Mallory," Charlotte said.

The younger woman nodded. "And Greg and Austin. They're just starting to heal. Nothing good is going to come out of stirring up the past." She twisted the bottom edge of her sleeve with one hand. "Please. Let Mallory down easy and stop your investigation."

"It must have been very painful to lose Gina," Charlotte said. The concern in her voice was genuine.

"Not as painful as it was for the children. Please. What you're doing isn't helping anyone."

Charlotte nodded. "You care about them."

"Of course I do," Katy said, as though she were offended that anyone would think any differently.

"Then you can understand better than a lot of people why it's so important to Mallory to help her father."

Katy took a deep breath and let it out slowly. "I know Mallory doesn't want to believe that Mike left Gina to die in that fire and I'm not saying he wanted that to happen, but he'd given her so many second chances I just don't think he had it in him anymore. And you must have heard about Judge Halloran. He certainly had no reason to lie about what he saw."

"What was Gina like?" Charlotte asked. "I didn't really get a sense of her as a person from Mallory."

"Gina was the only mother Mallory really knew. Her own mother died when she was barely more than a toddler. They were very close until Gina started drinking." Katy stared off into space just past Charlotte's right shoulder as though she was looking for something in the past. Then her gaze came back to Charlotte. "We met in our senior year of high school. I used to call her Goldie because she was one of those golden people for whom everything went right. She fell in love with Mike and he was crazy about her. And Mallory adored her. There was no wicked stepmother stuff. Then she had the boys. And she had a job she really liked. She had everything." She looked away again. "I tried to make her understand that."

"You were a good friend," Charlotte said, her voice gentle as though she were trying to get close to a skittish animal.

Katy shook her head. "It was after she got promoted at work that everything went wrong. She worried about every little detail. She'd come home so stressed out and she started having a couple of drinks to relax. Pretty soon it was more than two. I kept trying to find the right words that would make her realize what she was doing to her children but she only cared about her next drink." She narrowed her gaze at Charlotte. "You're not going to stop this, are you?" she asked, her expression troubled.

"No," Charlotte said. "Mallory asked for my help. I'm sorry. I can't just walk away from her."

"You're making a mistake." Katy's voice was shaky. She lifted a hand and then let it drop. "I have to go." She was out the door before Charlotte could say anything more.

I put a hand on Charlotte's shoulder. "Are you all right?" I asked. Katy's reaction had been unsettling.

She nodded. "I'm fine. But I don't think Gina's friend is."

We started back toward the workroom. "She seems very . . ." It took me a moment to come up with the right word. "Wounded."

"Did you see her face when she spoke about Mallory and her brothers?" Charlotte asked. "It was the only time she even came close to smiling. She obviously cares about them."

"You care about Mallory, too," I said. "That's why you're trying to figure out what really happened to Gina."

"So you don't think this investigation is a mistake?" There was a hint of both a question and a challenge in her voice.

"I never thought it was a mistake," I said. "I didn't— I don't want to see those children hurt because it's hard to look at what we know about Mike Pearson's case and not think that he may have killed his wife. He had motive and he had opportunity." I held up a hand because I knew there was an objection coming. "At least, it's hard for me. But you're a good judge of character and so is Rose and don't get me started on exactly how the stars aligned so that she and Nick are working together."

Charlotte smiled.

"The thing is, Mallory and her brothers deserve the truth and maybe it *will* bring their dad home." I felt like I'd just given a speech.

"I hope so," Charlotte said. She took a step closer to me and lowered her voice. "And I'm glad I'm not the only one who finds Rose and Nick on the same side a little disconcerting. Sometimes I have the feeling I've fallen into a parallel universe."

I grinned at her. "Don't worry. There's no way it can last."

Charlotte grinned back at me. "I'm not sure if that's a good thing or a bad thing!"

I gave her a hug and went back to the shop. Avery was arranging a collection of flowerpots—the ones Liz had asked me about—in the center of a long wooden trestle table. This was her latest project. She'd painted the terra-cotta pots with a flat black paint, then used spray adhesive to randomly fasten cheesecloth to them. Avery had followed with a coat of metallic gold paint. When the cheesecloth was removed the pots were left with a black-veined design highlighted against the gold. They made an elegant collection on the dark tabletop.

"I'm just going upstairs to grab a cup of coffee," I said to Avery. "I'll be right back."

"Sure," she said, lifting a hand but not even turning in my direction. All of her focus was on the table. I could have told her I was going to put on tap shoes and do a dance routine in the parking lot and she would have nodded absently and said *sure*.

I was adding sugar to my coffee when my cell phone rang. I glanced at the screen. It was Liz.

"Hi, toots," she said when I answered.

"Toots?" I asked.

"It's a perfectly good word," Liz retorted. "Which I'm not debating you on right now. What are you wearing?"

I leaned against the counter. "My bathrobe and slippers."

"Don't get saucy with me, missy," she said.

"Why do you care what I'm wearing?" I asked.

"Because we have an appointment with Judge Halloran at four o'clock."

I sighed. "Please don't tell me that you think he can be swayed by a pretty face."

Liz gave a snort of laughter. "I'm perfectly capable of charming Neill Halloran if that's what's called for, thank you very much. I just wanted to make sure you weren't wearing jeans and a sweatshirt because you were cleaning out that storage unit. I didn't think you'd want to go see the man if you were dressed like a hobo."

"I'm not dressed like a hobo," I said. "I'm wearing black pants and the red shirt I bought when we were in Boston."

"That's fine then," she said. "I'll be there at quarter to four."

"Why are *we* going to see the judge?"

"You'd rather Rose and Nicolas went to visit him?"

I couldn't help grinning. "They do seem to be a pretty good team at the moment."

"Ha-ha, you're hilarious," Liz said. "I'll see you later. Wear lipstick." She ended the call before I had a chance to say anything else.

It was exactly three forty-five when Liz walked into

the shop. Since I'd talked to her I'd also learned that she'd arranged for Rose and Charlotte to close the store if we weren't back in time. Rose came down the stairs and handed me a small cardboard container, tied with red-striped twine. "The cookies," she said. "Don't forget to tell Judge Halloran that they came from Isabel."

"Maybe you should go instead of me," I said.

She shook her head. "The judge went to school with your grandmother. That kind of connection matters to him. And he and Liz were on the board of directors at the theater. You two are the right choice."

"Wait a minute—did you organize this meeting?" I asked.

"I may have suggested to Liz that she was the best person to go see Judge Halloran."

I knew that quasi-innocent look on her face.

I narrowed my gaze at her. "And did you also suggest that I should go along as her sidekick?"

She gave an offhand shrug. "Actually I suggested myself."

Which pretty much guaranteed that Liz would ask me to go with her.

"You are a devious little woman," I said.

"I guess sometimes I am," she said with a self-satisfied smile. It seemed I'd given her a compliment.

"You can drive," Liz said, tossing her keys in my direction as we stepped out the back door. "And no comments about Driving Miss Daisy."

"Yes, ma'am," I said. I managed to swallow down a grin.

"So where are we going?" I asked after I'd fastened my seat belt and started the car.

"Bayview Street," Liz said. She held the box of cookies on her lap.

"There aren't any houses on Bayview Street," I said, adjusting the rearview mirror.

"We're going to the judge's office. Remember where Swift Holdings' offices were?"

I nodded. Liz and I had had a meeting once with Daniel Swift at his very impressive office. He'd tried to intimidate her. It hadn't gone well.

For him.

"It's the same building," Liz said.

"I can get us there," I said.

The three-story office building was located almost at the end of Bayview Street, at the far end of the harbor. There was no boardwalk on this end of the waterfront, no businesses catering to tourists, no slips for harbor cruises or kayak rentals. We pulled into the parking lot just a few minutes before four o'clock.

The receptionist at the judge's law office was a young woman whom I guessed was in her early twenties. She was conservatively dressed in a simple navy blue dress but the deep fuchsia streak in her fair hair suggested there were more layers to her personality. "Hello, Mrs. French," she said. "I'll let Judge Halloran's assistant know you're here."

"Thank you," Liz said, a glint of approval in her eye. The fact that the young woman knew who she was had made a good impression.

The young woman gestured toward a grouping of several chairs around a low wooden coffee table. "Please have a seat."

We sat but we weren't there for long. A middle-aged

man appeared from the hallway to the right of the reception desk. He crossed the floor to us and smiled at Liz, offering his hand. "Mrs. French? I'm Henry Davis," he said. "I'm Judge Halloran's assistant. We spoke on the phone."

Henry Davis was maybe two or three inches taller than my five foot six. He had dark skin and dark eyes. His head was shaved smooth and he had a closely cropped beard and mustache.

Liz shook his hand then turned toward me. "This is my friend Sarah Grayson."

"A pleasure to meet you, Ms. Grayson," he said. We shook hands as well and then he indicated the hallway. "Come on back to the judge's office."

I stepped back to let Liz go ahead of me. She was running the show, so to speak. She reached for her purse, which she'd left on the chair when she stood up.

"Thank you for putting your influence and your money behind something that's so important to Judge Halloran," Henry Davis said.

What?

I put a hand on Liz's shoulder as she straightened up. "Is there something I should know?" I asked just under my breath. Davis was already halfway across the reception area.

Liz adjusted the scarf at her neck. "Just roll with it," she murmured.

I didn't really have a lot of other options.

I had been expecting Judge Neill Halloran to be a large, imposing man given how people had talked about him, but in reality he was of average height with thinning hair, wire-framed glasses and two discreet hearing aids. He had keen blue eyes that took in everything and a serious expression that was chased away when he smiled, which he did when Liz and I walked in to his office.

The office had a lot of the trappings I would have expected from a lawyer's office: wood paneling three-quarters of the way up the walls, a large credenza under the windows behind the desk, and two chocolate-brown leather chairs for visitors. But there was also a large fish tank on the wall to the left of the desk, which was a modern curve of wood, metal and glass.

"Elizabeth French, it's a pleasure to see you," Neill Halloran said.

There was a small circular table and two chairs to the right of the office door. The table held a laptop, a yellow legal pad and two mechanical pencils. Henry Davis wrote something on the pad before sitting down at the computer.

"It's good to see you, as well, Neill," Liz said. She indicated me. "Neill, this is Sarah Grayson. I want to put together a book on the history of the Emmerson Foundation. Sarah is helping me with the research."

"It's nice to meet you, Judge Halloran," I said, shaking his hand. He had large hands and a firm handshake.

"I brought Sarah with me to introduce her personally because she may have a few questions for you at some point." Liz smiled. "I didn't realize you were a board member many years ago."

The judge returned her smile. "Your grandfather could be a very persuasive man."

Liz rolled her eyes. "I would have said stubborn as a mule, but I appreciate your tact."

"Your grandfather did *not* take no for an answer."

So that's where Liz got her stubborn streak.

As if she could read my mind Liz shot me a warning glare. I gave her my best innocent smile.

"Neill, Sarah is Isabel Grayson's granddaughter," Liz said.

His smile got even wider. "How is Isabel?" he asked. "It's been a long time since I've seen her. I heard she got married again."

"She's well," I said. "And yes, she did get married. She just got back from a very extended honeymoon." I held out the box of cookies. "She sent these for you."

He took the box and opened the note Gram had attached to the top. Bringing the cookies had made me feel a bit like we were trying to manipulate the judge, but he seemed so genuinely pleased to get them and Gram's note that I was reconsidering. He peeked inside and then looked at me. "Please thank your grandmother for the cookies and tell her that I would love to get together."

"I will," I promised.

He turned to Liz. "Now, how am I going to be able to say no to your book project?"

She laughed. "I'm hoping you'll find it pretty much impossible, but if all it takes is cookies I'll be happy to"—she paused—"buy you some."

The judge laughed.

Liz was flirting. Not the first time she'd done that to get information. She reached into her bag then and handed him an envelope.

He opened it, pulled out a check and his eyes widened. "Thank you, Elizabeth," he said. "That's very generous of you."

I glanced around the office, looking for a clue to this mysterious project.

"Well, I don't want to see all of North Harbor's past disappear, either," Liz said.

Okay, so the project had something to do with the town's history. That really didn't narrow things down a lot. "Do you mind if I ask how you got involved in this project in the first place?" I asked the judge.

"Not at all," he said. He gestured at the chairs in front of his desk. "I've forgotten my manners. Please, sit down."

Liz and I took a seat and Judge Halloran moved back behind his desk. He sat down, leaned back in his chair and looked at me thoughtfully. "I guess the real reason I got involved is because I've always had a soft spot for the old library building. My mother would take my brother and me to get a week's worth of books every Saturday after lunch."

So the project had something to do with the former library building, which I knew was about to be torn down. It had deteriorated so much over the years that it just wasn't structurally sound anymore, but it would be sad to see it turned into a pile of rubble.

"I understand that it's not possible to save every old building, nor should we. But I hate the idea that the sunflower window would leave town or even worse, the country," he said.

The sunflower window was a round stained glass window that had been in the old library from the time it was built in the late 1800s. It had gotten the name from the different varieties of yellow glass in the flowerlike design. I'd heard that there was someone in Singapore interested in buying the window. Like the judge, I'd spent many happy Saturday afternoons during summer vacation in that building. I didn't want to see the window leave town either.

"When I was little I liked to stand in the colored patches of light on the floor," I said, smiling at the memory.

"I very much wish they had moved the window when they built the new library," he said. "That was the original plan."

"So why didn't they?" Liz asked.

The judge shook his head. "There was some concern about removing it safely. I think part of the reason was also that it didn't fit with the vision the library board at the time had for the space. But hopefully we'll be able to match the offer that's already been made for the window and find it a new home here in North Harbor."

"I hope so," I said. It struck me that this was a project Liam needed to get involved with.

Judge Halloran tapped the envelope Liz had given him with one finger. "You know Sarah, I think you should work into this book project of Elizabeth's how much she's done for North Harbor that no one actually knows about."

"I like that idea," I said, shifting in my chair to grin at Liz. "I may need some details from you, however."

"You're a fine one to talk, Neill Halloran," Liz said tartly. "You're far more modest than I am. Do you remember what my grandfather used to say? Don't hide your light under a bushel."

She looked at me and gestured across the desk at the judge. "Neill is the driving force behind the building of the outdoor ice rink *and* he funded the hot lunch program for the entire first year until it got on its feet."

The hot lunch program in the elementary school was one of my pet projects thanks to Gram. I knew someone had kept it running through the bumpy first year but I had no idea it had been Judge Halloran. Given that he had a soft spot for my grandmother, it made sense.

He inclined his head in Liz's direction. "A word of warning, if Elizabeth knows your secrets they aren't going to be secrets for long."

I laughed. "Liz has known me since I was a baby so I don't have any secrets at all."

Liz's expression grew serious now. "Are you still involved with Haven House?" she asked.

Haven House. That was the name of the treatment center Gina Pearson had been waiting to be admitted to, and had been to before.

"You really do know all my secrets," the judge said. I noticed just a touch of wariness in his voice.

"Years ago, Michael Pearson was a summer student at the foundation," Liz said. "I suspect you pulled some strings to get a place at Haven House for his wife just before she died."

"I'm sure you know that I'm the one who told the police that I saw Michael walking away from their burning house." He took hold of the frames of his glasses. "For the record, I need these only for close work. My long-distance vision is fine."

Liz adjusted her own glasses. "I need mine only when I need to see," she said lightly.

He smiled.

"Michael Pearson is a good man."

"I know that," Judge Halloran said. "We were neighbors for five years. He loaned me his leaf-blower when mine stopped working. Two winters ago, when I broke my wrist, he kept my steps and driveway clear and he wouldn't take five cents for doing it. I didn't take any pleasure in telling the police what I saw." He held up a hand as though trying to forestall any objections Liz might have. "Mike was wearing the ball cap Gina had given him. I recognized him and that hat. He wore it all the time. It was a replica of the 1956 red and blue cap that the American team wore in Melbourne at the Olympics. Baseball was a demonstration sport that year. He was wearing it earlier in the day when we talked about Gina. He was wearing it that evening when he walked away from the house."

"Did you use your connections to get Gina into Haven House?"

"I told Mike I would see what I could do. They found a bed for her. She would have left the morning following the fire."

Gina Pearson had been so close to a chance to turn her life around. I had to swallow down the lump that was suddenly in the back of my throat.

Liz sighed softly.

The judge leaned forward, propping his elbows on the desk. "Elizabeth, if you have the idea that you can somehow help Mike Pearson, you're taking on a losing battle."

Liz looked at him for a long moment and I wasn't sure if she was going to say anything. "Thank you, Neill," was all she finally said. She got to her feet and extended her hand. "I'll see what I can do to generate more support for saving the sunflower window."

"I appreciate that," he said. He came around the desk, took my hand in both of his and smiled. "It was a pleasure, Isabel." He hesitated for a second then shook his head. "I'm sorry. It's just for a moment you reminded me so much of your grandmother."

"I'm honored by the comparison," I said.

"If I can be of any help with your book project please call Henry," he said. "He takes care of my schedule."

I smiled. "Thank you."

Henry Davis was already on his feet. He handed me his card. "That has my direct number," he said. "Please call me if there's anything you need from Judge Halloran."

I thanked him and we left.

"You lied to me," I said to Liz once we were in the elevator.

"No. I just didn't tell you everything."

"I could have messed up *everything*."

"You didn't," she said as the elevator doors opened to the main floor.

"Why all the elaborate subterfuge?" I asked as we headed for the door.

"Do you really think Henry Davis would have given us an appointment in this century if I'd told him I wanted to question the judge about whether or not he saw what he says he saw the night of that fire?"

I shook my head. "No. He probably wouldn't have."

"So I did what I had to."

"It was nice of you to write a check for that fund-raising campaign to save the old library window," I said.

"I think it would be a shame to see it end up halfway around the world. It's a piece of our history."

We were approaching the car. I pulled out the keys to unlock the doors. "It occurred to me that Liam might be able to help in some way. You want me to talk to him?"

"That's an excellent idea," Liz said, pointing at me with one finger.

"I'll see what he says and get him to call you." I slid behind the wheel and started the car, then turned to look at Liz. "The judge's ID seems pretty solid to me. He lived next to Mike for years. It wasn't like he forgot his glasses. He even recognized Mike's hat. Where do we go from here?"

Liz shook her head. "Damned if I know," she said.

Chapter 9

We got back to Second Chance just before five. Liz brought everyone up to date on what we'd learned from Judge Halloran while Avery and I closed up.

"Can I show you something?" Avery asked as we put the vacuum cleaner away.

"Sure," I said.

She led the way out to the workshop. On the far corner of the workbench were two of the small pails she'd been covering with maps. These two, however, had been covered with some kind of festive snowman paper.

I picked one up. She'd done a meticulous job as usual. Avery might forget to wear socks in her boots or to cut the tags off her thrift-store finds but she was exacting at any project she took on for the shop.

"Where did you find the paper?" I asked. I didn't recognize it.

"It was at the bottom of that box of stuff Charlotte was sorting. You know, all that fabric stuff. Was it okay that I used it?"

I nodded. "Very okay."

She smiled. "I thought I could do a few more and when it gets closer to Christmas we could fill them with those shiny tree ornaments we didn't sell last year. If people don't buy them then, hey, we still have some great decorations for here."

I set the festive pail back on the workbench. "I like that idea," I said. "But I'm not sure where those ornaments are."

"They're in a blue bin on the top shelf out in the garage. It even says 'Ornaments' on the top of the box. And I wasn't out there making a mess looking for them, if that's what you're thinking."

"I wasn't thinking that," I said. "I'm just impressed that you found them so easily."

She shrugged. "I asked Mr. P. to ask Mac where they were when he texted him. That's how I found them."

"Very resourceful," I said.

"When's he coming back?" she asked, turning the pail closest to her so the handles lined up exactly.

"I don't know."

She seemed baffled. "Well, what did Mac say when you asked him? I know you talk to him."

"I didn't ask him," I said, feeling a twinge of embarrassment at the admission. "Mac has a lot to take care of in Boston."

"But you told him we miss him, right?" There was a hint of a challenge in her voice.

I let out a breath. "Yes, I've told him we miss him."

"So then you should ask him when he's coming back so he knows that we want him back." She didn't say, "duh," but it was implied.

"Mac knows we want him back," I said.

"Okay, whatever." She didn't sound convinced.

Rose, Liz and Charlotte were standing by the front window still talking when Avery and I came back into the shop. Rose smiled at the teen. "There are some cookies left in the staff room upstairs. You can take them home with you."

"Oatmeal raisin?" Avery asked.

Rose shook her head. "Jam-jams."

Avery smiled. "Thanks," she said. She cocked her head to one side. "You know, if there's something you don't want to say in front of me you could just tell me to leave the room."

"Fine," Liz said. "Avery, leave the room."

"Okay," she said, heading for the stairs. "But I'm still getting the cookies." She took the steps two at a time.

I turned to Rose. "Liz told you about our conversation with the judge?"

She nodded. Then she looked up at me. "So what do you think about what he said?"

I brushed a bit of dust off the arm of my shirt. "I was going to ask you the same thing."

"Did you ever read that article I sent you about the validity of eyewitness testimony?" she asked. I knew from experience that Rose had very strong opinions on the subject.

"I read *both* of the articles."

"So you know that the judge's confidence in his ID doesn't translate to it being any more accurate?"

"You think he's wrong," I said.

"I think we need to find some evidence that either

backs him up or that proves he's mistaken." I knew that determined set to her chin. Behind Rose both Liz and Charlotte were trying not to smile.

"And how do you think we should do that?" I asked.

Rose reached over and plucked another dust bunny from my shirt. "We're going to do what we do best." She smiled sweetly.

"Refresh my memory," I said, struggling and failing not to smile back at her. "What is it exactly that *we* do best?"

"We act like nosey little old ladies." She gestured at Liz and Charlotte.

"Speak for yourself," Liz muttered.

"Of course not you, dear," Rose added, patting my hand and ignoring Liz's comment.

"So what am I then? Window dressing?" I asked.

"Exactly," she said with a grin. "And you drive." She caught sight of Avery coming down the stairs. "No, no child, that's the wrong tin," she said, hurrying over.

Liz came and put her arm around me. "It appears that you are just another pretty face," she teased.

I fished her keys out of my pocket and handed them to her. She leaned over and kissed my cheek, then started for the back door. "Love you," she said over her shoulder.

"Love you too, toots," I said.

Rose, Mr. P. and Avery left with Liz. I gave Charlotte a ride home. Elvis conceded the entire front seat to Charlotte and hopped into the back to sit in the middle of the seat.

"Were the cookies a hit?" Charlotte asked.

"I think so," I said. The judge seemed touched to get

them and the note from Gram. I glanced over at her. "I think he had a bit of a crush on her."

"It wouldn't surprise me," she said with a smile. "But what did he say that makes you think that?"

"When we were leaving he called me Isabel. He caught himself and said I reminded him of Gram."

"I can see that," Charlotte said. "You have Isabel's smile and her stubborn streak."

"I'm not stubborn," I said, maybe a bit more vehemently than was necessary.

A loud meow came from the backseat.

"I'm sorry. There seems to be some dispute about that."

I looked over at Charlotte again. She was laughing.

I glanced in the rearview mirror. Elvis was the picture of innocence on the backseat.

"You're actually right about the judge," Charlotte said. "From what I remember he was a little smitten with your grandmother. Of course, once she met your grandfather there was no one else for her, but I suspect for Neill Halloran, Isabel may be the one who got away."

I pulled onto Charlotte's street. "It sounds like Gram was a bit of a heartbreaker when she was young. First I find out that Clayton McNamara was romancing her when they were both just six years old and now there's Judge Halloran. Are there any other romances in Gram's past that I should know about?"

I turned into Charlotte's driveway. She smiled at me. "Isabel doesn't kiss and tell and I don't tell at all so I think you're out of luck." She unfastened her seat belt and reached for her bag. "Have fun tonight and tell Nicolas that if he doesn't come over this weekend and change the lightbulb in the garage I'm going to drag a kitchen chair out there and do it myself."

"I have lots of time," I said, unfastening my seat belt. "I can do that for you right now."

Charlotte was shaking her head before I finished speaking. "Thank you, but I really want Nick to change that lightbulb. If you do it for me all I'll get is a working lightbulb, but if Nick does it I'll get a working lightbulb and three boxes of his junk out of my garage."

I smiled and refastened my seat belt. "I'll pass on the message," I said.

I had just enough time to head home, shower and change. When I got to The Black Bear I found Jess holding court with Liam and Nick. I slid onto the chair they had been saving for me and looked around for a waiter but couldn't seem to catch one's attention.

"Do you want food?" Jess asked. She had her hair up and she was wearing a hot pink boat-neck sweater that kept slipping down over one shoulder—which was probably why she'd decided to wear it.

"Yes," I said. "I didn't have any supper."

She looked around, somehow caught a waiter's eye and raised a finger. The waiter immediately headed toward us.

"How do you do that?" I asked, slumping against the back of my chair.

"I just have a naturally commanding presence," Jess said with a grin.

More like she had a killer smile and lots of confidence.

I ordered two fish tacos and coleslaw. Then I briefed

Liam on the judge's sunflower window project. "Can you help?" I asked.

"Yeah, maybe," he said. "I'll call Liz in the morning and get some more details."

"Thanks," I said.

He nodded but his focus had shifted from me to someone he'd spotted across the room. "I see someone I need to talk to," he said, getting to his feet. "I'll be right back."

Nick reached out and swiped a chunk of tomato from my taco.

"I didn't know you asked Liam to come," I said. "Why didn't you say something? We could have had supper."

"*You* didn't have supper," he pointed out, nicking a bite of fish from my plate.

I smacked his hand. "Apparently neither did you."

"I invited Liam," Jess said. "I told you. Remember?"

I looked at her. She *had* told me that. "I do now."

"Sarah, do you have a problem with that?"

"No," I said. The moment the word was out of my mouth I realized how less than enthusiastic I sounded.

One eyebrow went up. "You sure?" Jess asked.

Nick took advantage of what I'm sure he thought was my distracted focus to swipe another chunk of fish from my plate.

"Yes, I'm sure," I said. I didn't sound very convincing even to myself.

"Sarah is afraid you're sleeping with her brother," Nick said.

I yanked my plate out of his reach with one hand,

made a fist with the other and slugged his shoulder. Hard. "You're not helping, and stop eating my food!"

"Are you afraid I'm going to break Liam's heart or something?" Jess asked. She seemed amused by the idea.

I hesitated, exhaling slowly to buy a little time. "No. I'm mostly afraid he'll break yours." Liam didn't seem interested in a serious relationship with anyone.

She laughed. "There's nothing to worry about, Sarah. Liam and I are just friends." She gave me a wicked grin. "Actually we're perpetrating a ruse."

"A ruse?" I said.

"Oh, this should be good," Nick chortled. He leaned against the back of his chair. "Do tell."

Jess rolled her eyes at him before turning her attention to me. "You know how Rose and the others were trying to pair you off with Nick and"—she glanced at him again—"well, pretty much just Nick?"

I nodded.

"Well, now they seem to have switched their efforts to Liam's love life. So he told them we were going out."

I pressed my lips together, but the laughter escaped anyway.

"C'mon, it's not funny," Jess said. "You know what they're like."

Nick was grinning as well.

"I know exactly what they're like," I said, shaking with laughter. "And it's hilarious."

Nick and I had had Rose and Liz and his mother inquiring and poking in our love lives for years. Liam, on the other hand, had pretty much been exempt from their . . . advice. I couldn't help being tickled that the tables had been turned.

Liam came back to the table then. "What did I miss?" he said.

"Nick was stealing my food." It was the first thing that came to mind.

Liam frowned at his friend. "Hey, don't do that."

I smiled at him sticking up for me. Meanwhile, he leaned over and grabbed a chunk of fish out of the taco I was holding. "Only I get to swipe Sarah's food," he said with a grin.

I made a show of looking around the pub. "Is there anywhere else I can sit?"

Jess grinned and held up a hand. "Okay, guys," she said. "No more teasing Sarah."

I jabbed a finger in Nick's direction. "I almost forgot. If you don't go and change the lightbulb in your mother's garage this weekend I'm going to go and do it for her and at the same time I'm going to take the three boxes of your junk that are still in the garage and give them to Cleveland."

"You can't do that," he said, setting down his beer. "That's all good stuff."

I folded my arms over my chest. "If it's such good stuff then why is it all in Charlotte's garage and not your apartment?"

He made a face. "You are so mean." I knew he wasn't really mad. The corners of his mouth were twitching. I also knew he'd get over to his mother's on Saturday and get those three boxes because he wasn't a hundred percent sure that I wouldn't give his stuff to my best trash picker.

"And you stole my food," I retorted.

The band came out then and there was no more time to talk.

By the time the first set was over my face was flushed and I was pulling at the neck of my T-shirt. It was warm in the bar and I'd spent most of the time dancing. Both Liam and Jess got up to stretch their legs. Once they were out of earshot, Nick turned to me. "How did the visit with Judge Halloran go?" he asked.

I shrugged. "I learned he had a thing for Gram when they were young and he's convinced he saw Mike Pearson walking away from that burning house."

Nick made a face. "Okay, I don't even know what to do with that first part, and as for the rest, well, we pretty much knew that was what he'd say." He picked up his beer, realized it was empty and set it back down again. "So what do you think?"

"You mean do I think this means Mike Pearson killed his wife?"

He nodded.

I rubbed a hand over the back of my neck. "The truth is, I'm less sure than I was before."

His eyes widened in surprise. "Why?"

"First of all there was a bed for Gina in rehab," I said. "The judge had pulled some strings and told Mike there would be a place for her in Haven House in the morning. Mike had been trying to make that happen. He was desperate for any kind of help for his wife. Why on earth would he kill Gina now that she was about to finally get that help?"

Nick nodded slowly. "Okay, that makes sense."

"The other thing is, one of the reasons the judge is so credible is because he knew Mike. He even described the ball cap that Mike was wearing. Apparently he wore it all the time."

Nick held up a hand. "Hang on," he said. "Why does that matter?"

"From what I've learned about Mike Pearson, he's not a stupid man. So if he'd just killed his wife and set the fire that ended up destroying his house, why didn't he make an effort not to be seen as he left? It's not like he didn't know the judge might see him. He'd talked to Judge Halloran earlier when the judge was just starting to clear out his driveway."

"Are you trying to say you think someone was impersonating Mike?" Nick asked. He looked a little skeptical and I didn't blame him.

I shrugged. "I don't know but I think we should keep digging and maybe we'll find out."

"I think you're right," he said.

I looked around the room.

"What are you looking for?" Nick asked.

"Zombies," I said.

"Zombies?"

I nodded. "Because you and Rose agreeing on everything has to be a sign of something ominous like a zombie apocalypse."

Nick laughed. Then his expression turned serious. "Can I tell you something but we keep it just between us?"

"I don't know," I said. "Can you?"

He recognized his mother's expression and gave me a wry smile. "I'm serious, Sarah. For now this isn't something I want to share with the rest of your band of merry detectives."

I hesitated. "Okay. We can keep whatever it is between us. For now." I stressed the last two words.

"I told you I was going to talk to Claire again."

I nodded. Had the medical examiner decided to change Gina Pearson's cause of death?

"She said that if I can find more evidence—something that indicates Gina didn't try to hang herself or that some other person started the fire, she'll change the cause of death."

"That would get the case reopened."

He nodded. "It would."

"That could potentially get Mike out of jail," I said.

"Or put him there for a lot longer," Nick added. "You can see why I don't want to get Rose's hopes up just yet."

I shifted in my seat. "You're right. I won't say anything." I eyed him for a moment.

He frowned. "What? Do I have food on my face or something?"

"No," I said. "I was just wondering how you do it every day. How do you not get overwhelmed by all the investigations?"

Nick ran a hand back through his hair. "I try to look strictly at the facts and not emotions."

I laughed. "And how's that been working lately?"

He gave me a bit of a shamefaced grin. "Let's just say it's a work in progress. What keeps me going is knowing that I speak for the dead. I hear what they say through the evidence and I'm their voice." He gave me a sideways look and said, "Sounds hokey, I know."

"It doesn't sound that way at all," I said. "I just wish we could figure out what Gina Pearson is trying to say to us."

Jess and Liam came back to the table then, heads together laughing about something. More plotting for their ruse? I didn't get a chance to ask because the band was coming back to the stage just then as well. Sam was carrying an extra guitar and he looked in our direction.

Nick shook his head. "No," he said.

I grinned and poked him with my elbow. Jess was already smiling and pointing at the stage.

"This is an ambush," Nick said over the clapping and hooting of the crowd. He looked at me.

"I didn't know Sam had this planned. I swear," I said, my mouth close to his ear. "I mean, I would have helped if I had known. But I didn't." I smiled at him. "Please play. I haven't heard you play in ages."

Nick rolled his eyes. "You owe me," he said. "And don't expect a lot. I'm really rusty." Then he got up and went to join the band, to even more clapping and cheers.

Nick played three songs with Sam and the boys and if he was rusty it didn't show. He came back to his seat to even more clapping, hoots and cheering. His face was flushed and he was grinning from ear to ear.

I suddenly remembered what Mallory had said about her stepmother, how much fun Gina had been before she started drinking all the time: *She'd put on music and dance with us with that sparkly sort of look in her eyes and her hair swirling all around.* I looked at Nick, still smiling as Jess gave his arm a squeeze and all around us people still clapped. If he lost the look that was on his face right now, I wouldn't give up until it came back. Was it fair to think Mike Pearson had given up on his wife? Maybe Rose was right. Maybe Neill Halloran was mistaken about what he saw. Or maybe he'd been deliberately misled. Either way, I knew I couldn't quit until I got some answers.

I was in my office with Elvis the next morning, checking Web site orders, when Mr. P. knocked on the half-open door and stuck his head around the door frame. "Am I interrupting, Sarah?" he asked.

"No, you're not," I said. "He, on the other hand . . ." I pointed at Elvis, who had just squeezed himself in between me and the laptop keyboard, which made it pretty much impossible for me to type.

The cat blinked his green eyes at me. I made a shooing motion with one hand. "Go downstairs and help Rose in the shop," I said. To my amusement he took a couple of swipes at his face with one paw, then jumped down from the desk, and moved behind Mr. P. out into the hallway.

I shook my head. "Sometimes I think he knows every word I'm saying to him, but he ignores it all just to mess with me."

Mr. P. smiled. "Cats are very intelligent animals," he said. "I'm sure you remember that they were worshipped in ancient Egypt."

I laughed. "That might explain why Elvis acts like royalty."

"It may indeed," he agreed.

"So what's up?" I asked, leaning back in my chair.

"The high school has a cross-country race after school today."

I felt a little confused and it probably showed on my face. "I didn't realize you followed high school sports," I said.

He smoothed down the few wisps of his hair with one hand. "Well, the women's hockey team does look like it's going to be very competitive this year, but the reason I mentioned the cross-country race is that Hannah Allison is competing."

It took a moment but then I made the connection. "Hannah Allison is the teen Gina Pearson hit with her car."

Mr. P. nodded. "Yes. It would be a good opportunity to talk to her parents. I have it on reliable authority that both of them will be there."

"Then so will we," I said.

Liam and Nick showed up at lunchtime. Liam stuck his head around the workroom door just as I was putting a guitar back on the wall. "Hi," he said. "Nick has the afternoon off so we're going to start in the sunporch if that's okay with you."

"It's fine with me," I said. "Just make sure it's all right with Mr. P."

No surprise, it was all right with Mr. P. I helped the three of them move what little furniture there was in the sunporch out into the workroom. We made a space for Alfred's makeshift desk near the workbench so he could plug in his computer.

"How can I help?" he asked Liam once Nick had moved his desk chair.

Liam fished a piece of paper from his pocket. "These are the Web sites for a couple of salvage places. They have their inventory online. What I need is enough trim to go around the windows and enough baseboard to finish the walls under the windows." He looked at me. "I know you don't care if the trim matches the rest of the place but I do."

I held up both hands. "That's fine with me."

Liam pointed to the bottom of the paper. "That's how

many feet I need of both, and you know what both the trim and the baseboard look like."

Mr. P. nodded. "I'll get right on it." He nudged his glasses up his nose. "I have some sources of my own as well." Then he disappeared into the workroom.

Liam looked at me. "He has sources?"

"Yes, he does," I said with a smile, "and you probably don't want to know about them."

I spent the first part of the afternoon in the garage work space removing moldings and plaster medallions that had been added to a beautiful Shaker-style armoire, which had also been painted a bilious shade of pea soup green. It had been meticulously put together with thick shelves and a shiplap back. I had no idea why anyone had wanted to paint it and then add so much decoration. For me the beauty of the piece was in its simple lines and beautiful wood.

Liam had taken a look inside and said he thought the wood was cypress. I had decided to refinish the piece as a Christmas gift for Gram and John. Gram had mentioned that she could use more storage space in the apartment.

Around three thirty I put everything away, brushed my hair and my teeth and put on a little lip gloss. Then I went in search of Rose and Mr. P. I found the latter standing in the middle of the sunporch, which no longer had drywall on two sides but did have a new window facing the street. Rose and Nick were standing by the back door, their heads bent over what looked like a small notebook. Nick had bits of drywall dust in his hair.

"Are you ready, Rose?" I said. She and Nick stepped apart—somewhat guiltily, it seemed to me.

"I just need to get my sweater," Rose said. She didn't make any effort to do that, though.

"What are you looking at?" I asked.

Nick looked at Rose. Rose looked at Nick. I noticed that neither of them was looking at me. I cocked my head inquiringly to one side. Nick looked like he was about to say something but Rose kicked his leg with her foot. He jumped, made a bit of a grunt and then tried to turn it into a cough to cover.

Rose gave me a totally insincere smile. "Dear, you know how sometimes you decide it might be better if you didn't know exactly how Alfred acquired a certain piece of information?"

I nodded.

"This may be a similar circumstance."

"I'll see you in the car in five minutes," I said.

We got to the park where the cross-country meet was being held just a few minutes before four o'clock. It was the kind of September afternoon the coast of Maine is known for: streaky clouds overhead, just a hint of a breeze coming in from the water and on the trees all around us the leaves were starting to change. I took a deep breath of the fresh air. It was good to be outside for a change. Rockwell Park had close to eight miles of trails, many of them through old-growth forest with trees that were close to four hundred years old. There was a waterfowl pond and outdoor rink in the wintertime. I made a mental note to come for a run in the park sometimes soon.

"How exactly are we going to find Hannah Allison's parents?" I asked, looking around. There were more people than I'd expected. Most of them were parents, I was guessing. "I don't even know their names."

"Ben Allison and Jia Kent-Allison," Mr. P. said. "Don't worry. I know what they look like."

The cross-country course had been marked off with stakes and yellow tape. We walked in the general direction that most of the people seemed to have gathered as Mr. P. scanned the spectators. No one paid any attention to us and I realized that we probably looked like the mom and grandparents of one of the kids. Finally Mr. P. put a hand on my arm. "Over there, Sarah," he said, inclining his head in the direction of a man and woman standing by themselves where the trail curved up the hill.

I took a minute to study them. Ben Allison looked to be in his early forties, average height and build, in jeans and a red and black hoodie. Everything about him was unremarkable except for his hair. It was on the longish side, thick and wavy, a mix of dark and silver. It was the kind of hair that belonged in a shampoo commercial.

Jia Kent-Allison was five eight or so with a lean build that made me suspect she was a runner herself. She was of Asian ancestry and she wore her dark hair in a cropped pixie that showed off her cheekbones and long neck. She was dressed in leggings and a gray zippered running jacket. Her arms were folded over her chest and there was a frown of concentration on her face as she watched the runners on the course.

We stood a little way away from the Allisons and waited until their daughter ran by. Hannah Allison was easy to spot with a similar runner's build to her mother and her dad's thick hair in a high ponytail. She ran at a steady pace, grinning at her parents as she passed them. I had no idea how good her time was, but I noticed that she had an excellent stride. Ben and Jia clapped and called out encouragingly as Hannah disappeared on the wooded part of the course.

Mr. P. and Rose exchanged a look. Then Mr. P. nodded and they started over to the Allisons. I tagged along behind them wondering what his approach was going to be.

It turned out Mr. P. had decided on a direct one. "Mr. and Mrs. Allison," he said. "My name is Alfred Peterson. I'm a private investigator." He showed them his license from the state. "These are my associates, Mrs. Jackson and Ms. Grayson."

"What do you want with us?" Ben asked. He seemed wary, shoulders squared, hands stuffed in the pocket of his hooded sweatshirt.

"I'd like to ask you a few questions about your daughter's accident," Mr. P. said.

"Why?" Jia Allison asked, a challenge in her dark eyes. She looked familiar. I had the feeling I'd seen her in a couple of 10K races that I'd done recently.

"Gina Pearson's name has come up in an investigation," he said. "We're looking into her background." Alfred Peterson may have been a balding little man who wore his pants a bit too high, but his quiet confidence and intelligence won people over.

"She's dead," Jia said bluntly.

Mr. P. nodded. "Yes, we're aware of that. But we still need to learn more about her."

"She damn near killed my daughter driving drunk," Ben said. There were deep lines around his eyes and mouth. "Running was Hannah's life and for a while, after her leg was injured in that accident, they weren't sure if she was going to be able to walk again, let alone run."

Jia looked at me. "You run," she said. "I do the hills loop a lot. I've seen you running it a few times."

I nodded. "Yes I do that one on occasion."

"Then you know what it was like for my daughter not to be able to run."

Two young women running in tandem passed us and I felt a sudden urge to join them, to feel my muscles working, feet pounding against the ground, lungs pulling in air. "I can guess," I said.

"Gina Pearson did that to my child," Jia said. She'd folded her arms across her chest with her fingers tucked into her armpits and she shifted her weight restlessly from one foot to the other as though she might suddenly turn and sprint away.

"This is probably going to sound cruel," Ben interrupted, "but as far as I'm concerned Gina Pearson could have drunk herself to death for all I cared, but she had no right to get into a car and drive." He pulled one hand out of his pocket and raked it back through his hair. "Her husband is partly to blame as well."

"Why do you say that?" Rose asked. As usual, her genuine curiosity got an answer.

"Mike Pearson was an enabler," Ben said. "He made excuses for his wife. He got her second and third and fourth chances." His voice was getting louder and rougher and his anger was apparent in every gesture he made, both hands moving, punctuating his words. "Gina Pearson's drinking never really cost her any of the things that mattered to her so she never hit bottom. And since she never hit bottom, she never had any incentive to climb back up. That's on him." He swiped a hand over his mouth and walked away from us.

His wife's eyes followed him but she didn't. Jia Allison looked at us. "Gina Pearson died in a fire that she started because, once again, she was drinking. Because she learned nothing from what she did to our daughter. Neither Ben nor I wanted her to die like that." She looked past us, took a deep breath and exhaled slowly. *"Any man's death diminishes me,"* she said softly.

"Because I am involved in mankind," Rose finished in a gentle voice. "John Donne."

Jia nodded. She dropped her arms to her sides. "Gina is dead because her drinking finally caught up with her the night she set her house on fire. And if you're thinking that somehow my husband confronted her and drove her to get drunk that night, sorry. As usual she got that way by herself, but for the record Ben was with Hannah the night of Gina's death, exercising in the pool at the Y. I was on a training run for the winter half marathon—in other words, I have no alibi."

It was apparent from the closed expression on her face that the conversation was over.

"Thank you for your time," Mr. P. said.

Jia nodded and walked off to join her husband.

We headed back to the SUV. "You'll check Ben Allison's alibi?" I asked Mr. P.

"I'll get to it as soon as we get back," he said.

"He's very angry."

"But his wife is the more likely candidate to have done something," Rose said.

I leaned around Mr. P. to look at her. "Are you saying that because she's a mother?"

Rose shook her head. "No. I'm saying that because her husband's anger is so easy to see. Look how it spilled over when he spoke to us. His wife on the other hand, all of her anger is inside." She patted her chest with the palm of her hand. "Her feelings go very deep."

"Deep enough to have killed Gina?" I asked. I was afraid I might know the answer. I'd seen Jia's right hand flexing and then clenching into a fist at her side.

Rose looked troubled. "Maybe," she said.

There wasn't anything else to say. We headed back to the shop.

That evening, about eight thirty, there was a knock on my door. Elvis and I had just settled in for an exciting Friday night of TV and nachos. It was Mr. P. with his laptop.

"I'm sorry for interrupting your Friday night," he said.

I smiled at his words. My Friday night was a plate of cheesy tortilla chips, a cat and a TV remote.

"No problem," I said. "Come in."

"I confirmed Ben Allison's alibi." He was wearing a pair of yellow fuzzy slippers. It wasn't the first time. I decided I didn't want to know why.

From the corner of my eye I could see Elvis eying the nachos. "Don't even think about it, furball," I said.

Mr. P. smiled. "Could you look at some numbers for me?" he asked, setting the computer on the counter.

I checked the columns of numbers on the screen and realized that what I was looking at were times and standings from the winter marathon that had been held just weeks after Gina's death. I found Jia Kent-Allison in the left-hand column of names. I compared her previous and subsequent times with her time in that marathon.

"She didn't do very well," I said, shaking my head. "In fact, her time was awful."

"I came to the same conclusion," Mr. P. said, "but I wanted to see if you agreed."

I shook my head. "It's possible she had some kind of an injury."

He nodded.

"It's also possible she just didn't put in the miles?"

Mr. P. looked thoughtful. "Well, if that's the case, what was Jia doing when she should have been training?"

I had a bad feeling I might have an answer.

Chapter 10

Liam and I were loading an antique pie safe into a customer's SUV the next morning when Liz pulled into the parking lot. He had the top of the cupboard and was leaning in the back passenger door trying to maneuver the padded piece into place while I held the legs.

"You need to go about an inch to your left," he said.

The pie safe—made of oak with the original hardware and punched tin doors was heavier than it looked. With a fair amount of grunts from me and a couple of muttered swear words from Liam, we managed to get the piece of furniture secured.

I was sweaty and rumpled and my hair had come loose from the ponytail I'd pulled it into. I blew my bangs back out of my face. "Thank you," I said to Liam. "I don't know how I would have done that without you."

"Anytime," he said with a smile. "I'll put it on your tab." He headed back to the sunporch, where he and Nick had already replaced a second window. I had a feeling my tab was getting pretty high.

I walked over to Liz, pulling loose the elastic that had been sort of holding my hair. "Hi," I said. "What did Avery forget? Her phone? Her lunch? Her eyeliner?"

"I'm not here because of Avery," Liz said. "Alfred called me. He's found Wilson's former assistant at the foundation. Remember I told you about her? Marie Heard."

"I remember," I said. "So where is she?"

Liz shook her head. "I don't know. Alfred said he'd explain when I got here."

"Let's go find out then," I said.

We found Mr. P. at his temporary desk. "Hello, Elizabeth," he said, getting to his feet and setting his coffee cup on the end of the workbench.

"Hello, Alfred," Liz said. "So tell me. Where's Marie? Is she still in Arizona? Is she in Florida?"

Mr. P. shook his head. "No. It turned out she was in Arizona."

I caught his use of the past tense. "Was?"

"I'm sorry," he said. "Mrs. Heard is dead."

Liz closed her eyes for a moment and sighed. "Dead? When did it happen?"

Alfred glanced down at the notepad next to his laptop. "About six months ago. I do have the contact information for her son, if you'd like it."

She nodded. "I would. Thank you, Alfred, very much."

He tore the top page off the pad and handed it to her. "If there's anything else you need, let me know."

"I will," Liz said. "I appreciate this." She folded the paper and stuck it in her purse.

We started for the shop. "I can't believe Marie is dead," Liz said. "I can't believe Wilson didn't stay in touch with her. We should have sent flowers or made a donation in her name or something."

I gestured at her purse. "You have her son's address and phone number. You can still make a donation and you can send a note to her son."

"I think I'll do that," she said. She made a face. "I know this is selfish of me, but this doesn't help us figure out what was going on at the foundation."

"I know," I said. "We'll just have to figure it out some other way." I wished I had even an inkling of what that other way was.

Just then John came through the door from the shop carrying a large cardboard carton. We'd found a beautiful 1930s vintage pink blush and clear pressed-glass shade in a closet in the spare bedroom at Clayton McNamara's house. Clayton had no idea where it had come from but he guessed it was likely something that had belonged to his brother, who was even more of a pack rat than Clayton was. When Gram had seen the shade she'd decided it was perfect for the ceiling fixture in the living room. Clayton wanted to, as he put it, "just give the danged thing to her," but Gram would have none of that. After some give-and-take on both sides I'd come up with an amount both of them could live with. John had arrived to pick up the shade and give Nick and Liam a hand taking out the run of windows in the sunporch that faced the parking lot.

"Hello, Liz," John said. Something about her expression made him frown. "Is everything all right?"

"Yes," Liz said, mostly, I think, out of reflex. Then she sighed. "No, John, it isn't. Do you remember Marie Heard from your time on the board?"

"I do," he said. "She was Wilson's assistant. She took the notes at the meetings." His brown eyes narrowed. "Why? Did something happen to her?"

"She died," I said.

"Six months ago," Liz added.

"I'm sorry to hear that," John said. "She knew when I first joined the board that I didn't have a clue about how that sort of thing worked. She always made sure I had what I needed to do the job—reports, spreadsheets, notes from previous meetings."

"We were hoping she could help with the book project," I said. "I don't suppose you kept any of that old paperwork?"

He shook his head. "I'm sorry, Sarah. It's long gone."

I nodded, hoping my disappointment didn't show on my face. Turns out it did.

John turned his attention to Liz. "How long have we known each other?" he asked.

"I don't know," she said. "Thirty years maybe. Whenever Jack took you on as his grad student."

"Closer to forty," he said. "So how about both of you stop this song and dance about writing a book and tell me what the hell is really going on?" I saw a brief flare of anger in his eyes.

"Tell him," I said.

Liz glared at me. "Fine," she said. She looked at John. "I think that Rob Andrews was set up. I don't think he embezzled the money from the camp."

John blew out a breath. He set the box on the corner of the workbench and then gave us his full attention.

"You need to go to the police," he said.

"Sarah and I are trying to find enough evidence to do

NO ESCAPE CLAWS 151

that," Liz said. I noticed she hadn't mentioned Michelle. "So I need you to keep this to yourself for now. Please."

John made a face and rubbed his jaw. "If you're right about this, then who did take the money?"

"We don't know," I said. "We were hoping Marie Heard might be able to help."

"Do you have any notes from the board meetings back then?" John asked. "Or copies of the annual reports?"

"I have both." Liz flicked a bit of lint from the dark purple tunic she was wearing. It seemed that I could feel the frustration coming off of her.

"If it will help, I can take a look at them again. Maybe I'll see something this time now that I know what I'm looking for."

"Thank you," I said.

He gave me a tight smile and looked at Liz. "I'll keep your secret for now—but not from Isabel."

"I'm sorry, I should have been honest with you from the start," she said.

"You really think Rob Andrews was innocent?"

"I do."

"I'll look at everything," he said. "Maybe there's a connection I didn't see." He eyed Liz for a long moment. "You're going to have to bring the police in on this at some point."

"Just not yet," Liz said. "Please."

John hesitated for a moment, then nodded. "All right." He picked up the box holding the light shade and headed for the back door.

"He's right," Liz said. "I should have told him what was going on from the beginning."

"You've told him now," I said. "And maybe he'll see something in those papers that we didn't."

"I hope so," she said, "because without Marie I'm not sure what my next move should be." She shook her head. "I feel bad that she died and none of us knew. I can't believe Wilson didn't stay in contact with her."

"What if you tell Wilson what you're trying to do?" I said. I looked down at my shoe and realized I had what looked like chocolate sprinkles on the toe, probably from the back of that customer's SUV. "Maybe he would have some idea who could have taken the money and set up Rob." There were also bits of dried grass and what seemed to be dog hair stuck to my sleeve. I brushed them away. That SUV could use a good vacuuming, which reminded me that my vehicle probably could as well.

"Do I look like I've taken leave of my senses?" she asked.

"No," I said a little uncertainly. This had to be a trick question.

"First of all, Wilson is incapable of keeping a secret." Her mouth twisted to one side. "He's my brother and I love him but sometimes I'd like to whack him on the back of the head with my purse. If something doesn't affect him directly it could be happening right under his nose and he wouldn't notice. And no, that short attention span is not because I knocked him with a swing when he was four."

"You knocked your brother off a swing?" I said.

Liam had once spun me so fast on a roundabout at the park that I'd thrown up.

On him.

"I didn't knock him off a swing," Liz said. "I might have knocked him in the head *with* a swing. But honestly, it hardly left a mark. Though you would have thought he'd fractured his skull the way he fussed."

I laughed and slung an arm around her shoulder. "Did I ever tell you about the time Liam spun me on the roundabout at that little park down the street from Mom and Dad's house?"

Liam and Nick headed out for lunch about twelve thirty. Rose and Mr. P. went with them. Mr. P. had managed to find enough trim and baseboard from Cleveland to finish the sunporch. In return we'd given the picker a box of old tools that had been in the first of the two storage units. Everyone was happy.

Charlotte and Avery were working in the store. Charlotte was showing china to a young woman who was getting married at Christmastime while Avery was ringing up a sale at the cash desk. To my surprise a man was buying two boxes of old first-grade readers that had to have been hanging around the shop for at least six months. Elvis was sitting in the tub chair being his usual charming self.

I went up to my office, dropped into my desk chair and picked up my coffee. It was cold. I could go get a cup and then add a few items to the store's Web site, I thought. I could go downstairs and talk to Avery about ideas for a new window display. I could eat the last blueberry streusel muffin in the staff room—assuming Nick or Avery hadn't already inhaled it. But what I really wanted was one of Mac's pep talks where he told me that Rose and crew would in fact pull this investigation out of the fire the way they'd saved every other case they'd taken on.

I looked at my phone lying on the desk. Mac had said if I needed anything to call him. "So why don't you call him?" I said.

There was a loud murp from the floor in front of my desk. Then Elvis launched himself onto the desktop. He licked a paw and ran it over his ear, then cocked his head and looked inquiringly—at least that's how it seemed—at me.

"He might be busy," I said. I rubbed the space between my eyebrows. I was having a conversation with a cat. A cat who probably had no clue what the heck I was even talking about.

The cat in question ducked his head and nudged the phone a bit closer to me. Okay. Maybe he did know what I was talking about.

I picked up the phone, punched in the number Mac had given me and wished I didn't feel like I was back in high school.

Mac answered on the fourth ring. "Sarah. Hi," he said.

I couldn't help smiling. "Hi yourself," I said. "Is this a bad time?"

"No, this is a good time." I heard the squeak of what sounded like a desk chair. "I'm eating a piece of coffee cake and drinking a cup of coffee and thinking how much better Rose's coffee cake is and how much I like the coffee made from the beans Mr. P. gets from that roaster in Kennebunk."

"So you miss us," I teased. "Or at least the food and the coffee."

Mac laughed. "Rose's coffee cake is very good, but I do miss all of you. What's up?"

Elvis had stretched out on the desk. Now he rolled on to his side and closed his green eyes. Cat for *My work here is done.*

I swiveled around in the chair and leaned back, propping one foot on the edge of the desk. "Liam is here working in the sunporch."

"That's good," Mac said.

"There are two new windows in and a big hole covered by a tarp because Liam, Nick, Rose and Mr. P. have gone to lunch."

He laughed. "They'll be back. I swear."

"I have visions of coming in Monday morning to find a raccoon sitting in the tub chair and a family of seagulls on top of that big gold standing mirror."

"In other words, you'd have the display for the front window for next month all worked out."

This time I was the one who laughed.

"So is the détente between Nick and Rose still holding?" Mac asked.

I swung slowly from side to side in my chair. "It is. Although sometimes I feel like I've been transported to some other version of this planet."

His question reminded me that I wanted to ask Nick what he and Rose had been looking at the day before. Even though Rose had said I didn't want to know, the more I thought about it, the more I realized I probably did.

"It would be great if they actually have stopped butting heads, but . . ."

". . . that's probably not the case so I should enjoy the calm before the storm so to speak," I finished.

"Based on past experience, probably." The chair or whatever it was squeaked again. "So what's happening with the case?" Mac asked. "In your last text you said you were going to talk to the parents of the girl this Gina Pearson hit with her car."

"The father is very angry still," I said. "Not that I blame him. But he has an alibi. As for the mother, Rose thinks she's a possibility. And she doesn't have an alibi."

"You don't agree with Rose?"

I sighed softly. "I guess I don't really want Jia—that's her name, Jia Allison—to be a possibility. There are already three kids who have lost their mother. I don't want it to be four."

"It'll work out, Sarah."

"You always say that," I said.

"And I'm always right."

I thought about what Avery had said about Mac. *You should ask him when he's coming back so he knows we want him back.* Instead I said, "I should probably go check on Avery and Charlotte."

"Tell them I said hello," Mac said.

"I will." I turned back around to face the desk. Elvis was gone.

"I'll talk to you soon," Mac said and he was gone, too.

I went downstairs. Charlotte had an armful of pillows and Avery was just coming in from the workroom with a tray of teacup planters—little Haworthia plants in china cups and saucers. They were a perennial favorite with tourists.

"Rose just texted Avery," Charlotte said. "She's sending a bus full of tourists from Quebec our way. They'll be here right after they finish lunch."

Rose and Mr. P., along with Liam and Nick, were back about ten minutes later.

"How was lunch?" I asked.

"Excellent," Rose said. "We went to Natalie's Chowder House." She looked at me as though she was expecting some kind of reaction.

"Good," I said, fairly certain that was not the response she was looking for.

"Molly Pace works there," Mr. P. said.

Molly Pace. Who the heck was Molly Pace?

Liam was leaning against the workbench while Nick was standing feet apart with his arms crossed. They seemed to be enjoying my bewilderment.

"Have you forgotten that Molly Pace is Gavin Pace's wife?" Rose said. "He's the man Gina Pearson had the affair with. Try to keep up, dear."

"I'm with you now," I said, glaring over her shoulder at Liam and Nick, who smirked back at me. "So did you talk to her?"

"Well, it would have been silly to go there and then not talk to her, don't you think?"

"Yes, it would," I said, nodding like a bobblehead doll stuck to a car dashboard. "What's she like?"

Luckily Mr. P. stepped in to save me. "Not what I expected," he said.

"What were you expecting?" I asked.

"Someone angrier, I guess, given what Sammy told me about her confrontation with Gina outside the pub—which wasn't their only encounter, by the way."

"Do you think she could have hurt Gina?"

Rose shook her head. "First of all, Molly isn't any taller than I am and she doesn't have my upper-body strength."

I had no idea what Rose's upper-body capacity was and it didn't seem like a good time to ask so I just nodded.

"And second, she wasn't even in town the weekend of the fire. She was in Portland with friends, Christmas shopping and indulging in the festivities."

"So we cross her off the list," I said.

"Yes, we do," Mr. P. said.

"But right now we need to get ready for those tourists," Rose said. She pressed her thumb to her lips and looked around the workroom.

"Charlotte already got the pillows," I said.

Rose nodded. "Good. What if we put out some of those fancy pots Avery did and maybe some of those old bottles from Clayton's?"

"Good idea," I said. "I'll go get the bottles. They're under the stairs."

"I'll get the flowerpots," she said. She looked at Mr. P. "Alf, could you give me a hand?"

"Of course," he said with a smile.

"Liam. Nicolas," Rose said over her shoulder, "I think that's enough lollygagging. Don't you two have work to do?"

Nick ducked his head. Liam cleared his throat. "Yes, ma'am," he said. They started for the sunporch.

The next hour was busy. The tourists from Quebec were friendly and full of questions about everything. And none of them laughed at my very rudimentary attempts to speak French. It turned out to be a good thing that Charlotte had brought out all the pillows and

Avery had carried in her planters. We sold them all, along with dishes, about half the bottles, books, vintage postcards and a large mahogany framed mirror and a chamber pot the purchaser insisted would fit under her seat.

Rose was already rearranging the remaining bottles. The pale green vintage Coke bottles were the first that had been snapped up. I was always amazed by the things people liked to collect.

I put my arm around Rose and kissed the top of her head. "Thank you for telling the tour bus operator about Second Chance. We did well and I think she'll be back next time she has a tour in this area."

"You're welcome, dear," she said. She put a hand up to her neck. "It helps that I'm wearing my lucky scarf."

Rose's lucky scarf (purple with a silver Aztec design) had been given to her by Steven Tyler—yes, that Steven Tyler—after she'd danced in the aisle with him at an Aerosmith concert and kissed him, so long and so deeply that teenaged me had wished for the earth to open up and swallow me alive, especially since Tyler had made it clear he'd enjoyed the encounter.

I went out to the garage to bring in a box of teacups. We never seemed to run out of them. I'd find a few in a yard sale or buy a couple from one of my regular pickers. And I'd purchased two dozen of them from one of Rose's friends who was giving up her house for an apartment and a very limber yoga instructor who was twenty years her junior.

When I came back into the workroom Avery was lifting a bin down from one of the shelves. "I thought I should reset those two tables," she said. "Maybe I'll use those white ghost pumpkins and some of those branches with the little red berries for a centerpiece."

I nodded. "That's a good idea." The place settings of china and the glassware on both of the tables in the shop had sold. The smaller table had even lost the starched linen tablecloth, napkins and silver napkin rings.

Avery set the bin on the floor. She eyed me and shifted from one foot to the other. I waited. "Sarah, would it be okay if my friend Greg stops by at the end of the day to look at some of those old classroom maps we have? We're working on a project."

"It's fine with me," I said. "Do you know where they are?"

She nodded, fidgeting with her arm of bracelets. "I pretty much know where everything is. I've been kind of making a map of back here."

I set the box of cups on the workbench. "Why didn't I think of that?"

"Probably because you and Mac are usually the ones who put things away so you know where it all is."

She was right. The garage work space was more Mac's domain than mine, and more than once in the last month I'd found myself out there searching for something he would have been able to put his hands on in less than a minute.

"So it's really okay for Greg to stop by?" Avery said.

I looked at her, more than a little confused. "Like I said, it's fine."

She was looking at me as if I was as dense as a bag of sand. Then I got it. "Wait a minute," I said. "Your friend Greg? Do you mean Greg Pearson?"

Avery nodded. "Yeah. Took you long enough." She pushed the bin across the floor to me.

"Are you two really working on a project?" I asked. I gestured at the small stepladder she'd been using and she went back to put it away.

"Yes," she said over her shoulder.

"How did that happen?"

"I knocked my stuff off my desk."

She seemed to think that was enough of an explanation.

"And?" I prompted.

"And by the time I'd picked everything up most of my friends had found partners. So I ended up with Greg." She shrugged. "Easy-peasy."

I had to swallow down a smile because she suddenly reminded me so much of Rose.

"And you know what the cool thing is?" she asked.

"No," I said.

She hung the ladder on its hook and walked back over to me. "I like working with him. He's smart and he has good ideas and he doesn't dump all the work on me."

I did smile then. "I'm glad it worked out."

"He should be here about four thirty or so. He doesn't drive so he has to wait for his grandmother to bring him."

"A teenage guy who doesn't drive? That's an anomaly." Avery drove Liz's car every chance she got.

I grabbed one end of the bin and Avery picked up the other. It was heavy.

"Yeah, I know," she said. "I think he was doing driving lessons when his mom . . . died. I figured maybe they couldn't afford them anymore and he was too embarrassed to say."

Mr. P. had already learned that the insurance company had refused to pay out on both the Pearsons' fire insurance and Gina's life insurance policy. Maybe if we could prove that someone had murdered her that would change.

Greg Pearson showed up just a couple of minutes after four thirty. He gave me a shy smile when Avery introduced me as her boss, but he looked me in the eye and thanked me for letting them look through the maps. Someone had taught him good manners.

He was tall and lanky in that way that teenage boys often are. He had the same brown eyes as his sister and the same guarded look in them. His hair was dark instead of blond, but he looked very much like Mallory, which meant they both took after their father. He wore khakis, a blue and red flannel shirt over a gray T-shirt and black Chuck Taylor's.

"Did I get here too early?" Greg said to Avery.

"No," I said. I smiled at Avery. "You can go take a look at those maps right now. I can help Charlotte."

"Okay," Avery said. "If you need me, yell or something."

I'd made a point of staying away from the sunporch ever since Liam and Nick came back from lunch—my resolve made easier by the blue plastic tarp they'd hung over the door. But now I wanted to see how much work they'd gotten done and I wanted to tackle Nick about his conversation with Rose the day before.

I poked my head around the side of the tarp. "Can I come in?" I asked.

"As long as you don't mind the mess," Liam said. A pair of safety goggles was pushed up on the top of his head and a dust mask hung below his chin. All four windows facing the parking lot had been replaced and he was screwing what looked to be the last piece of drywall to the studs.

"What do you think?" Nick asked. He was still wearing his safety glasses and there were bits of wood and drywall dust in his sandy hair. He'd pushed his own mask down off his face, too.

"I think it looks terrific," I said with a grin. "I can't believe you got so much done in just one day."

Liam grinned back. "It made a big difference having John here to help when we were taking out the old windows. And Nick's an okay assistant."

Nick held out one hand and waggled his fingers from side to side. "Your brother's an okay boss," he said.

I rolled my eyes. "It's good to know that the two of you have been striving for okay-ness."

Liam set the drill on the floor and straightened up. Nick reached for the broom that was leaning in the far corner of the room and began sweeping up the debris and dust on the floor. Liam picked his way over to me and draped one arm over my shoulder. "The plan for tomorrow is to pull down all the remaining drywall, insulate behind it and put up new stuff. I know an electrician who's coming to add a couple of outlets and install the lights. After that, it's just a matter of taping, mudding, sanding, trim and paint."

"That sounds like a lot of work."

Liam shook his head. "Once the drywall is up, the worst is over, as far as I'm concerned. He frowned. "Is

Alfred around? I need to find out when the trim is getting dropped off."

"He was helping Charlotte change the filter in the vacuum," I said.

"I'm just going to go talk to him," Liam said. "I'll be right back." He pushed the tarp aside and disappeared into the workroom.

Nick had just about swept his way over to me. "Thank you for helping Liam with all of this," I said.

"You're welcome," he said, looking around for something to pick up all the bits he'd collected.

There was a rectangle of brown cardboard—it looked like the top flap from a box—leaning against the wall where normally Mr. P.'s desk sat. I grabbed it. I knew it was Liam's version of a dustpan. I'd also seen him use the newspaper and the top of an egg carton for the task, much to Mom's annoyance.

"Here," I said to Nick, holding the cardboard so he could sweep everything onto it. The cardboard made a pretty good dustpan. I dumped everything into a black garbage bag without spilling anything back on the floor.

"Seriously," I said, turning back to Nick. "I appreciate this. I owe you."

He grinned and nodded. "I know."

I folded my arms over my chest and eyed him. "Am I going to regret that?"

"There's a pretty good chance of that," he said, still grinning.

I bent down and picked up a drywall screw from the floor. Liam and I hadn't talked about floor covering, I realized.

"I need to ask you something," I said to Nick.

He was eyeing the back wall, lips silently moving, probably doing more drywall calculations in his head. "About the room or about the case?"

"The case." That got me all of his attention.

"Problem?"

I shrugged. "That depends. What were you showing Rose yesterday?"

"I thought everyone agreed that was something you didn't want to know."

"Rose said that and in the moment I agreed, but now I'm not so sure I should have."

His mouth twisted to one side, but he didn't say anything.

"C'mon, Nick," I said. "I thought we were on the same team."

He let out a breath. "We are." Another momentary silence. "Fine. I uh . . . I know the officer who investigated that car accident Gina Pearson had. It was in Rockport. He let me take a quick look at his report. I can't show it to anyone else."

There was a "but" coming. I waited.

"But he let me have a look at his rough notes. He has stacks of those six-by-nine memo pads, in boxes in his basement, every one with a black cover. New case, new notepad. I showed the notes to Rose. I thought maybe there might be someone—a coach, a teacher, another parent—who might be a viable suspect."

So it hadn't been a notebook they'd been looking at. It had been a memo pad.

I pulled my left shoulder with one hand. "And?" I said.

Nick looked confused. "And what?"

"And did you learn anything?"

"No. No, I don't think so."

I caught just the briefest hesitation between the first and second no. "You're not certain."

He closed his eyes for a second and shook his head. "You're as bad as Rose, Sarah," he said.

I didn't say anything.

Nick pulled the eye protectors off the top of his head and turned them over in his hands. "I didn't see anything in those notes. Hannah Allison was the only one hurt. One of the coaches did first aid. Another took charge of the rest of the runners. As far as I could see, neither one of them had any kind of exchange with Gina Pearson or her son."

"So why the lack of certainty?"

"Okay, this is going to sound weird and I can't actually believe I'm saying this but I think Rose noticed something in those notes."

"Okay," I said.

He frowned. "You don't seem that surprised."

I smiled at him. "This is not my first rodeo. What makes you think she found something?"

"She went back and read the same page twice."

"Did you ask her about it?"

Nick gave me a wry smile. "She said she just wanted to make sure she hadn't missed anything."

"And that could be all it is," I said.

"Or?"

"Or it could be she discovered something she doesn't want the rest of us to know, at least for now.

He bent down, picked up the drill and snapped out the battery pack. "So what do we do?"

"*You* don't do anything," I said. "Right now you're on her nice list and I'd like to keep it that way at least for a little while longer. I'll talk to her."

He narrowed his dark eyes. "You really think she'll admit anything to you?"

I shook my head. "Not a chance. But she will tell Mr. P. and I'm pretty sure he'll tell me."

"What do you think she saw that I didn't?" Nick asked.

"You know Rose's mind doesn't work like anyone else's," I said.

He smiled. "Oh yeah, that's true."

Liam came back then. Cleveland would bring the trim first thing in the morning.

"What time do you want to start?" I asked.

"Is eight too early?" Liam asked.

"Not for me," I said. "I'll see you then." I ducked under the tarp. Nick hadn't noticed that I hadn't actually answered his question. What had Rose seen in those notes that Nick hadn't? She didn't want me to know, whatever it was. Was it something that might incriminate Mike Pearson?

I stopped at the Emmerson Foundation offices on the way home to pick up the papers Liz had promised to John. The foundation was located on the second floor of the old soap factory, an L-shaped brick building close to the harbor front. I took the stairs because I loved to look at the old photos of North Harbor that hung in the stairwell. I was expecting to find Liz in her office but instead discovered her assistant, Jane Evans, who was also mom to Josh Evans, the Angels' de facto lawyer.

"Hi, Sarah," she said. She was just putting two file

folders into a cardboard banker's box. Jane was about my height, albeit a lot curvier, with blond curls courtesy of Phantasy. At the moment a pair of half-frame glasses was perched on the end of her nose. She was wearing a green and black dress with heels, although not as high as Liz generally wore. Jane and her son had the same slightly mischievous smile.

"Hi, Jane," I said. "What are you doing here?"

She put the lid on the box. "I came in to bring coffee and cream for Monday morning and found Liz trying to sort this box of papers into some kind of order."

"And ended up doing it yourself."

She ducked her head and smiled. "Liz has a lot of skills, but dealing with paperwork isn't one of them. I sent her home."

"You're the only person on the planet who could do that. She'd never listen to anyone else," I said. "How do you do that?"

The smile got a little wider. "I'd really love to tell you," she said.

"But then you'd have to kill me," I finished.

"Maybe not kill you. But certainly incapacitate you for a while." She pushed the box across the tabletop toward me.

"Thank you, Jane," I said, reaching for the carton.

"I was sorry to hear about Marie," she said.

"Did you know her?"

Jane nodded. "We both started off working in the office at the chocolate factory. That was a long time ago."

"What was she like?" I asked.

Jane smiled. "Liz said you were helping her with this book project." She took a minute to consider my question. "Marie was a dynamo," she said finally. "She was organized and efficient and she could keep a more complicated schedule in her head than most of us could keep with a datebook and a calendar. And I know it's cliché, but she was married to her job after her husband died. Working for the foundation, for Wilson, was her life." She pushed the chair next to her under the long wooden conference table. "I think it's wonderful that you offered to help Liz with this project, Sarah, but don't fall into the trap of work being your whole life."

She laughed then, well aware that she was standing in her office on a Saturday. "I've been telling Josh the same thing. And I know I'm a fine one to talk."

"I'll keep your advice in mind," I said, giving her a smile. "As long as you promise to do the same."

"You have a deal," she said.

I picked up the box, thanked her and headed for the stairs. I hoped John could find some answers in the contents.

I knew that Liz considered the Emmerson Foundation her family's legacy. The thought that someone had tampered with it cut her deeply and I knew she'd do whatever it took to protect her family. I thought about Mike Pearson then. What had he done to protect *his* family?

Chapter 11

It hadn't taken much effort for Mr. P. to find out that Gina Pearson had worked for a marketing consulting firm in Rockland until her drinking had become just too much of a problem for them. And it was one of her former coworkers who had told him about the affair with Gavin Pace. Molly Pace had admitted she'd had two different confrontations with Gina, but it was Charlotte who unearthed more details about their second encounter. Before he transferred to Avery's progressive private school, Greg Pearson had been a student in the North Harbor school system. One of his teachers had told Charlotte about the confrontation in the school drop-off area between Gina and Molly. Although Molly seemed to have put her marriage to Gavin behind her now, back then she'd been very angry.

"Everyone within earshot heard Molly tell Gina to keep her hands off her husband," Charlotte said as she made the tea Monday morning. "It got uglier after that."

"I can't imagine what that must have been like for

Greg," I said, leaning back against the counter with my coffee mug.

Charlotte shook her head. "I guess he tried to drag his mother away. One of the vice principals had had to step between the two women and some other parent called the police."

"That is ugly," I said.

"Is there any chance Molly Pace isn't telling the truth about where she was the night of the fire?"

I took a sip of my coffee. "No. Mr. P. checked her Facebook page. There were lots of photos of Molly and her friends getting in the holiday spirit, if you get my drift."

"I do," she said.

"I'd like to talk to Gavin Pace," I said.

A small smile played across Charlotte's face. "I might be able to help with that."

"Really?" I said. "Do tell."

Charlotte reached for a cup. "The high school has an alumni newsletter."

I took a sip of my coffee as her words sank in. "Wait a second," I said. "Where did Mr. Pace attend high school?"

That got me an approving smile. "Here in North Harbor."

I waited as she poured her tea.

"He now works as a sales rep for a company that markets flyers."

"That's a step down from account executive," I said.

Charlotte nodded as she tried the tea and then added a tiny bit more milk.

"According to what Alfred could find out, Mr. Pace

resigned from his former job about a month before the fire."

I raised an eyebrow.

"It does seem as though it was suggested he resign."

"Because of the affair with Gina?" I asked.

"Possibly," Charlotte said. She picked up her cup and we headed for the stairs. "But I think it's even more likely it was because Gavin Pace is also an alcoholic. Alfred tracked down Gina's former assistant. She was very reluctant to talk about Gina but she did admit that the relationship between Gina and Gavin was probably more about alcohol than romance."

"So we know Gavin lost his job—"

"—and his marriage, remember," Charlotte added. "Molly Pace filed for divorce just a couple of weeks before Gavin left that consulting firm job." She glanced at her watch and went to open the front door.

I took a sip of my coffee. "For some people either one of those things would be enough to want to get revenge. The question is whether Gavin Pace is one of those people."

"Liz and Rose are going to talk to him right before lunch," Charlotte said. "Why don't you go with them and find out?"

There were plenty of other things I could have been doing on a Monday morning. None of them stopped me from saying yes.

It was about a fifteen-minute drive from North Harbor to the business in Rockport where Gavin Pace now worked.

"We have an appointment at eleven fifteen," Liz said when she walked in at ten thirty. She dangled her car keys in front of me. "You can drive. Watch your lead foot."

I grabbed the keys and took a giant step backward.

She frowned at me. "What on earth are you doing? Have you suddenly taken up the tango?"

"No," I said. "It's just that I was afraid that *you* commenting about my lead foot might nudge the universe to remind you that I'm not the only person around here who sees speed limits as suggestions, not firm rules." I patted my hair. It was pulled back in a smooth knot held by two elastics, probably two dozen bobby pins and a lot of gel. "I didn't want any lightning bolts to singe my hair."

"You're hilarious," Liz said. "You could also be replaced with an Uber and one of those robot things that vacuums."

I was already on my way to the workroom. I didn't even try to hide my laughter.

"So what pretense did you use to get an appointment with Mr. Pace?" I asked Liz once we were on the highway.

"I did not use a pretense," she said somewhat indignantly.

"I'm sorry," I said. "What completely legitimate reason did you use to make an appointment with Gavin Pace?" I sent a quick sideways glance her way.

She adjusted the sleeve of her orange sherbet–colored shirt. "I simply told him that I was interested in more information about possibly sending out a flyer next spring about the Sunshine Camp."

"You deceived that young man," Rose said from the backseat. It didn't seem like a good idea to point out that she had been known to leave out a few details on occasion.

"I did nothing of the sort," Liz retorted.

"When has the camp ever needed to advertise? In fifty-plus years has there ever been a year you didn't have a waiting list?"

Okay. I could see that we were already starting to veer off track.

"It never hurts to have information. Times are changing. You don't know that we won't want to advertise in the future."

"I don't like lying to people," Rose said stubbornly.

I knew if I looked in the rearview mirror I'd see that determined jut to her chin. "None of us do, Rose," I said. "But I doubt Mr. Pace would have agreed to see us if he knew we wanted to talk to him about Gina Pearson. And technically Liz isn't lying. She didn't say she was going to send out flyers, just that she wanted information about doing it."

There was silence for a moment. Then Rose spoke. "Sarah's right. I'm sorry."

Liz waved away her words. "It doesn't matter. However, for the record, I do have a plan and it does involve telling Pace the truth."

Out of the corner of my eye I could see a self-satisfied smile on her face. It didn't give me a good feeling.

We arrived about five minutes early for our meeting. I found a place to park in the lot behind the small office building where Metromedia was located. I didn't ask Liz what her plan was; I figured there was a pretty good chance she wouldn't tell me anyway.

Gavin Pace kept us waiting a good ten minutes and

didn't apologize for it when he finally came to collect us. If Liz had really come looking to advertise in one of his flyer bundles, he would have already blown the sale. But the man's biggest mistake was not taking the time to look her up online, which was why when the receptionist gestured in our direction he walked over and held out his hand *to me*.

"Mrs. French, it's such a pleasure to meet you," he said in an overly hearty tone.

It was completely inappropriate, but a bubble of laughter filled my chest. Before I could say anything, Liz stepped between us. "*I'm* Elizabeth French," she said icily. "This is Sarah Grayson and Rose Jackson."

"My bad," he said with a boyish laugh and a head tilt that had probably been getting him out of trouble since he was six.

I put a hand to my mouth and turned the laugh that escaped into a cough. Given the look that Rose shot my way it might not have been that convincing.

Gavin Pace led us back to his office. It was small, which wouldn't have mattered so much if it hadn't been so cluttered. There were papers all over his desk and a couple of boxes stacked on one of the two visitors' chairs. Gavin moved the two boxes to the floor. Liz and Rose sat down, in Liz's case after carefully brushing off the seat, to make a point, I was sure, although I thought it was most likely wasted on Mr. Pace. I stood.

"Sorry, I don't have another chair," he said to me with a smile and an offhand shrug.

Gavin Pace was a good-looking man. He was tall with thick blond hair and great teeth, assets he seemed very much aware of. His dark blue suit was of good quality, and his tie was silk. He didn't stand by his desk so much as pose for a moment before he sat down. He brushed a hand back through his hair—not out of frustration or because it was in his eyes, but because I suspected he wanted to draw attention to it. As he'd moved past me I noticed he smelled like a mix of mouthwash and breath mints. I told myself not to read too much into that.

"So you're interested in putting a flyer in our North Harbor/Camden/Rockport bundle?" he said to Liz. He looked over the top of his desk, then pulled open his bottom desk drawer, fished around for a moment and pulled out a pen. His hands were soft, I noticed, no calluses, or scrapes. His nails were neatly trimmed and looked like they'd been buffed.

"Actually Mr. Pace, I'm more interested in talking about Gina Pearson," Liz said. She leaned back in her chair and gave him a polite smile. It seemed the unvarnished truth was her plan.

For a moment he didn't say a word. "I'm sorry. I uh . . . I don't know what you mean," he said finally. Given that he looked like he'd just seen a ghost, it seemed likely he probably did know what Liz meant.

"Gina Pearson," Liz said. "The woman you had an affair with."

The muscles along his jawline tightened. "I don't discuss my personal life with clients," he said stiffly. He set the pen down on the desk and got to his feet.

Liz stayed seated, crossing one leg over the other as though she was prepared to sit there all day. "I'm not your client," she said, her tone conversational as if they were simply chatting about the weather. "However, I am the chairman of the board of the Emmerson Foundation and former chairperson of the Midcoast Chamber of Commerce. I know every business owner in a fifty-mile radius of this office."

Pace understood what she was getting at. He sat down on the corner of the desk, pushing a pile of paper out of the way. A file folder toppled to the floor. He ignored it. "Gina Pearson is dead."

"I know that," Liz said. "What I don't know is what the relationship was like between the two of you."

He shrugged. "You said it yourself. We had an affair. I'm not proud of it."

Liz didn't say anything. I'd seen her do that before.

After a moment he made a face. "Look, we were both drunks then. There's no other word for it. The affair destroyed my marriage. I left my job because I needed a new start. We weren't in love. There was no relationship."

"You must have been very angry at Gina," I said. "Her marriage did survive and she didn't have to leave her job the way you did."

He glanced over at me. "For a while yeah, I was pis— pretty mad at her. But in the end, no one made me pick up a drink. And no one made me get involved with Gina, either."

"When was the last time you talked to her?" Liz asked.

"I don't know," he said after taking a moment to seemingly think about it. "A couple of months before she died. That was, I guess what you'd call an eye-opener for me."

"What do you mean?" I asked. I glanced at Rose. Usually she wasn't this quiet. All I could see was the back of her head.

He rubbed the side of his face with one hand. "I mean, she looked like she was living on the street. It was like she hadn't been sleeping. The coat she had on just hung on her; she was so damn skinny, like someone who had an eating disorder or something. I couldn't get the picture of her out of my head. I stopped drinking cold turkey. I'm sober. I go to the gym. I've got a pretty decent relationship now with my ex. So I guess in a way you could say she did me a favor."

"So you didn't see Gina the day that she died?" Liz asked.

Pace reached across the desk and straightened his pen, which had rolled sideways almost to the edge. It struck me that it was a gesture to buy time before he answered. "Like I said, the last time I saw Gina was a couple of months before she died. If I'd seen her again I would have told her to get some help. In fact, I wish I *had* seen her. Just maybe she would have listened. I don't know."

That was pretty much the end of the conversation. Pace didn't bother walking us out.

No one said anything until we were in the car. I shifted in my seat to look at Liz.

"Well?" I said.

"That young man has only a passing acquaintance with the truth," she said as she fastened her seat belt.

I nodded. "I agree. He was definitely lying. Did you notice how he kept pausing before he answered? And how he touched his face and straightened his pen?"

"What I noticed is that he couldn't look me in the eye for any length of time," Liz said.

"I saw that too," Rose chimed in from the backseat.

"I think it's possible Mr. Pace might be drinking," I said. "I don't want to jump to conclusions but he smelled like mouthwash and breath mints. It was kind of overkill."

"Oh, he's definitely drinking," she said.

I turned around to look at her. "Did you notice the mints and mouthwash, too?" I asked

"Actually no dear, I didn't," she said. "But I did notice the half-empty pint of vodka in the bottom-left-hand drawer of his desk."

"What!" I exclaimed.

"Very nice, Rose," Liz said with an approving smile.

"I'm not certain but I believe it was pickle flavor."

I grimaced. "That just sounds wrong," I said, not that I knew anything about vodka.

"How did you notice that bottle and we missed it?" Liz asked, looking over her shoulder.

"You were both paying attention to Mr. Pace," Rose said. "I wasn't. And I'm little so people tend not to pay attention to me. He closed that desk drawer pretty quickly, but I did see the bottle."

"Do you think Gavin Pace could have killed Gina and set that house on fire?" I asked.

She shook her head. "I honestly don't know. He has a rather weak chin and yes, I know that speaks more to genetics than character."

I looked at Liz. "What do you think?"

"I think he went out of his way to lie to us. He's hiding something." She gave a sly smile. "Let's find out why and what."

Chapter 12

On the drive back to the shop we decided the next step was to ask Mr. P. to get in touch with Molly Pace and see what she could tell us about her former husband.

"Do either of you know anyone who lives on the Pearsons' street other than the judge?" I asked. "It would help if we could find out if anyone remembers seeing Gavin Pace around the time of the fire."

Liz shook her head.

"I'm sorry. I can't think of anyone," Rose said.

"I thought you two knew just about everyone in town," I said.

"Not everyone, dear. I can't keep up with all the grandchildren." She leaned forward. "Can you, Liz?"

Liz waved a hand in the air. "Good heavens, no. And I don't always get to the Chamber of Commerce meetings, although in my defense Monday is a terrible night to have them."

I wasn't sure how the Chamber meetings were connected, but I was afraid that if I asked Liz might tell me.

"You know, I could ask Elspeth," Liz said. "She might know someone."

"And doesn't Charlotte know somebody at Shady Pines who used to live in that area?" Rose asked.

I stopped at the corner before turning onto our street, clearing my throat loudly at Rose's referring to Legacy Place, the senior citizen's apartment complex where she had once lived, as Shady Pines.

"Oh sweet girl, I think you're coming down with something," she immediately said. "Is your throat scratchy?"

So this was how we were going to play it.

"My throat is fine," I said.

"You can't be too careful this time of year," she said. "Once the children go back to school all sorts of terrible bugs start making the rounds." I could hear her fishing in her bag. Then she tapped me on the shoulder.

"Here, dear. Try this," she said. Something dropped into my lap.

I glanced down. It was a Fisherman's Friend lozenge.

"Pop that in your mouth. It'll cure whatever you might have picked up." Fisherman's Friend were Rose's cure-all for everything—extra-strong menthol lozenges that would make a cough lie down and surrender and clear every sinus cavity in your head.

It was impossible to miss the challenge in her eyes.

"Well, put it in your mouth," she said. "It won't do you any good sitting on your lap."

"Let me help you," Liz said.

From the corner of my eye I watched her unwrap the cough drop. The gleam in her eyes told me she was enjoying this way too much.

"Hold out your hand," she instructed. I took my hand

off the wheel long enough for her to drop the lozenge into my palm. I popped it into my mouth.

"Thank you," I said. My eyes immediately began to water. Point, set and match to Rose, with an assist to Liz.

I parked the car in the lot and gave Liz back her keys.

"I'm going to stop by Channing's office," she said. "It occurred to me that he might have a contact at that consulting firm where Gavin Pace used to work. I'd like to know more about that young man."

"You've been spending an awful lot of time with Mr. Caulfield lately," I teased. "I'm not going to have to start calling him Uncle Channing, am I?"

She narrowed her blue eyes at me and waggled one finger. "Remember what I told you. An Uber and a robot vacuum cleaner, Sarah," she said. "And you'd be replaced. Don't say you weren't warned."

Liz came around the car and slid behind the wheel. Rose and I walked toward the back door. She put an arm around my waist. "Don't worry, sweetie," she said. "I would never replace you with a robot vacuum."

"You don't like robot vacuum cleaners," I pointed out.

She nodded. "That's true, but it's not the only reason. I promise."

I laid my head against the top of hers for a moment.

She stopped when we reached the back door. "Sarah, do you think it would be a mistake to show Mallory a photo of Gavin Pace and ask if she saw him around the time of the fire?"

I folded one arm up over my head, digging my fingers into my scalp. "I don't know. She's going to ask us who he is and why we want to know. Are you ready for those questions?"

Rose looked thoughtful. "I think so. I know we agreed not to tell Mallory that we believe her mother was murdered and I still agree with that, but we can tell her we're talking to people, including people Gina worked with, trying to find out if she had any enemies. That's not a lie."

"That should work," I said. Rose's idea made me a little uneasy in truth, but Mallory might have seen someone in the neighborhood and we couldn't afford not to find out.

I knew this was as good a time as any to tackle Rose about those notes Nick had showed her. She was about to go in the back door. I put a hand on her arm. "I need to ask you something."

"Of course. What is it?"

I shifted from one foot to the other, suddenly feeling uncomfortable. "I know you said it would be better if I didn't know what you and Nick were talking about the other day, but I don't think it is."

She made an annoyed sound. "Honestly, Nicolas could not keep a secret even if you put duct tape over his mouth. Not that I would." She looked up at me and I thought once again how she reminded me of a tiny, inquisitive bird. "He told you about that investigator's notes, didn't he?" She gave her head a little shake.

I squeezed my eyes shut for a second, counted to three and opened them again. "He did," I admitted. "But to be fair, Rose, I pressured him."

She all but rolled her eyes at me. "Sweetie, you smiling and batting your eyelashes can hardly be called pressure."

I felt my cheeks get red. She knew me too well. "Okay,

how exactly I pressured Nick is not what matters here. What matters is that something in those notes twigged for you. Please tell me what it was."

"It might be nothing," she hedged.

"So no harm done in telling me then."

"You're not going to let this go, are you?" she asked.

I raised an eyebrow. "I learned at the feet of the master."

She smiled. "All right." She took a deep breath and exhaled slowly. "Did you know that Greg Pearson was in the car that day with his mother?"

"No," I said. I shook my head. "That's awful."

"It had to have been," she said. "And not just the accident itself, which was bad enough. There was an . . . incident afterward. The ambulance had just arrived. Greg had been arguing with his mother. One of the police officers who had responded had separated them. He took Gina over to the police car. Greg was sitting on the back bumper of Gina's car. He got sick. The officer went to help him and when she turned back around a woman was . . . attacking Gina. She yelled and . . . and hit her."

I kicked a rock and sent it skittering across the pavement. "It was Hannah's mother, Jia, wasn't it?" I remembered the way Jia's hand had clenched into a fist, almost involuntarily it had seemed, when she talked about Gina.

Then I noticed Rose was slowly shaking her head. "No, dear," she said. "It wasn't her. It was Mallory."

"Ah crap!" I muttered. I looked at Rose. "That's ugly."

"I can't believe that that sweet child could have done anything to hurt her stepmother," Rose said.

"Just because Mallory lost it with her stepmother after the accident doesn't mean she had anything to do with the fire."

"I know," Rose said. She still looked . . . troubled.

"What am I missing?" I asked.

"What if the reason Mike Pearson agreed to the plea deal is because he thinks Mallory was the one who started the fire?"

For a long moment I just looked at her. "I don't know what to say," I finally said.

Rose nodded. "I know. But it explains why he took the deal and why he instructed his lawyer to tell us to back off. It explains why Gina's friend Katy Mueller came here to try to get us to drop the case."

"It explains a lot of things."

I tried to imagine Mallory being responsible for her stepmother's death. And I couldn't reconcile the young woman who had pleaded with Charlotte to help her father also being the person who had killed the only mother she could remember. Yell at Gina because she drove drunk with one of the kids in the car? Yes. Hit her because Gina had run someone down? Yes. I was no different than Rose, who had insisted she just knew Mike Pearson wasn't guilty. I just didn't believe Mallory Pearson was guilty, either.

"But nothing is different," I said, hoping the conviction I felt came through in my voice. "I have no idea whether Mike Pearson thought Mallory had played any part in what had happened and it's not like he would tell us anyway. So the only thing we can do is figure out who did kill Gina."

Rose stood on tiptoe and kissed my cheek. "I love you, sweetie," she said. "Let's do it."

As usual Rose was a dynamo. She put Mr. P. to work getting in touch with Molly Pace. She got Charlotte to make a list of anyone they knew who might have a connection to the street where the Pearsons had lived. And she even had Avery make a pot of tea.

The teen came down the stairs looking quite pleased with herself. She was carrying a small tray holding three cups of tea and a coffee mug. She stopped in front of me. "That's for you, Sarah," she said with a shy smile.

"You made me coffee?" I said. "Thank you."

"It might suck," she said. She pressed her lips together for a moment. "I mean, it might not be very good."

I reached for the stoneware mug and took a sip. "Hey, this is good," I said.

She narrowed her gaze at me. "Good for real or good so you won't damage my fragile self-esteem?"

"Good for real," I said, taking another sip. "How did you learn to make coffee? You're much more of a smoothie person."

"Yeah," she said with a shrug. "But I've seen Mr. P. make the coffee about a dozen times. It's not rocket science, although it is math."

"Well, thank you," I said. I watched her head for the workroom with the tea and it occurred to me that being around Avery could only be good for Greg Pearson. I hoped their friendship would keep going.

The rest of the day was busy. Liam's electrician came and finished the wiring work in the sunporch. Liam came by to put another coat of mud on the drywall late in the afternoon.

"If everything goes well, the office should be ready

by the end of the week," he said, shaking drywall dust out of his hair and all over the workroom floor.

"So what do I owe you, anyway?" I asked.

He named an amount that was way too low.

"C'mon, that can't be right," I said. "What about all the time you and Nick put in on this?"

"We're going to put that on your tab," he said, a teasing gleam in his eyes.

"In other words I'm going to owe the two of you. You're going to get as much mileage as you can out of me owing each of you a favor."

"That's the plan," he said with a grin.

I grabbed the collar of his flannel shirt, catching him by surprise. I pulled him sideways and gave him a noogie on the top of his head, just as Rose came by on her way to the garage—or somewhere.

"Sarah, dear, don't do that," she said. "You're making a mess all over the floor."

"Why do I put up with you?" I hissed at Liam, who wasn't even trying to hide his grin. I didn't need to whisper. Rose was already gone.

"Because I'm your brother and you love me," he said, pulling away from me and putting one hand dramatically over his heart.

I nodded. "Yeah, I do, even though sometimes you drive me crazy." I smiled. "And I really like how you're not making a big deal over that bald spot."

He put a hand on top of his head, frowning. "What bald spot? I don't have a bald spot. You're just screwing with me, right?" He looked around the workroom for a mirror.

"I'm going to go get the vacuum cleaner," I said, gesturing in the direction of the shop. I started for the door then looked over my shoulder. Liam was trying to check out the top of his head in the shiny surface of a huge lobster pot.

"Gotcha!" I whispered.

Mr. P. was just coming down the stairs and Avery was at the cash desk, shining part of our collection of mismatched spoons with a soft cloth, bouncing up slightly on her toes as she worked. She glanced over at Alfred, then her eyes flicked to me. She seemed to be a ball of barely contained energy, which I knew meant something was up.

I walked over to join her.

"Hey, Sarah, do you want me to vacuum or finish these first?" she asked.

"Finish what you're doing," I said. "I'll get the vacuum out."

She nodded. "Okay."

It seemed to me that I could almost feel the energy radiating off of her. "Avery, is there anything you want to share with me?" I asked.

Her gaze immediately darted to Mr. P., who had just joined us. I leaned to one side, folded my arms over my chest and raised a quizzical eyebrow at him.

A hint of a smile flickered across the old man's face. "I hope it wasn't presumptuous of us, Sarah. Avery and I have been doing a little digging into the history of your casket."

He didn't need to tell me that they'd discovered something. I could tell that from Avery's fidgeting. "So what did you find out?" I said.

"Avery did most of the digging," Mr. P. said, smiling

at the teen. He gestured at me. "Tell Sarah what you learned."

Avery set down the spoon and the cloth she'd been using and propped her elbows on the counter. "Okay, first of all we tried to find the guy who rented that storage unit and then skipped on the bill, but he's gone." She made a fluttering gesture with one hand. "He blew off some other people too, and—"

Out of the corner of my eye I saw Mr. P. narrow his gaze at her.

Avery stopped and shook her head. "And you probably don't care about that stuff." She brushed a strand of hair away from her face. "So anyway, we talked to a bunch of people and finally we talked to the guy's mother and it turns out that he was just storing the coffin for another guy he knows."

"Do you know who built it?" I asked.

"Uh, yeah, the guy he was keeping it for." She frowned at me as though that should have been obvious.

"Do you know why it was built?"

Mr. P. cleared his throat. I looked at him. "I'm afraid this is going to sound like the punch line to a bad joke, but it turns out that coffin was built for the carpenter's mother-in-law."

I shook my head. I'd been hoping for a more heart-warming story. "He disliked her that much?"

I knew there were people who loathed their in-laws but it hadn't been my experience. My grandmother had technically stopped being my mom's mother-in-law when my father died and several years later Mom married my stepfather, Peter. But Gram had embraced the new family members. She was Liam's grandmother as much as mine. She'd been the one who'd taken him out to practice driving when everyone else's patience was fried, and taught him how to tie a necktie. Then again, there weren't a lot of people like Gram. It struck me that she was practical enough to appreciate a casket as a gift.

"Ms. Hall says she's cheap," Avery said. Her eyes flicked to Mr. P. for a moment. "And cheap is the word she used, not frugal."

"I remember," Alfred said.

"She" had to mean the carpenter's mother-in-law. I wasn't exactly sure how Stella Hall—we had cleared out her late brother's house—had slipped into the conversation. It had taken a turn that had gotten me lost. It was like talking with Rose. The last time we'd been cooking the topic had changed from Swedish meatballs to Steven Tyler and I still didn't know how.

I held up both hands. "Hang on. What does Stella's friend's frugality have to do with the casket in my workroom?"

"I don't think she's Ms. Hall's friend," Avery said, wrinkling her nose at me. "She didn't talk about her like they were friends. She held her mouth funny when she said 'cheap.'"

The last comment was directed at Alfred.

"I have to concur with Avery," he said. "There was a little disdain in Stella's manner when she spoke about the woman."

Rose was definitely rubbing off on both Avery and Mr. P.

I took a deep breath and let it out slowly. "Okay, so this

woman is *not* Stella Hall's friend and she *is* tight with money." I circled one hand in the air in a let's-get-on-with-it motion. "And?"

Avery picked up her cloth again. "And so she was supposed to be dying and because she's cheap she didn't like the idea of a lot of money going for her funeral so her son-in-law made her that coffin and then before he could give it to her it turned out she wasn't dying after all—and she really wasn't, cause she's still alive—and so he couldn't give it to her because she might take it the wrong way so he got his friend to keep it for him and Mr. P. talked to the dude and he doesn't want anything to do with it." She finally took a breath and smiled at me as she reached for a spoon.

None of the scenarios I'd come up with for how the wooden casket had ended up in that storage unit were anywhere near that mundane. I felt a little bit disappointed. "Well, at least we won't be selling anyone's family heirloom," I said.

"You know, I've always fancied the idea of having some of my ashes launched into space," Mr. P. confided.

"There's a place in England where you can do that." Avery frowned at the back of the spoon she was holding. "They use a hydrogen balloon. Your ashes would be up in the stratosphere. You could even make it out into space."

"That would be remarkable," Mr. P. said.

The conversational train had jumped the track again. I thanked them both and headed for my office.

I drove home at the end of the day with just Elvis for company. Rose and Mr. P. "had plans." They didn't share what those plans were. Charlotte had left with Liz. I was going to pick up Gram and we were going to have supper at Charlotte's. John had some kind of meeting. Elvis had been included in the dinner invitation at Charlotte's.

I changed, took off my makeup and pulled my hair back in a loose knot. Elvis stretched, did a quick walk-through of the apartment and washed his face. We were ready at the same time.

Gram was just coming down the stairs as I was locking my door. "Perfect timing," I said.

She smiled. "The key to a happy life." She was carrying a small cookie tin and a book.

"John told me what you and Liz are doing," she said. "I'm proud of both of you."

"Thanks," I said. "But we really haven't done anything yet."

"It was horrible for Rob Andrews's family when he went to prison. Nothing will change that but if you could clear his name maybe that would help a little."

I thought about Michelle and her unwavering belief in her dad's innocence. "I hope so," I said.

When we got to Charlotte's house we found her in the living room with Mallory Pearson.

"Mallory brought me a journal Gina started keeping while she was in rehab," Charlotte said after she'd introduced the teen to Gram. She indicated a small leather-covered book on the coffee table. The cover was singed.

"We found it after the fire," Mallory said. "I thought it might help. It was probably a stupid idea."

"No, it wasn't," Gram said. "That journal will give Charlotte some insight into how your mother thought. That can be very helpful."

Charlotte nodded. "Yes, it can."

"I tried to read it but I couldn't. She wrote about how things were going to get better but they didn't. Not really." She didn't seem to know what to do with her hands.

Elvis jumped up onto the sofa beside her. I moved to get him down, but Charlotte shook her head. The cat nudged Mallory's hand and she began to stroke his fur.

"It was a lot worse for my brothers," she said. "The only happy day we had in the year before the fire was one day in the fall when Dad took us to a Patriots game in Foxboro." A smile pulled at her mouth. "She didn't drink. Not that whole day. She bought Austin this stuffed bear in a Patriots jersey he slept with every night. Greg got a Patriots hat that he never took off. Gina was always ragging on him for wearing it in the house." She looked away from us. "He hasn't worn the hat since . . . and Austin stopped sleeping with the bear because it was in the house at the time of the fire and he kept saying it smelled funny even though Katy washed it three times."

I thought about what Rose and I had talked about earlier. "Mallory, how were things between you and your stepmother?"

She shrugged. "Not good."

Elvis had settled himself on her lap.

"We were fighting all the time. Mostly about her drinking, but about other things, too, like school and my clothes and what time I got home."

She went very still then except for the hand stroking Elvis's fur. "You don't think I had something to do with what happened, do you? I swear I would never have burned down our house."

I couldn't help it. I glanced at the cat. He was blissfully settled in her lap. Mallory Pearson was telling the truth.

I had no explanation for it, but Elvis could tell when someone was lying if they happened to be petting him at the same time. His ears would flatten and he'd look at the person with half-lidded eyes, pupils narrowed, the picture of skepticism. Mac seemed to think the cat could sense the same kind of physiological changes that a polygraph measured. I had no idea whether he was right. I'd just seen Elvis do it enough times to know it wasn't a coincidence.

"No, no," I said. "None of us think you had anything to do with what happened. It's just the more we learn about Gina the better chance we have of figuring out what really happened."

It was a pretty lame explanation but luckily she didn't question it.

Mallory looked at Charlotte once more. "Please don't give up. You have to prove that it wasn't Dad's fault. I'm okay, but . . . but Greg and Austin need him."

I pulled out my phone and scrolled through to a photo Mr. P. had found online of Gavin Pace. "Mallory, do you remember seeing this man anywhere in your neighborhood any time before the fire?" I asked, holding out the phone to her.

She studied the image. "He looks familiar, but I don't remember seeing him anywhere in our neighborhood. Who is he? Do you think he's the person Mr. Halloran saw?"

Charlotte put a hand on her arm. "He's just someone who worked with Gina. We're trying to track down her friends."

Mallory picked at the hem of her *Hey Violet* T-shirt. "She pretty much didn't have any friends left at the end. Except Katy. They'd been friends forever." She looked at Charlotte. "Have you talked to her? Do you want me to call her or something?"

"We've already talked to her," Charlotte said.

"She asked you to stop trying to help my dad." The words weren't a question.

Charlotte looked at me.

"I think Katy really cares about you and your brothers," I said.

Mallory sighed. "I know she does. She stuck by . . . Gina when all her other friends walked away. And she even said if my grandmother really does want to move back to Washington we could move in with her."

I waited for the "but" I knew was coming.

"But Katy tries to act like she's our mother sometimes and there's no way she could ever be that. Greg and I are having lunch with her on Thursday and she'll probably start bugging us about this. She keeps saying we need to heal." She put a hand on Charlotte's arm. "We can't heal without Dad."

"We'll figure it out," Charlotte said.

I nodded. I wished I knew how we were going to do that.

Chapter 13

Mac called about eight thirty that evening. I told him about the visit with Gavin Pace and the conversation with Mallory. "I've gotten sucked into this way more than any other case the Angels have taken on," I said.

"That doesn't have to be a bad thing," he said.

"We're not any closer to figuring out what happened the night of the fire. What if we can't? What if Mike Pearson spends the next four and a half years in jail?" I slumped in the corner of the sofa. "The problem is we're trying to prove a negative."

"What do you mean?" he asked.

"Judge Halloran says he saw Mike walking away from the burning house. How do we prove the judge is wrong?"

"Where was he?"

"The judge? On his front steps, as far as I know."

"No, not him," Mac said. "Where exactly was Mike Pearson? If he wasn't at the fire, where was he? He had to be somewhere. Wherever that is, maybe someone saw him."

I blew out a breath. "I can't believe I didn't think of that before now." I pictured Mac smiling.

"You would have gotten there eventually."

"I don't know," I said. "I think we've all gotten a little too invested in this case. It started out that we were just looking for a way to get Mike out of jail and then suddenly we were investigating a murder that no one else is willing to say was a murder. No wonder we can't seem to find any answers."

"Hey, you're on the team with Rose Jackson and Alfred Peterson," Mac said. "They might know what the word 'can't' means, but most of the time they just ignore it."

I laughed in spite of myself. "I wish you'd been here to see Rose with the electrician Liam sent."

"Let me guess: He told her she couldn't have something the way she wanted it done—"

"Wall sconces," I said.

"And Rose just kept going like the poor guy hadn't said anything."

"With just a pinch of befuddled little old lady thrown in."

He laughed. "So how do the wall sconces look?" he asked.

"Good, actually."

"Sarah, do you remember what you said to me when the Angels' case involved my life, my future? You said, *'We have a secret weapon. We have Rose. She's a pit bull with sensible shoes and a tote bag full of cookies.'*"

At the time I'd been trying to lighten the mood, but part of me had also been serious. Rose, Mr. P., Liz and Charlotte and their unorthodox methods of solving crime had worked in the past and deep inside I'd wanted to believe they could solve Mac's case, too.

I could hear a sound on the other end of the phone. "Are you clapping?" I asked.

"Yes, I am," Mac said. "I believe in you. I believe in Rose. I believe in the Angels. So I'm clapping."

He was referencing *Peter Pan*, I realized.

"You clap if you believe in fairies, not angels."

"Close enough."

"This is silly," I said.

"I've got all night and a cup of coffee at my elbow."

I couldn't help smiling. Mac always did that to me. I held up a hand in a gesture of surrender even though he couldn't see me. "Okay, okay. I get your point."

"Good," he said. "It'll work out. I mean it."

I really hoped he was right.

After Mac and I said good night, I called Nick. "Hey, Sarah, what's up?" he said. I could hear voices, noise in the background.

"I have a question," I said. "You've read pretty much all the reports on Mike Pearson's case, right?"

"Yeah, I have."

"If it wasn't Mike who Judge Halloran saw, where was he? Rose said he told the police he was just driving around. But where? Maybe someone saw him or maybe a security camera picked him up."

Nick was quiet for a moment then he said, "That's a good question. Let me see what I can find out to-morrow."

I thanked him and said good night.

I woke up the next morning feeling a lot more posi-tive. Talking to Mac—even though it was over the phone and not in person—had helped, and I had my fingers crossed that Nick might come up with some piece of information to help prove where Mike had really been the night of the fire.

Rose and Mr. P. had spent their evening looking for a connection with one of the Pearsons' former neighbors and I knew from the gleam in his eye and the smile on her face that they'd had success.

Rose explained the connection as we drove to work. As far as I could follow things, it seemed to involve someone she'd known at Legacy Place who'd had a failed romance with a bit of a senior lothario, whose son's former girlfriend had and still did live on the street. There was also something about a tuna casserole and the request for risqué photos, which had led to the throwing of said casserole. Rose had made a clucking sound and said, "There's no fool like an old fool."

The upshot was they were going to talk to the former girlfriend and see if she'd seen Gavin Pace—or anyone else—in the neighborhood around the time of the fire.

"I talked to Molly Pace," Mr. P. said.

"What did you find out?" I asked.

"The word she used to describe her ex-husband was 'useless.'"

"That's harsh."

"I agree," he said. "Although given the circumstances you can see why she might say something like that. Overall, she seems to think he's a bit of a spoiled mama's boy who tends to take the easy way out of things."

"It wasn't him," Rose said.

I glanced at her in the rearview mirror. "You sound pretty certain."

"I am," she said.

"How would killing Gina and setting that house on fire be taking the easy way out for Mr. Pace? What did he gain? Nothing. I think this is more about anger, revenge. That's not Gavin Pace's MO. I told you: weak chin."

I nodded. Having met Pace I tended to agree with her but since we didn't have a lot of suspects I wasn't ruling him out just yet.

Late morning I headed down to The Black Bear to see Sam. Once again I had a guitar I needed his opinion on.

As I cut through the restaurant I saw Liz having an early lunch with her brother, Wilson. Wilson Emmerson had what Gram would call a lived-in face. There were lines bracketing his mouth and pulling at the corners of his piercing blue eyes, which were topped with bushy white eyebrows. Even when he was smiling he looked a little stern. Now he looked downright angry, gesturing across the table at Liz with his fork. I wondered if they were talking about the "book project."

Sam was waiting for me in his office. It only took him a moment to tune the guitar. He played a couple of songs, his dollar store reading glasses low on his nose, and I watched his fingers fly over the strings.

Finally he looked up at me. "Very nice," he said. "Where did it come from? There's really no wear on the body."

"An indulgent rock-and-roll grandmother and a grandson who decided he liked the clarinet better. There are no clarinets in rock-and-roll."

Sam took off his glasses. "'When I'm 64' by the Beatles, 'Dance to the Music,' Sly and the Family Stone, Van Halen, 'Big Bad Bill.'"

"Okay, so there aren't a *lot* of clarinets in rock-and-roll," I said.

He smiled. "How much are you going to ask for it?"

The handmade Bourgeois Slope D steel string had a sitka spruce top and sides and a neck and back made from mahogany. The fingerboard and bridge were ebony. And just a few chords showed off its beautiful tone. I told him my price.

"That's fair," he said. "I'll take it."

"Are you serious?" I said.

He ran a hand over the top of the guitar. "Absolutely, kiddo. I've always wanted one of these guitars. And I'm not getting any younger."

I smiled, wondering if I could sneak in a 15 percent discount because it was Sam.

"And don't even think of trying to give me some kind of friends and family discount," he said as though he'd read my mind.

I tried to make a case for one as a way of thanking him for all the guitars he'd looked at for me since I'd opened Second Chance but Sam wasn't having any of it. He could rival Rose for stubbornness. In the end I gave in and took his check after getting him to promise he'd play the guitar at the next jam.

When I came out of Sam's office Liz was alone. She caught sight of me and waved me over to her table.

"What are you doing here?" she asked.

I inclined my head in the direction of Sam's office. "I brought a guitar over for Sam's opinion."

Liz looked at my empty hands. "And?"

"And he bought it."

"Good for him," she said. "Did you get him to let you give him the friends and family deal?"

"No," I said, rolling my eyes. "He's as stubborn as Rose."

"Or my brother," Liz said darkly.

"I saw Wilson with you when I came in. It looked like the two of you were having a disagreement."

"I was trying to find out more about those projects mentioned in those old minutes but I can't get him to take any of this seriously. He thinks our book idea is a vanity project and he's not taking it seriously." A waiter started in our direction and she waved him away with one hand.

"What if you told him the truth?" I said.

Liz was shaking her head before I got the words out. "I already told you. No. Too many people know what's going on as it is."

"We can't keep everything secret forever."

"We can for now," she said. She pressed her lips together in annoyance. "The problem is Wilson thinks he's the crown prince because that's how our mother treated him, like the sun rose and set on his lily-white backside." She looked at me. "We'll just have to do this without his help."

Since we already were I didn't see how anything had changed. "Works for me," I said.

Gram called midafternoon to invite me to supper. Actually to invite Elvis and me to supper.

"I'd love to," I said. I hadn't bought groceries and my cupboards were looking like Old Mother Hubbard's.

Gram had made potato scallop—one of my favorites— along with ham and a big salad. About halfway through the meal I caught Gram and John exchanging a look. I set my fork down.

"What's going on?" I asked. "You two remind me of Elvis right before he tries to stick his face in the popcorn bowl."

"I've started going through that box of papers you brought me," John said.

"You found something," I said.

"That's the thing," he said, putting his own fork down. "I'm not sure if it is something."

"Was it some kind of accounting irregularity?"

John shook his head. "No. It was something I noticed in the minutes from the board meetings." He looked at Gram.

"Tell her," she said.

"I read through the minutes from several different meetings and there are notations about several projects I don't remember."

My pulse quickened. "What do you mean by 'projects you don't remember'?"

"Those meetings were a long time ago and if you'd asked me what we talked about in any particular one I wouldn't have been able to tell you, but as I read through the minutes they nudged my memory."

I nodded.

"For example, at one of the board meetings we talked about a new roof for the dining hall at the Sunshine Camp. Reading that on the agenda reminded me about how heated the discussion got about whether we should use asphalt shingles or invest in a metal roof."

"But I'm guessing not for those projects you don't remember."

"Exactly."

I tucked my hair back behind one ear. "Do you remember the names of those projects?" I asked.

Gram got up, went over to the counter and came back with a piece of paper. She handed it to me. There were six names on it. They were the same projects that weeks ago Liz and I had discovered had never been implemented or even documented anywhere other than those minutes.

I knew this had to be important. I just wasn't sure how.

I looked up at John. "Have you given these names to Liz yet?"

"I was going to call her tonight."

I rubbed the back of my neck with one hand. "These projects that you don't remember. They have to mean something," I said.

"I could see myself forgetting one or maybe two," John said. "But not six." He smiled at Gram, who had reached over to give his shoulder a squeeze.

"Has Liz considered having a full audit done, at least of the camp's books?" Gram asked.

"Channing Caulfield found a forensic accountant," I said. "It's already being done."

"That might be where the answers are," John said.

Gram picked up her fork. "What's going on with Liz and Channing?"

I was glad for the change of subject. "She says nothing, but I'm not so sure. They've had dinner several times—all 'business,' according to Liz. Of course that hasn't stopped me from needling her about him." I grinned across the table at Gram.

She smiled back at me. "I think they'd make a very nice couple."

"Not everyone wants to be part of a couple," John said. "If that's the case, no amount of matchmaking is going to work."

I almost choked on a bite of scallop. I reached for my water and Gram patted my back.

"What did I say?" John asked, a frown creasing his forehead.

I took another drink of water. "You and Gram wouldn't be married if it wasn't for Rose and Liz playing matchmaker, Mr. Single and Happy. And Charlotte . . . and maybe me."

"Sarah Grayson, what on earth are you talking about?" Gram said.

It occurred to me that I'd said too much.

"I'm waiting," she said.

I held up both hands. "It's just that we all thought you two were perfect for each other. You talked to John for maybe five minutes that day in the library and then he was all you talked about for the next week."

He smiled at her over his glasses. "Is that true, Isabel?"

Gram's cheeks were pink. "You weren't *all* I talked about."

"Yes, you were," I said. I pointed a finger at John. "And you pestered Liz with questions about Gram."

Gram looked down at her plate and smiled, her blushing more pronounced.

John looked at her with so much love my chest ached.

"I couldn't help it," he said. "I'd been struck by Cupid's arrow."

"Actually I think it was a history textbook."

Gram narrowed her eyes at me. "You're not going to let that go, are you?" she said.

I grinned. "Not a chance."

John leaned over and kissed Gram's cheek. "So what exactly did you do?"

I picked up my knife and fork. "Didn't you ever question how you both ended up at Sam's for lunch on the same day?"

"No," Gram said. "Charlotte asked me to have lunch with her and Rose because she was worried about Rose's decision to move into Legacy Place."

"She was worried about that," I said. "And it turns out for good reason, but that was just a ruse to get you there."

"And I'm guessing you really weren't that interested in the history of the MaineWorks Alliance?" John said.

"I was interested," I said. "I joined after we had lunch that day, but I was really just doing what Liz had told me to do."

Gram was smiling and shaking her head. "That's why Rose made such a point about finding the perfect table. She wanted to make sure John saw us."

"That was the plan."

"I saw you," he said. "The moment you came in the door I couldn't take my eyes off of you. You were wearing that same little gray hat with the feather that you'd been wearing at the library.

They exchanged that look again.

I picked up my plate and got to my feet.

"What are you doing?" Gram said.

"I'm thinking I should just take my supper and go home and leave you two lovebirds alone."

"Sit," she said. There was still a touch of color in her cheeks. "Let's talk about your love life instead of ours."

Elvis meowed loudly from the floor at my feet. "It'll be a short conversation," I said.

"Nothing happening between you and Nick?"

I shook my head. "He's more like my brother than anything romantic."

"What about Mac?" John said.

"I don't know when he's coming back. I don't even know *if* he's coming back."

"Have you asked him?" Gram said.

"No."

She got up from the table and patted my shoulder as she moved behind me. "You can't get the right answers if you don't ask the right questions."

Chapter 14

Nick called me about a half hour after Elvis and I got home.

"I did a little digging to see what Mike Pearson had said about where he was when the fire started."

"And?"

"And basically he didn't offer any explanation other than one of the firefighters remembers him saying he'd just been out driving around. But no one else heard him say that and as far as I can find out after that, he didn't say anything. It was just one more detail that made him look guilty."

"Crap," I muttered. "I was hoping you might come up with something that would give us another direction to go in."

"Sorry," he said. "If I come up with anything else I'll let you know."

Liz came in the next morning at about ten o'clock carrying a small bag from McNamara's. I was just coming down the stairs. "Is there something in that bag for me?" I asked, linking my arm through hers.

"Why would I bring something for you?" she asked. "Have you done anything to deserve a treat?"

"Yes," I said, squaring my shoulders and tossing my hair. "I'm a joy to be around. I spread sunshine wherever I go."

"You spread something," Liz said. "I'm not sure it's sunshine." She glanced at the top of the stairs. "Do you have a couple of minutes?"

I nodded. "Sure. I was going to call you."

We headed up to my office. I got Liz a cup of tea and a fresh cup of coffee for myself. The bag from McNamara's held two blueberry muffins.

"So what's up?" I asked.

"I had supper with Channing last night," she said. She narrowed her eyes at me and pointed one French-tipped finger at my face. "And don't start with me, Miss Sunshine."

I broke my muffin in half. "How's Channing?" I asked.

"Fine," Liz said. "He found some more interesting information about Gavin Pace."

"How interesting?"

"He couldn't find a job for several months after he lost his. It turns out Sam's pub and the school weren't the only places his wife chose to make a scene. Word got around."

"So he has some incentive to keep this job," I said. The muffins were good. I licked a bit of blueberry from my thumb.

"A little more than you'd think," Liz said. "He's still in a probationary period. He could still be let go."

"So he lost his job and Gina kept hers, at least for a while."

Liz took a sip of her tea and nodded. "And from what Channing could find out Pace is up to his eyeballs in debt from his divorce."

The office door moved and Elvis came into the room. He launched himself up onto the desk and settled himself on one corner. "Mrr," he said to Liz.

"Hello, cat," she said.

"Do you think he might have blamed Gina for any of what happened?"

"Try all of what happened."

"Excuse me?" I said.

"Channing talked to a couple of people who used to work with young Mr. Pace, all on the understanding that what they say would stay off the record."

I nodded.

"It seems that he was pretty vocal about putting the blame for all of his problems squarely on Gina. Sounds like a motive for murder to me."

I wasn't sure, although I tended to agree with Rose's assessment of Gavin Pace.

"Rose and Mr. P. are talking to someone who lives near the Pearsons' former house," I said. "Maybe she'll remember seeing him."

"I think we're going to have to pay him another visit."

I nodded. "I think you're right."

"So what did you want to talk to me about?" Liz asked.

I explained what I'd learned from John at supper the previous night.

"I knew there was something off about those so-called projects," she said.

"I think you should tell Wilson what's going on," I said. I realized I was beginning to sound like a broken record on that subject.

She waved my suggestion away. "And let the culprit get away with it because my brother can't keep his mouth shut? I don't think so. I do have an idea, though."

I popped a piece of muffin in my mouth and made a go-on gesture with one hand.

"I'm going to get in touch with Marie's son. Marie was a meticulous record keeper. She kept Wilson's files just so and I know she kept a journal. Maybe she kept some kind of notes, maybe she wrote about what was going on."

"It's worth a shot," I said.

Liz drank the last of her tea and got to her feet. "Bring Rose and Alfred up to date, please," she said.

I looked at my watch. "They should be here anytime now."

"I can't stay," she said. "I've got places to go and things to do."

"Is one of those things Channing?" I asked. A crumpled paper napkin whizzed past my head as she left.

I knew the moment Rose and Mr. P. walked in that they'd had some kind of success.

"So what did you find out?" I asked as Rose took off her sweater and unwound the gauzy scarf from around her neck.

"Well, Denise makes a lovely zucchini bread," Rose said. "She uses pecans instead of walnuts."

Denise.

I was pretty sure she was the woman who lived near

the Pearsons, the former girlfriend of the son of the senior Casanova who had lived in Rose's old apartment building. Or something like that.

"I'll, uh, remember that," I said. "Did she recognize Gavin Pace?"

Rose shook her head. "No, she didn't."

Then why did she look so pleased? It had to be more than just the pecans in the zucchini bread.

"But she did remember seeing a homeless man wandering around the neighborhood," Mr. P. said. "It seems he relieved himself in someone's yard and the police came and rousted the man."

"And you think *he* may have seen something?" I said.

"Yes I do," she said, brushing a bit of sparkly thread that had probably come from her scarf off of the front of her pale yellow top. "I suspect that being homeless, just like being old, means people don't really pay attention to you. So who knows what he might have seen?"

I straightened a pillow in the tub chair and brushed a clump of cat hair from the seat, making a mental note to ask Avery to give the chair a good vacuuming. "But how are we going to find this man? Were there any security cameras?"

"I've already taken care of that," Rose said airily. "And no, as far as Alf could find out no one had a security camera. But I called Nicolas. There should be some kind of report since the police were called. The man, whoever he was, would have had to have given them his name and told them where he lived. We'll find him."

She seemed confident and I hoped Nick came through for her.

"Liz was here," I said. I told them what Channing had unearthed about the precariousness of Pace's job.

"I knew he wasn't being straight with us," Rose said. "Everything he said was nothing more than twaddle." She looked at Alfred and me. "I think another visit to that young man is in order."

It was about a half hour later and I had just finished selling an iron bed frame and helping the customer fit it into the back of her car when Nick pulled into the lot.

"Hi," he said, walking over to me.

"Hi yourself," I said. I studied him for a moment. "I know that look. You found Rose's homeless man."

"In a way."

I brushed a bit of dirt off the front of my gray pants. "What does 'in a way' mean?"

"Is Rose here?" Nick gestured at the shop. "I'd rather just tell the story once."

"She's here," I said. "When I came out she was showing a customer a set of dishes. By now she's probably sold him the dishes and the flatware."

It turned out Rose had sold the man dishes, flatware, a tablecloth and napkins. He was just walking out with two large paper shopping bags. Avery was with him carrying a large cardboard box.

Rose turned to Nick, a gleam in her gray eyes. "What did you find out?" She beckoned to Charlotte, who was fitting pale pink tapers into a cut-glass candelabra. She joined us, still holding one candle.

"What about Alfred?" I asked.

"He's in the office with Liam," Rose said.

"Liam's here?" I said. I seemed to be losing control of my day.

"He just got here." She gestured toward the street. "He found a blackboard."

"A blackboard? What for?"

"The office, dear," she said with just a hint of impatience in her voice.

I decided to stop while I was ahead. A bit confused but ahead.

Nick cleared his throat. "First of all, your homeless man wasn't—isn't—homeless."

Rose frowned. "But Denise said he relieved himself on the rhododendrons across the street from her house."

"Yes, he did," Nick said. "Because he was drunk. Not because he was homeless. They threw him in a cell until he sobered up. Because it was so close to Christmas they didn't charge him with anything."

"But you know his name. We can talk to him."

Nick swiped a hand over his chin. "You already did. It was Gavin Pace."

Charlotte and I just stared at each other. I hadn't expected Nick to say that.

Rose was nodding. "I told you that young man had a weak chin."

"And a taste for pickle vodka apparently," I said, sotto voce, to Nick.

The phone rang then. Charlotte touched my arm. "I'll get that," she said.

"I'll call Liz," Rose said, patting her pockets in search of her cell phone. She spotted it over on the cash desk and started toward it. "Sarah, are you coming with us?" she called over her shoulder.

Nick swiped a hand over his mouth again and hissed, "It's go or probably have to post their bail."

"I'm coming," I said.

Rose grabbed her phone and turned to look at Nick. "What about you, Nicolas? Would you like to come along?"

He smiled. "Thank you, but I have to go to work."

It registered then that he was wearing his work clothes, a knit shirt and dark pants with a multitude of pockets.

"Thank you," I said.

"You really should thank Michelle. She's the one who looked up the report."

"I didn't know she was back."

"Last night." He hesitated. "I told her what's going on. I hope that's okay."

I nodded. "It is. I don't like keeping this kind of a secret from her. And she'd find out anyway." I gestured at his mom and Rose. "They're not exactly subtle."

Nick followed my gaze. "Try to keep them out of trouble."

"Hey, this is not my first rodeo," I said.

"I take it that means you have rope and know how to make a lasso."

I grinned at him. "Yes on both counts."

"Let me know how it works out," he said. He stopped to give his mother a kiss and he was gone.

Liz arrived about a half hour later. "I thought you had places to go and people to see," I said.

"I've gone and I've seen," she said. "And you have entirely too much time on your hands."

"Do we have an appointment?" I asked as she tossed me the car keys.

"We don't need an appointment," she said.

"What if he isn't there?"

She gave me a look. "Mr. Pace isn't exactly lighting the work world on fire. I don't think we need to worry about that."

And we didn't. Gavin Pace came out to the reception area to meet us. He didn't look very happy to see us. "I already answered your questions," he said. "I don't have anything else to tell you."

"Would you like me to tell you what your ex-wife said about you, young man?" Rose asked. "I'll give you a hint. She called you something that rhymes with 'glass bowl.' And that was the nicest thing she said."

I stifled a smile at her use of an expression Avery started using when Liz got after her to clean up her language.

"Could you please keep it down?" he said, looking around. The young woman at the reception desk was watching us, not even trying to hide her interest.

"Maybe we should talk somewhere a little more private," Liz suggested.

"Fine," he said. "Come back to my office."

The office was even more cluttered than our previous visit. Pace didn't make a move to clear off the chairs but we weren't going to be there very long so it didn't matter that we had nowhere to sit down.

Liz didn't waste any time. "You lied to me," she said. "I don't like that."

"I didn't lie," he said but his eyes slid off her face as he said the words.

"You said you hadn't seen Gina in months when in fact you were caught by the police watering someone's rhododendrons in her neighborhood the night she died.

Then you told a touching story of how she inspired you to stop drinking, which, judging by the contents of your bottom-left desk drawer was also a lie. Would you like to go three for three?"

"Fine," he said. "I saw Gina the day she died, but I didn't kill her." He pulled a hand back through his hair a couple of times. "She ruined my life. I lost my job. Molly wouldn't take me back. And Gina? Nothing happened to her. People were falling all over themselves to help poor little Gina." His voice had turned mocking and mean. "So yeah, I told her how she'd ruined my life and how I hoped she'd rot in hell. Then I had a couple of drinks—just to relax and the next thing I know the cops are hassling me."

Rose's phone had given a low buzz while Gavin was talking. Someone had sent her a text. She slid the phone out of her pocket, checked the screen and then silently handed it to me. Nick. *Based on the estimated time of death for Gina Pearson Pace is not your killer. He was still locked up.*

Somehow I'd known that all along. I looked at Gavin Pace. Rose was right about the weak chin and the rest of him matched it.

Liz, meanwhile, had reached her limit for listening to his complaining. She took a couple of steps forward so she was right in his face.

"You, young man, are a bum," she said, punctuating her words with one pointing finger. "Gina Pearson didn't ruin your life. Your problems are your own and unlike her, you still have lots of time to fix them. So get a haircut, lose the attitude, clean up this office, get to a meeting and stop bellyaching!"

She turned and stalked out of the office as only Elizabeth Emmerson Kiley French can. Rose and I trailed after her, leaving Gavin Pace standing in his office with his mouth hanging open.

"I feel a little like the man who walks behind the elephant," Rose confided.

We caught up with Liz at the main entrance. "Are we ready to go?" I asked.

"I am," she said. She looked at Rose. "Are you?"

"We may as well," Rose said, settling her purse over her arm. "I don't imagine we'll get any more information out of Mr. Pace now. And he's not our killer." She showed Nick's text to Liz.

"I suppose you think I should have kept quiet," Liz said. She patted her blond hair. Not a single one was out of place.

"Do you think your little outburst is actually going to make anything better?" Rose asked.

Liz smiled. "It made *me* feel better," she said. "Let's go home."

Chapter 15

We were about five minutes away from Second Chance when Liz's cell phone rang. I saw her frown at the screen before she took the call. I had no idea what was going on from the one side of the call I could hear but from the way her expression changed I could see she wasn't happy.

"Is everything all right?" Rose asked from the backseat after Liz ended the call.

"Not for some people," Liz said darkly.

Avery was just coming down the sidewalk as we pulled into the parking lot. Greg Pearson was with her. Avery was talking and I could tell by how animatedly her hands were moving that it was about something important to her. Greg nodded from time to time but wasn't saying anything. He liked her, I realized. I hoped she felt the same way. I didn't want to see him get hurt.

We got out of the car. Liz stood by the front fender. Rose nudged me with her elbow. "I think I know which people are in trouble."

Avery stopped in front of her grandmother. She reminded me so much of Liz in the way she stood with her feet apart and her chin lifted. Whatever she'd done, she didn't seem very sorry.

"You pretended to be your mother to get out of a field trip?" Liz said.

Avery shrugged. "Yeah, I can sound just like her. Not that the school would know what she sounds like anyway. It's not like she ever talks to them."

Avery and her parents had a difficult relationship. That was why she'd come to live with Liz.

"Field trips are part of the reason you're going to this school," Liz said. "They expand your horizons."

"Oh, c'mon, Nonna, that's a load of crap and you know it. How is ballet going to expand my horizons? It's so boring. And the reason I'm going to this school is because I got kicked out of two others."

"And are you going for the hat trick?" Liz retorted.

"It's not Avery's fault, Mrs. French," Greg said, shoving his hair off his face.

Avery gave him a look. "Don't," she said.

Liz held up a hand. "No, please, young man, explain how Avery lying to the vice principal, her teacher and me is your fault. I'd like to hear that."

"I know that Mallory asked you and your friends to help get our dad out of jail."

"How did you know?" Rose said.

Greg looked over at her. "I heard her arguing about it with my mom's friend." That had to be Katy. "I wanted to help. I went back to where we used to live. Avery came with me. That's why we ditched the field trip. It was my only chance without Mallory or anyone else knowing what I was doing." He picked at the strap of his backpack. "She'd just tell me to stay out of it."

"And if I'd told *you* what I was doing you would have made me go to the stupid ballet," Avery added.

"We'll never know because you didn't give me the chance to say yes or no," Liz said. Her stance had softened a little and so had her voice.

"Alfred and I were in that neighborhood this morning," Rose said. She walked around the front of the car. "We didn't see you."

"We saw you first," Avery said. "We just waited at that little playground around the corner until you were gone."

"Well, did you find out anything?" Rose asked. Liz glared at her.

"We went all around the neighborhood and the only person who remembers seeing my dad is Mr. Halloran, who was our next-door neighbor," Greg said. "Could he just be wrong because he's old? Maybe he needs glasses or something."

"We already checked," Liz said. "He doesn't need glasses, not for seeing things at a distance."

Avery shoved her hands in the pockets of her red hoodie. "If you're waiting for me to say I'm sorry, Nonna, it's not going to happen. Ballet is lame."

"Lying and impersonating your mother is a lot lamer," Liz said. She turned to me then. "Sarah, when was the last time your garage floor was cleaned—really cleaned?"

"I don't know," I said. "A month maybe. Before Mac left, for sure."

To my surprise Liz walked over to her granddaughter, wrapped her arms around Avery and kissed the top of her head. "Get going, missy," she said. "I want that floor clean enough to eat off of."

"Why do people always say that when they want something really clean?" Avery asked. "It's not like anyone would actually ever eat off the floor."

"Avery this would probably be a good time to stop talking," Greg said.

She shrugged and headed for the garage. "I'm doing this under protest," she called over her shoulder.

"I'll make a note in your permanent record," Liz said dryly.

"I'm helping her because she was trying to help me," Greg said. He hiked his backpack a little higher on his shoulder and followed Avery.

"I like that boy," Liz said. "Don't tell Avery I said that."

"That's a big space," Rose said eyeing the garage.

I came up behind her and wrapped my arms around hers. "Don't go there," I whispered. I watched the kids wrestle both big doors open and head inside. Rose was right. That was a lot of floor to clean. But Avery had been wrong to lie and impersonate her mother. It was wrong for a lot of reasons, but a small part of me admired her resourcefulness. Liz was the one who dealt with Avery's school. As she'd pointed out they didn't know her mother's voice so it was easy to pretend to be her.

Easy to pretend. I realized that I was standing next to the car by myself. Rose and Liz were at the back door. I hurried after them.

I caught up with Liz just inside the door and put a

hand on her arm. "Don't even think about pleading that child's case," she said.

"I'm not going to," I said. "Tell me what Mike Pearson looks like."

"I haven't seen him for years," Liz said. "I can tell you that he wasn't very tall."

"I could get Alfred to find a photo for you," Rose offered.

Charlotte came into the workroom just then. "You're back," she said. "Did you learn anything from Mr. Pace?"

"Just that he's a glass bowl," Rose said.

"And we already knew that," Liz added. She looked at me. "Charlotte could probably tell you what Mike looks like now."

"Can you describe him?" I asked. "Liz said he's not very tall."

"No, he's not," Charlotte said. "He's maybe two or three inches taller than you are."

That made him five eight or five nine. Just under average for a man in this country.

"Greg has his coloring," she continued.

"So dark hair and dark eyes."

She nodded.

"Heavy? Skinny? Muscular?"

Charlotte thought for a moment. "I guess I'd describe Mike as wiry."

Wiry. "Like a runner?" I asked.

She nodded. "Yes. Although I don't know if he was one."

"That doesn't matter," I said.

"Why do you suddenly care what Mike Pearson looks like?" Liz asked.

"Because if Avery can impersonate her mother, why couldn't someone have impersonated Mike the night of the fire?" They were all looking at me now. "We've been trying to show that Judge Halloran was mistaken. That he didn't see Mike. But maybe he did."

"He saw someone pretending to be Mike," Rose finished.

"Exactly."

"But who?" Charlotte asked.

"Someone who isn't very tall," Rose said, holding up one finger.

"And a lean build," Charlotte added.

Rose nodded and held up a second finger. "And he has to have short, dark hair." She had three fingers in the air now.

"The hair could have been dyed," Liz interjected.

"The man Neill Halloran saw was wearing a hat," Rose said. "I think height and build are what we should focus on."

The man Neill Halloran saw.

Man.

Jia Allison was a couple of inches taller than I was. She had the wiry build of a runner. She even had short, dark hair. And she had a reason to hate Gina Pearson.

The man Neill Halloran saw.

Had it been a man, I wondered?

Chapter 16

I hated the idea that Jia Allison could be responsible for Gina Pearson's death. I should have gone and talked to her, one-on-one, I realized. Until I did, I didn't feel I could share my suspicions with anyone.

Rose and Charlotte had already gone into the shop. I put my arm around Liz's shoulders. "How about a cup of tea?"

"That does sound good," she said. She glanced over her shoulder. "I can't believe that child actually thought she could get away with pretending to be her mother."

"I'm not excusing what she did," I said. "But you have to admit she was pretty creative."

"I don't have to admit anything," Liz said, but a hint of a smile played on her lips.

I made the tea. Elvis watched me, whiskers twitching when I found one lone oatmeal cookie in the can on the counter. I broke off a tiny piece and fed it to him. "You are so spoiled," I told him, giving the top of his head a scratch.

"Mrr," he said. It seemed he didn't care.

Mallory Pearson was in the shop talking to Liz when

I went back downstairs. Katy was with her. I walked over to them. It turned out that Greg had texted his sister to tell her he was helping Avery with her "punishment."

"I'm sorry, Mrs. French," she was saying. "This is my fault."

"No, it isn't," Katy said. She looked at Liz. "It's your fault. Please just stop this. I know you mean well but you're just making things worse, not better, for Mallory and her brothers."

Mallory put a hand on the woman's arm. "Thank you for the ride over here," she said. "You can go now. I can handle this."

"We can just get your brother and leave," Katy said. "You don't have to stay here."

Mallory forced a smile. She put her arms around Katy and gave her a hug. "Thank you for caring. But everything's okay. Go home. I'll call you later."

She was very mature for her age, probably because life had forced her to be.

Katy looked from Mallory to Liz. "If you need me, you call me."

Mallory nodded. "I promise." She kept the smile on her face until Katy was gone then she turned to Liz. "I'm sorry about that," she said. "Katy just doesn't know when to let go."

"Gina was her best friend," I said. "It's understandable that she'd worry about you and your brothers."

She gave me a wry smile. "She drives Greg crazy, but I kind of feel sad for her." She played with a strand of hair, twisting it around one finger. "A couple of months before the fire Katy was set to adopt a baby and it didn't happen because the birth mother changed her mind."

"That had to be very painful," Liz said.

Mallory nodded. "The night of the fire, the night Dad took us to her house, I slept in the living room because the baby's room was, well, still the baby's room with a crib and everything."

Katy's overprotectiveness toward her best friend's children made a little more sense now.

Mallory looked at Liz. "Would it be all right if I talked to Greg for a sec?" she asked.

"Of course," Liz said.

"They're out in the garage," Charlotte said. She put an arm around Mallory's shoulders. "I'll show you."

"I'll come with you," I said. I looked at Liz. "Go get some hot for your cup. I'll be right back."

Greg was moving things and Avery was wielding the shop vac when we got to the garage work space.

"They're doing a good job," I whispered to Charlotte. "This space hasn't been this clean in I don't know how long."

Avery caught sight of us and turned off the vacuum. She tapped Greg on the arm and he turned around. Mallory walked over to her brother. She hugged him and then smacked his arm. "What the heck were you thinking?" she asked. "Were you trying to get suspended?" She gestured at Avery. "Were you trying to get her suspended?"

"They don't suspend people at our school," Avery said.

Charlotte shook her head.

"Not helping," I said quietly.

Avery stared at her feet. "Fine," she muttered.

"I was doing the same thing you are," Greg said defiantly. "Trying to get Dad out of jail. Avery and I talked to most of the people at our end of the street and no one else saw Dad when the fire started, which means that judge guy is wrong. Why did they listen to him anyway?"

"He's a good witness," I said. "He's careful, not impulsive. He knew your dad as a neighbor. He even recognized your father's ball cap." I didn't say that I was starting to think that maybe someone had gone to a lot of effort to make Neill Halloran think he'd seen Mike Pearson.

Greg shoved his hair back out of his eyes. "Yeah, well, he isn't always careful. About a week before . . . before the fire, he had his barbecue going in the snow and then forgot about it. He almost set his house on fire."

Mallory wasn't following the conversation, I realized. She was eyeing me, a frown knotting her forehead. "So the judge said Dad was wearing his ball cap?" she said slowly, like she was testing each word.

I nodded.

"Which one? Do you know?"

"The baseball cap from the Melbourne Olympics."

"The blue and red one?" A smile was starting to spread across her face and she slowly shook her head. "He's wrong," she said. "He didn't see Dad." She grabbed Charlotte's arm. "Mrs. Elliot, the judge didn't see Dad. He's wrong. He has to be." She looked at us, the smile lighting up her face.

"Hang on a minute," Charlotte said. "What makes you so sure?" She looked at me over Mallory's head, a frown creasing her forehead.

"I know because I was wearing that hat," Mallory said. She looked at her brother. "Greg, do you remember?"

I saw his expression change and his face light up as the memory came back. "Yeah. Dad was mad because you were washing your hair instead of getting ready to go. I would have given you my hat but Mom had taken it."

Mallory nodded. "And my hair was still wet and then when we got outside it was cold and he put his hat on my head in the car on the way to Katy's." Her words were falling over one another. She turned back to Charlotte. "You see? This proves the judge is wrong. We can go to the police. We can get Dad out of jail!"

I could almost feel the excitement coming off of her.

"It's not that simple," Charlotte said.

Mallory looked confused. "What do you mean? I remember what happened and so does Greg. That's two against one. They can't keep Dad in jail now."

"But you two are his children. It's not the same as two strangers contradicting what Judge Halloran says he saw."

"We're not lying!" Greg said, a stubborn jut to his chin.

"We know that," I said. "But the police, the prosecutor, they'll say you two have more of a reason to lie than the judge does."

"That bites!" Avery exclaimed.

I nodded. "Yes, it does."

Mallory crossed her arms over her chest. "Okay fine," she said. "I'll just go talk to Judge Halloran myself. I'll tell him he's wrong. I'll tell him about the hat and he can just go to the police and take back what he said." She looked at the door and I realized she intended to go over there right now and confront the judge. From what I'd seen he was a kind man and I believed he'd listen to Mallory and treat her with respect, but he'd been a judge for a long time. He knew people would do or say anything to protect the people they loved and in the end I felt sure he'd dismiss Mallory's story.

The thing was, I believed her. "I'll go," I said.

Mallory shook her head. "I'm not a child," she said. "You don't have to go with me and hold my hand or anything."

"That's not what I'm saying," I said. "Let me go talk to Judge Halloran by myself." I held up both hands to hopefully hold off her objections. I saw Greg make a face and Avery roll her eyes. "I believe you. I think if this were some kind of made-up story to get your dad out of prison you would have used it months ago."

"So that's something, right?" Avery said.

I rubbed my neck with one hand. "It is. But just for a minute, think about how many people must have stood in front of the judge, sworn to tell the truth and then lied. Not because they're bad people, but because someone they loved was in trouble and they didn't know what else to do."

"But that's not fair," Greg said. "We're not lying."

"No it isn't," Charlotte said. "But sometimes that's how life works. I'm with Sarah. I believe you. But everyone else is going to be harder to convince. Fair or not, that's the way it is. Let Sarah go talk to the judge and make your case. If she doesn't get anywhere, then you go. We won't try to stop you."

Mallory was looking past us toward the open door. I was pretty sure she was chewing the inside of her lip.

"I know this has nothing to do with me, but let Sarah go talk to that judge guy," Avery said. She was still holding on to the vacuum cleaner hose, her other arm folded over her midsection. Her head was tilted to one side. "She's really good at talking to people, even when they don't want to listen. I've seen her do it. It's like her superpower."

I looked at Mallory.

"All right," she said. "But if he won't take it back—"

"__then I'll call my friend who is a police detective and you can tell her what you just told us."

"Okay," she said.

I looked at Charlotte. "We can handle things here," she said.

I went back inside, told Rose and Liz where I was going and promised Charlotte would fill in the blanks. I went upstairs and grabbed my purse and keys. When I came down Liz was waiting at the bottom of the steps.

She raised an eyebrow. "Need a sidekick, Warrior Princess?" she asked.

I had once gone with Liz to confront businessman Daniel Swift at his office, which ironically had been located in the same building as Judge Halloran's law office. She'd been fierce that day and I'd nicknamed her Xena after the heroine of the campy '90s TV show. This time it seemed I was the Warrior Princess.

Xena had Gabrielle. I had Liz.

"Let's go," I said.

We took my SUV. "Do you mind if I make a quick stop at Glenn's for a cup of coffee?" I asked. "I never did get one when we got back from Rockport."

"It's fine with me," Liz said. "And it's probably better that we don't go see the judge when you're down half a quart of caffeine."

"Charlotte told you what happened?" I asked, slowing down for the stop sign ahead.

"She did."

From the corner of my eye I could see that she was eyeing me. "You don't think those two are stretching the truth just to get their father out of jail?"

I shook my head. "No. I think if they were, well, lying, they would have done it a lot sooner."

"The same thing occurred to me," Liz said.

I shot a quick sideways glance at her. "If you'd seen Mallory's face when she thought she had a way to get her father out of jail . . . I don't think she was acting."

We drove in silence for a couple of minutes. Even though I'd decided to keep my suspicions to myself for the time being about Mike having been set up, I was having second thoughts. "I need your opinion on something," I said.

"That's what a sidekick is for."

I suddenly remembered what Gram had said about Rose wanting to find the perfect table at Sam's when I was teasing her about how we'd all conspired to get her and John together. *She wanted to make sure John saw us.*

"I think it's possible that someone set Mike up, wore the same ball cap as he did and made sure to be seen by Judge Halloran."

"I thought that might be what was in your mind when you asked what he looked like," she said. "The problem is, young Mr. Pace was sleeping it off in a jail cell, Ben Allison was with his daughter and a dozen other witnesses and Molly Pace wasn't even in town."

I blew out a breath.

"You have someone in mind," Liz said. "Don't you?"

"Ben Allison has an alibi. His wife doesn't."

I glanced at Liz again.

She was nodding her head. "It makes sense. Gina Pearson almost killed that child."

"Jia Allison keeps all her anger in here," I said, tapping the middle of my chest with a loose fist. "When it gets out I think she could be capable of anything."

"So what are you going to do?" Liz asked.

I pulled to the curb in front of McNamara's. "For now I'm going to see if I can float the possibility to Judge Halloran that the person he saw wasn't Mike Pearson. After that I need to talk to Jia Allison."

Glenn was at the counter when we stepped inside the little bakery and sandwich shop. "Perfect timing," he said with a smile. "I have two lemon tarts left."

"I actually came for coffee," I said. "Large, please."

Liz put a hand on my arm. "Let's not be hasty," she said. "Glenn will think we don't like his lemon tarts. Do you want to hurt his feelings?"

"Yeah," Glenn said. "Do you want to hurt my feelings?"

"Fine," I said. "One large coffee and two lemon tarts." I looked at Liz. "Would you like anything?"

She shook her head. "I'm fine, thank you."

Glenn nestled the two tarts in a small cardboard box. "Sarah, I keep meaning to say thank you for taking on Clayton's place. It's a hell of a lot more livable since you cleared it out and sold all that stuff."

"Clayton was easy to work with," I said. "We have a few more things left on consignment—a lamp, a couple of chairs and some dishes. They should sell once the leaf peepers show up."

Glenn smiled. "Most of those dishes belonged to Mary."

"Clayton's wife," Liz said.

He nodded. "Beth took a few pieces for sentimental reasons, but it's just not her taste. I'm glad things will at least be with people who appreciate them."

Beth was Glenn's cousin, Clayton's only daughter. She didn't live in North Harbor.

"She had a good eye for things," I said.

"Mary could set a table so it looked like something from a magazine," Glenn said. "And cook a meal to match." He shook his head. "It was so cruel. When her mind went, the first thing she forgot how to do was cook. She'd get out all the ingredients for a cake and not know what to do with them."

"She had dementia?"

He nodded. "I'd go to see her and she'd call me Clayton. That was one of the first things we noticed. She kept mixing people up." He handed me my coffee. I paid for it and the lemon tarts and we left.

We got back in the SUV and I set my coffee in the cup holder after taking a long drink. I looked at Liz. "Are you thinking what I'm thinking?" I asked.

She nodded. "I am." She looked sad.

"So what do we do?"

"What we set out to do. Get some answers."

I thought about something else Gram had said at dinner: *You can't get the right answers if you don't ask the right questions.*

Chapter 17

I didn't really have a plan for what I was going to do when I got to the judge's office. Luckily he had been as good as his word as far as helping with the nonexistent book project. His receptionist smiled at us. "Hello, Mrs. French, Ms. Grayson," she said. "It's good to see you again." She was wearing a crisp white blouse with three-quarter-length sleeves. The fuchsia streak was still in her hair.

"Hello, Chelsea," Liz said. "Would the judge have a few minutes for us?"

Liz knew the young woman's name. That didn't surprise me.

"Let me check with Mr. Davis," Chelsea said.

She reached for the phone, had a brief conversation and then hung up. "He'll be right out," she said.

It was no more than a minute before Henry Davis came into the reception area. "It's good to see you both again," he said.

"I'm sorry we didn't call first," I said.

"You caught us on a quiet day," he said with a smile. "How can I help you?"

He knows, I thought. I was willing to bet every visitor, not just us, saw Henry Davis first. He was more than an assistant. He was a protector.

"I don't know if you remember, but that last time we were here the conversation turned to a man named Mike Pearson," I said.

Henry stiffened. It was almost imperceptible but I was watching for a reaction and I saw it. "I remember."

"The judge is certain he saw Mike the night the Pearson house burned down."

"The judge's word is beyond reproach."

"No one is questioning Neill's word," Liz said.

I looked down at my hands. I felt as though I was shaking but they were steady. The sensation was all on the inside. "He also called me Isabel," I said.

Henry had recovered his equanimity. "It seems you resemble your grandmother."

"A little. I do," I said. "But that's not why the judge got my name wrong, is it?"

He didn't say anything.

"An innocent man doesn't deserve to be in jail, Mr. Davis."

"Mr. Pearson took a plea deal," Henry said.

"Because the police had a witness whose integrity *no one* would question," Liz said.

Just then Judge Halloran came down the hallway. He was in his shirtsleeves, carrying a yellow legal pad, his reading glasses sliding down his nose. "Chelsea, did I—" he began, then he caught sight of us. "Elizabeth, I didn't realize you were here." He joined us.

"Hello, Neill," Liz said. "You remember Sarah Grayson."

"Of course I do," he said. "It's good to see you again, Sarah."

"It's good to see you, too," I said. He had such a kind face. I suddenly had a lump in my throat.

He smiled at us. "Why are we standing out here? Come back to my office."

We followed the judge down the hall and I tried to tell myself I was wrong. So he'd called me by Gram's name. I'd gotten people's names mixed up before. And he started the barbecue in December. Lots of people liked to grill all year 'round.

Henry Davis was in front of me. He held himself stiffly, his shoulders rigid. He didn't want this conversation to continue. I knew I wasn't wrong.

We stepped into the judge's office. "Please, sit down," he said, gesturing at the two chairs in front of his desk where we'd sat during our last visit. He turned to me and smiled. "Now, Isabel, what can I do for you?"

I swallowed down that lump in my throat. "The last time we were here we talked about Mike Pearson."

He nodded. "I remember."

"You told us that you're certain you saw him after the Pearsons' house was on fire."

"That's right. I also saw him earlier in the day while I was shoveling my driveway."

Henry Davis took a couple of steps closer so he was in my line of sight. "Ms. Grayson, I don't mean to be rude, but Judge Halloran is a very busy man."

The judge looked at his assistant. "I'm not too busy for an old friend, Henry."

I felt the prickle of sudden tears, but I blinked them away. "What's my name?" I asked.

Henry sucked in a sharp breath.

Judge Halloran frowned. "Your name is Sarah," he said. "Now, how about you tell me what is going on?"

"Before, you called me Isabel."

He smiled then. "I'm sorry. You remind me so much of your grandmother."

"You called me by her name when I was here before," I said. I kept my eyes locked on his face.

"Are you trying to say there's something wrong with my memory?" he asked. "Is that the reason for all the questions about the fire?"

Liz leaned forward in her chair. "Neill, Mike Pearson is a good man, a good man I believe should not be in jail."

Henry cleared his throat. "As I said earlier, it's my understanding that Mr. Pearson is in jail because he took a plea deal."

Her gaze flicked to him for just a moment. Something in the look she gave him silenced the man. Liz turned her attention back to Judge Halloran.

I didn't like doing this. The judge was a good man, too. I didn't like forcing his secret from him. But I couldn't leave Mike Pearson in jail. I couldn't leave three kids without their father.

"Judge, we don't know each other," I said. "But my grandmother does know you. Her exact words to me were, 'Neill will do the right thing, always.' I'm going to trust that you're the person she says you are." I got to my feet and looked at Liz. "Let's go," I said.

I expected her to object, to say something more to the judge but she didn't. She stood up and slipped her purse over her arm.

I'd taken two steps when he spoke. "Please, don't leave," he said.

I stopped and turned around. Liz put a hand on my arm.

The judge was on his feet as well.

Henry Davis stepped in front of him. "Think this through, Judge," he said.

Judge Halloran smiled. "I have, Henry," he said. "That's the problem. All I've done is think . . . about myself." He gestured at the chairs. "Please, Elizabeth, Is—Sarah, sit down."

I glanced at Liz. She nodded. We took our seats again. The judge leaned against the edge of his desk.

"I'm in the very early stages of . . . dementia. According to my doctor, aside from some drop in my concentration levels—and some of that may just be a factor of getting older in general—and some small memory issues, mostly with names, which you noticed, I'm not suffering from any cognitive decline."

"I work with the judge every day," Henry said. "I haven't seen any loss of mental ability." He was angry. I could see it in the way he held his mouth and in the rigidity of his body. I couldn't help but like his loyalty.

"It's not a question of your mental function, Neill," Liz said.

"But you believe I'm mistaken about seeing Mike Pearson," he said.

I shook my head. "We think someone went to a fair amount of effort to set Mike up, to make you believe you saw him."

He frowned. "What do you mean?"

I leaned forward in my chair. "One of the details you mentioned was Mike's hat—a blue and red baseball cap."

"The replica of the Melbourne Olympics baseball team hat," he said. "Michael wore that hat a lot."

"He wasn't wearing it when the fire started," Liz said. "Because he didn't have it then."

"You're certain."

I nodded.

"So you believe I saw someone pretending to be Michael?"

"Yes."

He may have had dementia but his reasoning skills were still intact. "Which means you think there's a possibility that Gina Pearson didn't start that fire. You think someone murdered her."

"We don't have enough evidence right now to take to the police," Liz said. "But yes, we do."

"Would it help if I went to the prosecutor and explained about my diagnosis?" he asked.

The tight feeling was back in my chest. "At some point it might," I said.

He nodded. "You know, the one thing that always bothered me was that Michael didn't make any attempt not to be seen. His house was on fire and he just walked away. He was too smart for that." He looked at Henry, whose lips were pulled into two thin lines. "Henry, don't be angry with Elizabeth and Sarah." He smiled at me when he said my name. "I should never have kept this quiet like it was some dirty little secret."

I smiled back at him. "Judge, may I ask you a question? I'm only asking out of curiosity so I won't be offended if you tell me it's none of my business."

"What is it?" he said.

"Why did you care so much about Gina Pearson? Why did you go to so much trouble to help her?"

"Gina wasn't drinking when they first moved in next to me. She was a good mother. A good person." He exhaled softly. "She reminded me of my mother."

I hadn't expected him to say that.

"When my older brother, Connor, died, my mother started drinking. We didn't use the word 'alcoholic' very much back then, but that's what she was. Good people helped her find her way back to us. I just wanted to do the same thing for someone else."

I had to swallow a couple of times before I could speak. "I think you would have succeeded," I said.

Liz got to her feet and I followed suit. "Thank you, Neill," she said, extending her hand.

"You're welcome, Elizabeth."

I offered my own hand, which he took in both of his. "Thank you," I said. I cleared my throat. "Everything Gram said about you is true."

He swallowed to clear his own throat. "I'm honored by her faith in me, and yours." He smiled then. "And please, come back soon and I'll pull out a couple of embarrassing stories about Elizabeth for your book project."

"I will," I said. "I promise."

Neither Liz nor I said a word until we were in the elevator. I leaned my cheek against the top of her head. "Being the Warrior Princess bites sometimes," I said.

She laid a hand against my other cheek. "I know," she said. "And I'm proud of you."

We headed back to the shop, where we brought the others up to date.

"So now what?" I asked.

"Mallory and Gregory can give statements that Mike didn't have his ball cap," Mr. P. said.

"Do you think Katy Mueller remembers that Mallory was wearing it?" Charlotte asked.

"I think that's a long shot," I said, choosing my words carefully. Katy Mueller seemed convinced that Mike Pearson was responsible for her best friend's death. I had the feeling she wasn't going to be very helpful in getting him released.

I looked at Mr. P., who seemed to know what I was thinking. "I agree with Sarah," he said. "Judge Halloran's condition will add a little ambiguity to his ID of Mike, but it would help if we could come up with a little more evidence." He hiked his pants up. "There is one more thing we could try. It's a bit of a long shot, though."

"A long shot is better than no shot," Liz said. "What are you thinking, Alfred?"

"Maybe one of the neighbors had a security system."

"But Rose said you didn't notice any cameras," I said.

He nodded. "I didn't. But it's occurred to me that the fire happened just two weeks before Christmas last year."

Rose realized what he was getting at before the rest of us did. "Christmas parcels," she said with a knowing smile.

Charlotte and I exchanged a blank look.

"Want to clue the rest of us in?" Liz asked, making a get-on-with-it motion with one hand.

"More and more people are shopping online, especially during the holidays," Mr. P. said. "Which means there are more packages being delivered when everyone is at work and school."

Rose straightened the front of her apron. "Do you remember the story last December about the three friends who were stealing parcels all over Rockport?"

Charlotte began to nod her head. "They each dressed up as Mrs. Claus."

"I remember that," I said. "They didn't even need the money. They were just doing it because they were bored."

"And do you remember how they got caught?" Alfred asked.

"Someone set them up," I said, smiling as the details came back to me. "The guy left a box on his front steps and he set up some kind of temporary camera."

Alfred nodded as though I was his prize student who had just gotten all the test answers right. "That camera sent images to the man's phone and stored them in the cloud."

"And how does that help us?" Liz asked.

"Those cameras were very popular," Mr. P. said. "You could even rent them. A lot of people did that. In January they took them back. But unless they closed their account and deleted the images that were stored in the cloud, it's all still there. As I said, a long shot."

"Like Liz said, a long shot is better than no shot," I said.

He nodded. "I'll see what I can do."

Charlotte left with Liz and Avery. Rose and Mr. P. rode with Elvis and me. They spent the drive making a list of the neighbors in the immediate vicinity of the Pearson house. It seems Denise had mentioned the names of several of them when Rose and Alfred had talked to her about the fire.

I unlocked the apartment door, set my things inside and put Elvis on the floor. He stretched and headed for the bedroom. I followed him. He made his way over to my new running shoes, which were sitting by the bottom of the bed. He nudged one shoe with his nose, knocking it over onto its side. Then he looked at me.

"How did you know what I was thinking?" I asked.

"Merow," he said.

Jia Allison had mentioned she ran the hills loop, an almost-six-mile circuit with some easy-grade uphill work. I'd been thinking of running the route on the off chance that she might be out there herself.

I crouched down, leaned my face in close to Elvis and gave the top of his head a scratch. "Sometimes you're just a little bit spooky," I said. He murped in agreement and licked my chin.

I changed into my running gear while Elvis nosed around in the closet. "We'll have supper when I get back," I said. "Unless you were planning on cooking."

He yawned. I was pretty sure that meant no.

It was a good time for a run. There was very little traffic for some reason. Usually at this time of day I'd see other runners but I was the only one hitting the pavement. There was no sign of Jia Allison.

I was past the halfway point of the loop when I caught sight of someone running ahead of me. I spotted short, dark hair under a baseball cap, but it wasn't until the street curved that I knew for sure it was Jia. I upped my speed, pushing myself to catch her, which wasn't easy because her training pace was faster than mine. But I did manage to close the distance between us.

"Jia," I called when I judged I was close enough for her to hear me.

She looked back over her shoulder. I saw a flash of recognition and she slowed her pace. I closed the rest of the distance between us.

"Hi," she said. "You training for the Half Shore 10K too?"

"Actually I was looking for you," I said as I kept pace beside her. It helped that she hadn't speeded back up.

"Let me guess: You have more questions about Gina Pearson. I already told you everything there is to tell." Her eyes didn't quite meet mine.

I studied her for a moment, tried to imagine her in a dark coat and a red and blue ball cap. In the dark and the snow could Judge Halloran have mistaken her for Mike Pearson? It was possible. "You saw her before the fire, didn't you?"

It was a guess but I had a gut feeling I was right.

She pressed her lips together for a moment. "It was bad enough that she drove drunk and ran my daughter down. She also had her own child in the car. Did you know that?"

"You mean Greg."

Jia nodded. She was wearing a gray and yellow half-zip running shirt. It was inside out and something was hanging from the upper arm. A fabric softener sheet. I reached over and grabbed it. Jia started and pulled away from me.

"I'm sorry," I said, holding up my hand. "You just had a dryer sheet stuck to your shirt."

She glanced at her arm. "And my damn shirt is on inside out." She closed her eyes, her chin dropped to her chest and she stopped in her tracks. Her whole body sagged.

"Are you all right?" I said.

Jia shook her head. "No. I'm not. I know Hannah is better—better than we could have hoped for. And I'm grateful every single day but sometimes I have these moments where I panic that it's all going to be taken away again. I keep . . . I keep trying to run past the feeling, but I'm not doing a very good job of it." She looked at me then, shaking her head.

"We should walk," I said. "Your legs are going to cramp." We started moving and I watched for any sign that she was light-headed.

We walked in silence for maybe half a minute, Jia looking straight ahead. "I did see her," she suddenly said.

I realized she was talking about Gina.

"In fact, it was the day of the fire. I was at the grocery store. She tried to apologize again. I just . . . I pushed her aside and just walked away from her. I was afraid if I stayed there I'd hit her." She looked at me then, anguish etched on her face. "I keep thinking what if that was the one thing that pushed her over the edge, what if I drove her to kill herself because I wouldn't let her apologize?"

I was shaking my head before she finished talking. "You are *not* responsible for Gina Pearson's death," I said emphatically. I wished I could tell her that Gina had been murdered, that she hadn't killed herself.

"It's . . . it's more complicated than that, but it's not your fault in any way. It's not."

She nodded but I wasn't sure I'd convinced her. "I told you that I was out for a run that night," she said.

I nodded. "I remember."

"That night and all the other times I was supposed to be training, I was really just running as far as the lookout and then just sitting there on a bench and crying." Her mouth twisted to one side. "How dumb is that?"

I put a hand on her arm and this time she didn't flinch. "It's not dumb. I can't even imagine what it was like for you when your daughter was hurt. I think that now it's okay if you take care of yourself. You don't need to hold up everyone's world."

Jia gave me a small smile. "That's what it feels like some days. Like I'm holding up the world."

"Promise me when you get home you'll talk to your husband?"

It took a moment but then she nodded. "Okay."

"And I'm going to call you if that's okay?" I said.

The smile got a tiny bit bigger. "It's okay."

We ran the rest of the loop, albeit at a much slower pace.

"That's my house, right there." She pointed at a gray saltbox with a fire-engine-red front door. She glanced down at her feet for a moment then looked up at me. "Thanks for listening."

"Hey, anytime," I said. "Maybe we could go for a run sometime."

"I'd like that," she said. She took a couple of steps toward the house and then stopped, looking back over her shoulder. "You're going to watch me until I get to the door, aren't you?"

I nodded. "I am. And I *am* going to call you." I shrugged. "I spend a lot of time with a bunch of nosy, bossy, opinionated—wonderful—seniors. You met two of them the other day. I've picked up some of their behaviors."

Jia smiled. "I'll talk to you soon then," she said. She headed down the sidewalk, stopping to raise one hand before she opened the red door and went inside. I turned then and headed home.

When I got there, Liz was just getting out of her car parked at the curb.

"Hi, what are you doing here?" I said.

"I came to talk to John, to see if there's anything else he remembers about those projects that never happened." She eyed my running gear. "Did you talk to the Allison woman?"

"I did," I said, pulling the elastic out of my hair.

"It's not her, is it?"

We headed up the walkway. "I don't think so. She did see Gina the day of the fire. And she's carrying a lot of guilt because she just walked away from her. I just don't think she would have admitted that if she'd killed Gina."

She patted my arm. "Chin up, kiddo," she said. "We'll figure this out."

I held the door and then followed her inside. "Did you call Marie's son?" I asked.

"As a matter of fact, I did," Liz said. "He's overnighting a box of papers and things from his mother's desk that she'd had in storage."

"Maybe we'll find some answers somewhere in those papers," I said.

"Channing says the key to figuring out who set up Rob Andrews is to figure out who benefitted."

I opened my mouth but before I could say anything her index finger was in my face. "Think carefully before you speak," Liz warned.

I gave her my best guileless look. "I was just going to say that I think Channing is right. He's pretty savvy when it comes to financial issues."

I unlocked my apartment door. "And hot babes!" I added. I wiggled my eyebrows at her then ducked inside.

"You better hide, missy," Liz said from the other side.

I leaned against the door, laughing. I wasn't going to stop teasing her about Channing Caulfield. It was way too much fun. On the other hand I did make sure my door was locked. Liz wasn't above sneaking in while I slept and pouring a bucket of water over my head.

I kicked off my shoes and headed for the shower. Was Channing right? I wondered. If we could figure out who benefitted would we have the person who set up Michelle's father?

As I ran the water in the shower it occurred to me that maybe the same reasoning could be applied to Gina Pearson's death. The only problem was I couldn't think of anyone who had benefitted from her death.

Chapter 18

Liz called me late Thursday morning. "Could you take an early lunch?" she asked. "FedEx just delivered the box of Marie's things."

I looked at my watch. "Give me about twenty minutes," I said.

I headed downstairs. Rose was at the cash desk just ringing up a customer. I waited until she finished. The customer smiled as she passed me.

"Rose, what did that woman buy?" I asked. "She's not carrying anything."

Rose had a self-satisfied smile on her face. "The last bedroom set from Clayton McNamara's house."

"But we don't even have it set up," I said, looking around the room. The heavy, ornate black walnut bedroom set with a headboard and footboard, a chest of drawers and a mirrored dresser would have taken up a lot of space in the shop and I'd been debating how best to show it off.

"I took her out to the old garage so she could see the pieces. She's coming back with a truck."

I grinned at her. "Rose Jackson, is there anything you can't sell?"

"Lima beans in a casserole," she said. "And I can't take credit for selling that bedroom set. The woman came in here looking specifically for something just like it."

"Some days you eat the bear, some days the bear eats you," I said.

"I wonder who came up with that saying," she said, her expression thoughtful. "I can't actually imagine ever eating a bear, can you?"

I loved the way Rose's mind worked. "I'd rather eat the lima beans," I said.

She nodded in agreement.

"I need to go out for a little while," I said. "Can you handle everything?"

She smiled. "Of course I can, dear. Avery will be here soon and Charlotte is coming after lunch. And if it gets busy Alfred can help. Go."

I leaned over and kissed her cheek. "Thank you," I said.

The box was sitting on the coffee table in Liz's living room. She hadn't even peeled off the tape sealing the top.

"I swear if there are no answers in this box of papers I'm going to hire Alfred to go through every file the foundation has until he finds something," Liz said.

"Not the worst idea you've ever had," I said.

I picked up the scissors lying on the table next to the box and slit the packing tape. Inside we found a pile of file folders, each one held together with a couple of heavy binder clips. I took the top folder out and handed it to Liz. I took the next one, unfastening the clips.

We sat there in silence for a few minutes, the only

sound the pages being turned. Finally I looked up at Liz. "Am I wrong or are these more minutes from those board meetings?"

"You're not wrong," she said. "Except I think what we have is the real minutes from those board meetings." She turned the page she was holding around so I could see it. "Right there," she said, pointing with one finger. "See that?"

I squinted at the paper and then looked at her. "I don't see anything. None of those projects are listed."

Liz nodded. "I know. That's my point."

She took the rest of the files out of the box. Something in the fourth one caught her attention. "Sarah, look at this," she said.

It was a page of notes and numbers in neat, boxy handwriting. Marie Heard's? I wondered.

"That's an allocation of money for one of those projects." I read a little further. "What does viability next to the amount mean?"

"It means the idea was one step before the development stage. In other words, was it a viable project?"

I found a similar reference to one of the other projects on a page of notes in the file I had.

"So Marie was stealing money and covering her tracks by making it look like authorized expenditures if anyone checked," Liz said. Her eyes were sad but her voice was devoid of emotion.

"It looks that way," I said.

"I can't believe someone I knew so well was cheating the foundation and setting up Rob Andrews to take the fall," she said. She gestured at the box. "What else is there besides the files?"

I looked inside. "I think it's all personal items she had in her desk." I handed Liz two photos.

"That's Marie's son," she said of a framed photo of a young man grinning from ear to ear in his cap and gown.

The other photo was of Liz's brother, Wilson, with a tiny dumpling of a woman.

"That's Marie and Wilson when he was named Man of the Year by the Chamber of Commerce." Liz studied the photo for a long moment and then set it on the coffee table next to the box.

The only items left were an amethyst bracelet and a navy silk tie.

The tie lay across her knees as she fingered the bracelet and then set it next to the photo. For a moment she didn't speak. "Marie always had an extra clean tie in her desk in case Wilson needed it," she finally said. "I, uh, never saw her wear this bracelet."

I repeated what Jane said about Marie being wedded to her job.

"It's true," Liz said. "I don't ever remember hearing that Marie was seeing anyone after her husband died."

I could see how troubled she was. I put my arm around her shoulders. "I'm so sorry," I said.

"So am I."

"Why don't you take a couple of days before we tell Michelle what we know?"

She almost smiled. "I think I'll do that."

We both got to our feet. "Do you want me to put everything away?" I asked.

Liz shook her head. "Leave it." She walked me to the front door and wrapped her arms around me. "Love you, toots."

"Love you, too," I said.

I drove back to Second Chance feeling as though a large rock had settled in my stomach. Michelle was right. Her father had been innocent, but knowing that now really wasn't going to fix anything. Her father was still dead. Marie was also dead so there was no chance for any real justice, and Liz had learned a painful truth about someone she'd trusted.

I pulled into the store parking lot and just sat there. My head hurt and so did my stomach. I didn't want to go inside. I didn't want to pretend I felt okay when I didn't. I wanted Mac to be there. I wanted to hear one of his positive little speeches about how this would be all right. I wanted to hide in the old garage with my sander, working on the armoire for Gram and John while Mac ran interference. But Mac wasn't here. I headed inside, pasting on a happy face I didn't really feel.

I was up in my office about an hour later when Mr. P. knocked on the door. "Nicolas is here," he said. "He brought something I think you'll probably want to see."

I started downstairs with him. "Did you have any luck finding any security footage from the Pearsons' neighbors?" I asked.

"I guess my best answer would have to be, maybe," Alfred said. "It turns out their backyard neighbor did have one of those temporary cameras that downloads all its footage to the cloud. At least he thinks it does." He raised an eyebrow. "He'll get back to me."

I'd told Mr. P. and Rose about my conversation with Jia Allison and my belief that she'd had nothing to do with Gina's death. If the security footage was a dead end our only hope was Nick persuading the medical examiner to change Gina's cause of death.

Nick was out in the workroom with Rose, using the top of my storage unit casket like a desk. Their heads were bent over something and Michelle was with them.

"Hi," I said, making my way around the makeshift desk so I could hug her. "I'm glad you're back. How's your mom?"

Michelle smiled. "She's good." She gestured at Nick and Rose, who I realized were intently studying several photographs. "It seems I missed a few things," she said.

I gave an elaborate shrug. "Maybe one or two." I moved around her so I was next to Nick and poked him with my elbow. "What are you looking at?" I asked.

He glanced at Michelle. "Crime scene photos."

"Should we be looking at these?"

"I'm sorry," Michelle said. "I didn't hear you."

"I said should we—Ow!" Rose had just smacked the back of my head. I turned and glared at her. "Why did you do that?"

"Because your mouth seemed to be stuck on repeat, dear. Sometimes it takes a bit of a tap to fix that. It's not really that different from when the printer jams." I caught on then that Michelle really had suddenly gone hard of hearing, at least with respect to the photographs.

"Um, thank you," I said. I resisted the urge to rub the spot on the back of my head. It seemed Rose and I had different ideas about what constituted a tap.

I leaned over to look at the photos. They were of the Pearson house after the fire, specifically the basement family room. The walls were black with soot and I could make out scorch patterns on the floor. Part of the sofa had been burned to the springs,

After a moment Michelle leaned over as well. "That case never sat right with me," she said softly.

"I thought maybe you would see something the rest of us missed," Nick said.

What I saw was Greg Pearson's Patriots cap, which Gina had confiscated because he wouldn't take it off in the house. It was a bit singed but other than that it looked fine; there was barely any soot on it. I also saw what I was guessing was his little brother's teddy bear, and it *was* covered in soot like the wall behind it. I remembered what Mallory said about the bear.

I studied the two photos and the sensation was like a finger tickling my brain. Who would benefit if Gina Pearson were dead? The pieces began to connect like one domino falling over on another.

I looked at Rose and Nick. I looked across the wooden casket at Mr. P. Finally I turned and looked at Michelle. "I know what happened," I said. "I know who killed Gina Pearson."

Chapter 19

I laid out my theory even as I was putting it together in my head. Mr. P. began to nod almost at once. Michelle interrupted me twice with questions, Nick once. I waited for them to point out the holes in my reasoning, but they didn't.

"So?" I said when I'd finished talking.

"I think you're right," Mr. P. said.

I leaned around Nick to look at Rose. "I agree with Alfred, sweet girl," she said. "Although I wish you were wrong."

"I can't disagree," Nick said, shaking his head.

Finally I turned to Michelle. "I can't see any flaw in your reasoning," she said.

"So what happens now?" Nick asked.

I sighed. "I'm going to go tell Charlotte, and then before we do anything else we need to talk to Mallory."

Mallory and Greg Pearson arrived at Charlotte's house about quarter to eight. They'd had supper with Katy Mueller. Charlotte and I met them at the door. "You're welcome to join us," I said to Katy. "We're just going to bring Mallory and Greg up to date on what the Angels have learned."

"Thank you," she said. "I think I will."

We settled in Charlotte's living room. Mallory and Greg on the sofa with Charlotte, and Rose in the matching chair, Mr. P. sitting on the wide arm next to her. I gave Katy the other chair and took a seat on the footstool.

Charlotte reached over and took one of Mallory's hands in hers. "I'm sorry," she said. "There isn't any easy way to tell you this. Gina didn't kill herself. She was murdered."

"My dad didn't kill her," Mallory immediately said. Her chin came up. Beside her Greg swallowed hard, his face pale.

"We know that," Charlotte said. "We believe that Mike took the plea deal to end the investigation and protect someone he loved."

Katy leaned forward in her chair. "What are you talking about?" she said.

Charlotte leaned sideways. "Greg," she said. "Tell them."

Mallory's eyes widened and she shifted to look at her brother. She looked confused. "I don't understand. Do you know something?"

He looked away. His mouth twisted and finally he nodded. "I went back to the house that night," he said.

When I'd seen his hat in the photograph there was almost no soot on it, unlike everything else in the room. It looked like someone had tried to save it. Gina?

"But why?" Mallory asked.

His gaze met his sister's then. "I wanted to get my hat and because I was sick of what she was doing." His hands were clenched into tight fists, so tight his knuckles were white, the skin stretched tight over the finger joints. "Austin cried until he fell asleep. Did you forget that?"

Mallory shook her head.

"You know how Dad had talked about us going to stay at Gram's for a while? Well, I went to ask her to at least let Austin go. He was a little kid, Mal. He should have been having a normal life with a mom who made cookies and read him bedtime stories."

Tears were slipping down Mallory's face. My stomach clenched. If I'd been able to figure out any other way to do this I would have.

Greg raked his hand back through his hair. "I was pouring out all her bottles because I pretty much knew all of her hiding places—even some you and Dad didn't know. She grabbed my hat and pulled it off my head again. She was a freakin' drunk and all she cared about was me wearing my hat in the house. I was just so pis— so angry I stopped." He lifted his hands in the air and then just let them fall. "I gave her one of the bottles and I said, 'Go ahead and drink yourself to death. I don't care anymore.'" A couple of tears slid down his face and he swiped at them with one hand. "It's my fault she's dead."

Charlotte reached across Mallory and caught one of Greg's hands. "Your mother didn't kill herself," she said firmly. "What happened isn't your fault."

My throat was tight but I swallowed the sensation away and turned to Katy. "It isn't Greg's fault," I said. "Is it?"

Chapter 20

"I don't know what you're talking about," Katy said. She waved a hand in the air. "All this proves is what I've been saying all along: This investigation is a waste of time." She turned to Mallory and Greg. "It's time to go."

"I know you were at the house the night of the fire," I said as if she hadn't spoken.

I glanced at Mr. P., who gave me a small nod of encouragement. I reached under the footstool and pulled out an enlargement of a section of the crime scene photo that Nick had showed us earlier. Mr. P. had worked his computer magic on it and I had a fairly sharp image of Austin Pearson's teddy bear. It was clear from the photograph that the stuffed toy had been too burned to be salvaged.

"Mallory told me that Austin wouldn't sleep with his bear anymore because even though you'd washed it three times it didn't smell right. She thought it was because there was some lingering smoke smell from the fire, but that wasn't it, was it?" I said. "The bear smelled wrong because it was a different bear. It smelled *new*, not like smoke and not like the old one."

"I don't understand," Mallory said.

I turned to look at her. "My dad died when I was five. For months I dragged around one of his sweaters the way some kids drag around an old baby blanket. Finally my mother washed it and I cried for days. It smelled wrong to me because it didn't smell like him anymore."

"So I bought Austin a new bear," Katy said. "He treated it like it was a person. I didn't want him to know it had been destroyed in the fire."

"The night of the fire you went to the house to get that teddy bear," I said. "Greg said that Austin cried himself to sleep. You thought he'd feel better when he woke up if it was there."

She didn't say anything.

"Your hair was shorter then and you wore Mike's ball cap and a similar dark jacket. Was there a reason you didn't want anyone to know you were there?"

Once I'd seen the burned toy in the photo everything had fallen into place. Katy was the only person who had something to gain. Katy, who was always stepping in to take care of her best friend's children, Katy, who had lost another chance to be a mother.

"I think you got there just after Greg left," I continued. "Gina had seen Jia Allison in the grocery store earlier in the day and she'd had that confrontation with Gavin Pace. But I think it was Greg who finally got through to her. For the first time Gina accepted that she was a drunk."

I was guessing, speculating, but something in Katy's eyes told me I was right.

"Judge Halloran had gotten her a place in a rehab center in Maine. She told you that in the morning she was going and this time she was going to be the mother and wife her family deserved."

Mallory was on her feet. "What did you do to my mom?" she shouted.

Charlotte wrapped her arms around Mallory.

Katy was staring straight ahead, looking at nothing. "This was just like the other times; she wasn't going to change," she said. "I know she said she was, but once a drunk always a drunk." She looked up at Mallory then. "She tried to tell me that she could see in Greg's eyes just what she'd done to him and you and Austin. But she didn't mean it. She was just going to let you down again."

Tears were sliding down Mallory's face and dripping off her chin. Greg had gotten to his feet and, like Charlotte, folded his arms around his sister.

"I was just trying to shake some sense in to her," Katy said. "And then I don't know how it happened but she wasn't breathing."

"You started the fire to cover up what you'd done. You knew that Gina had tried to hang herself a couple of days before so you figured no one would look too closely at the bruises on her neck."

Katy looked at Mallory and Greg. "I'm sorry your father is in jail. I didn't mean for that to happen, but it's not for that long and I can be your mother, a better one than Gina ever was. You're better off with her dead. You'll see that." She got to her feet and made a move toward Mallory, holding her arms out.

Mallory shrank against Charlotte. "You're not my

mother," she said, shaking her head. "You're not my mother and you never could be. Get away from me!"

Michelle came out of the kitchen then and began to read Katy her rights. It was over. I just wished it felt better.

Chapter 21

The police took Katy away.

Michelle retrieved the microphone that had been hidden beside the chair Katy had been sitting in. "Tomorrow I'm going to need everything that you have," she said to Mr. P.

He handed her a brown envelope and a flash drive. "If you need anything else, Detective," he said with a smile, "please let me know."

Michelle turned to me. "I'll talk to the prosecutor and the medical examiner first thing tomorrow. I'll do everything I can to get Mike Pearson out of jail as fast as possible." She looked toward the front door, shaking her head. "Do you really think she went there to kill Gina Pearson?"

I laced my fingers on top of my head. "I'm not sure. But I do know that she went out of her way to make it look like Mike was there." I gestured at the flash drive. "Mr. P. got security footage from one of the Pearsons' neighbors. The camera caught Katy heading for the house. She's wearing a dark jacket and Mike Pearson's cap."

"Judge Halloran called me this afternoon," she said. "Did you have anything to do with that?"

"I actually didn't," I said. "But I'm not surprised he got in touch with you. He's that kind of person."

Michelle nodded. "His influence can only help."

I wrapped her in a hug. "Thank you for doing this."

"Without all of you the truth might never have come out." She smiled. "I'll talk to you tomorrow."

Charlotte was sitting on the sofa with Mallory and Greg. They looked shell-shocked. Rose had gone to the kitchen to make tea and hot chocolate.

As soon as I'd seen the burned teddy bear I'd realized Katy had bought a new one. Not a big deal, but why had she made a point of telling Mallory she'd washed the old one three times to get the smoke smell out? In fact, why not tell Mallory the truth about the toy? It was almost as if Katy wanted everyone to see what a good parent she could be.

Who benefitted?

The problem was all we had was a lie about a teddy bear and some footage of a person who might or might not be Katy cutting across the Pearson's backyard. As Nick had pointed out, it wasn't enough.

We'd needed to get Katy to confess and the only way to get her to talk to us was to let her stay while we talked to Mallory and Greg.

I went over to them now, pulled the footstool closer to the sofa and sat down. "I'm sorry," I said. "I can't imagine how awful that was for both of you."

Mallory shook her head. "You don't have to apologize for anything," she said. "If it wasn't for you, Katy would have gotten away with killing our mom."

"Do you really think this time would have been different?" Greg asked.

I knew he was referring to Gina going to rehab again. I nodded. "I do. I think that's why Katy felt so threatened. Your mother loved you. She just ran out of time to show you."

He nodded, swallowing hard.

Mallory flung her arms around me. Surprised, I hugged her back. "Thank you," she whispered.

"It gets better," I said. "I promise."

Charlotte and Nick took Mallory and Greg back to their grandmother.

I helped Rose tidy up the kitchen and wash our cups. As I wiped the counter I realized she was studying me. "Do I have spinach between my teeth?" I asked. "You're staring at me."

"I heard what you said about Gina to those two lovely young people," she said, as she dried the last cup. "Do you really believe this time was going to be different?"

I leaned against the counter. "Maybe Gina would have gone to rehab and it would have been no different from the previous times. Or maybe, as Gram likes to say, this time would have been the charm. I don't know. What I do know is that it doesn't hurt anyone to give her the benefit of the doubt."

Mr. P. was putting the cups away. He turned and gave me a smile. "You're right," he said. "It doesn't."

I stepped into the hallway the next morning to find Alfred holding Rose's cake carrier. "Good morning, Sarah," he said.

"Good morning." I eyed the large container. "Is that for us?"

He smiled. "It is. Blueberry buttermilk coffee cake."

I gestured over my shoulder at my apartment door with one finger. "Maybe I should just slip back inside and grab a fork? You know, just to make sure the cake turned out."

"Or maybe you should just march yourself out to the car, just to make sure it's going to start," a voice said behind me.

Rose. She was glaring sternly at me but I caught a hint of a smile play across her lips.

"I wasn't really going to eat any of that cake," I said.

"Well, I know that," she said, reaching up to pat my cheek as she bustled past. "Alfred could take you down with one hand tied behind his back." She smiled archly. "He has a number of talents you're not aware of."

Mr. P. smiled at her and raised one eyebrow.

I decided starting the car was a very good idea.

Rose kept the cake on the backseat with her. Elvis sat next to her and helped guard it.

Liam pulled into the shop's parking lot right behind me. He came around the back of his truck and took Rose's tote from her. "Is that for me?" he asked with a smile, gesturing at the coffee cake Mr. P. was carrying.

I shook my head. "I swear you're like one of those dogs they use in the Alps that can find people under the snow. How do you always know when there's cake?"

"I'm psychic," he said, bumping me with his hip as we started for the back door. "Some people can talk to the dead. I can find cake."

"Good to know if I ever have to send out a search party for a slice of devil's food," I said.

He gave me that grin that had been charming women since before he could walk. Then he slung his free arm around my shoulders. "How would you like to get your sunporch back today?"

"Seriously?"

He nodded. "I have to hang that blackboard, put some hooks on the end wall and do a couple of other things, but I should be done around lunchtime."

I hugged him. "I owe you."

"I know," he said. "One of these days I'm going to collect." He tipped his head close to mine. "Be afraid," he whispered. "Be very afraid."

Liam finished up in the office just before lunch. We all trooped in to take a look.

"Aw, Liam, this is great," I said, turning in a slow circle to take it all in.

The new windows had thermal shades, which would keep the heat out in the summer and in during the winter. The walls were painted a pale shade of off-white and I knew there was lots of insulation behind the new drywall. Liam had put down vinyl plank flooring and a baseboard electric heater for the coldest months.

The chalkboard was on the wall above Mr. P.'s desk, flanked by Rose's wall sconces, which, I had to admit, looked great. The long farm-style table we always seemed to gather around was at the far end of the room, surrounded by a collection of mismatched chairs.

"You did an excellent job," Mr. P. said. He couldn't stop smiling.

"It's perfect," Rose said, clasping her hands together.

"I can't take all the credit," Liam said. "It would have taken a lot longer if I hadn't had Nick's help."

"I live to serve," a voice said from the doorway. Nick and Charlotte were standing there.

"This is beautiful," Charlotte said. "You both do lovely work."

Rose was standing just to the right of the desk, frowning at the wall. She beckoned at Charlotte with one hand. "What do you think about a bookcase right here?" she asked.

Charlotte walked over to join her. Liam was showing Mr. P. how the blinds worked.

I smiled at Nick. "Thank you," I said. "Liam's right. This would have taken a lot longer without you."

"Anytime," he said. He tipped his head toward the workroom. I followed him out. "I just came from the police station. It looked like Katy Mueller will be sent for a psychiatric evaluation."

I'd expected that.

"It's going to take a little time, but the plea agreement will be voided and Mike Pearson will come home to his kids. They're going to keep him in the infirmary for now." He shrugged. "It's not a perfect ending, but it's not a bad one, either."

I nodded. "You and Rose make a pretty good team."

Nick smiled. "I'll try not to let that go to my head."

Rose decided we needed to christen the office by having our cake there around what had already been doubling as our meeting table.

"Does anyone know where Liz is?" I asked as I waited for Rose to cut a slice to set aside for Avery.

Charlotte shook her head.

"All I know is that she said she had some meeting she had to go to," Rose said. "Some kind of foundation business."

I nodded. I knew what that meant.

Liz never did show up. "Do you need a ride?" I asked Avery at the end of the day.

"No," she said as she pulled the vacuum out from under the stairs.

"Is your grandmother coming to get you?"

"No," she said again.

Okay. I needed to stop asking yes-or-no questions. "How are you planning on getting home, then?" I asked, grabbing the attachment for the vacuum.

"I'm not going home."

At the rate the conversation was happening, neither was I. Then I realized she had her earbuds in. I reached over and pulled one out of her ear.

She frowned.

"Where are you going and how are you getting there?" I wrapped my fingers around the wireless earpiece so she couldn't snatch it back.

Avery sighed. "I'm going to the library for the Jonathan Demme film festival. Greg is meeting me here and we're walking. We're going to McNamara's for supper." She made a point of enunciating each word like I was very young or very old.

I handed her back the earbud and started for the stairs.

"Sarah," she said.

I turned around. "Thank you for what you did for Greg and his family."

"I'm glad you're his friend," I said.

She smiled then. "Yeah, me, too."

Liz called after supper. I brought her up to date on what had happened in the last twenty-four hours.

"Michael deserves a happy ending," she said. "He's a quality person. In fact, I told him that."

"Wait a minute. You talked to him?"

"Yes," she said. "That's why I was gone all day. I went to the prison to talk to him. There were a couple of questions I wanted to ask him about the summer he worked for the foundation."

"Did you get the answers you were looking for?" I asked.

"Yes I did," she said. "And I have a favor to ask you."

"Anything," I said. I propped my feet on the edge of the coffee table. Elvis jumped onto my lap. I started to stroke his fur.

"I'm going to see Wilson tomorrow to tell him what I've learned about Marie. Will you come with me?"

"Of course I will. We make a pretty good team, you know."

"That we do, pretty girl," she said.

We agreed to meet at nine thirty the next morning at the foundation's offices and said good night.

I got to Liz's office about twenty-five minutes after nine. I was surprised to find Jane Evans there as well. She looked just as surprised to see me. "You're going to Liz's meeting with Wilson?" she said.

"I am," I said. Liz was at her desk, looking through some papers.

"I hope he'll find a little more enthusiasm for this book project."

So Liz hadn't told Jane what we'd learned. She'd be finding out soon enough.

I saw Liz glance at the gold watch on her left arm. She turned and looked at me. "Let's get this show on the road, toots," she said.

I followed her down the hall. The door to the end office was partly open. Liz knocked and didn't wait to be invited in.

Wilson Emmerson's office was full of rich colors and dark wood. The walls were painted a buttery yellow. An oriental rug in burgundy, cream and gold covered the center of the floor. Gleaming walnut bookshelves filled the end wall. To the right were his framed diplomas and a round, wooden wall clock. Underneath them was a small cabinet flanked by two armless chairs upholstered in a houndstooth fabric. The open desk was set slightly left of center. Everything about the room said money, which I suspected was the intended message. I thought how different Wilson was from Liz. He did have that crown prince entitled attitude about him.

Wilson was seated in a chocolate-brown leather chair behind the desk and talking to someone on the phone. He glanced up at his sister but didn't end the conversation.

I stood just at the edge of the carpet while she walked over to the desk. I knew what was coming. Liz reached over and took the phone right out of his hand. "I'm sorry," she said sweetly to whomever he'd been talking to. "Wilson's going to have to call you back." She ended the call and set the phone on the edge of the desk.

"Why did you do that?" he said.

"Because we have a meeting at nine thirty and it's nine thirty," she said.

Wilson leaned sideways and gave me a tight smile. "Hello, Sarah," he said.

I smiled back. "Good morning."

He turned back to Liz. "If this is about this book project of yours, I haven't changed my mind. I just don't see the point."

I noticed he hadn't offered either of us a seat.

Liz looked over her shoulder at me. "Sarah, would you get me a chair, please?" she said, indicating the two under the clock.

I picked one up and set it in front of Wilson's desk.

"Those chairs are there for a reason," he said, his voice laced with annoyance.

"I don't doubt that they are." Liz smoothed her skirt and sat down. I stood just behind her. She was in full Warrior Princess mode, which meant I was her trusty sidekick. She folded her hands in her lap. "There is no book, Wilson," she said.

"Well, I'm glad you listened to me for once," he said, leaning back in his chair. He wore a fog gray sweater over a white shirt. His clothes were no more expensive than anything Liz wore, I was guessing, so why did he seem so pretentious?

"You're giving yourself too much credit," she said. "There never was a book."

A frown creased his forehead. "What are you talking about? You've been working on the damn thing for weeks."

Liz crossed one leg over the other. She was wearing a pair of red peep-toe slingbacks that had to be at least three inches high. "No, I just told you that was what I was doing. What I was really doing was trying to figure out who framed Rob Andrews."

For a moment Wilson didn't so much as blink. He just stared across the desk at Liz. "Rob Andrews?" he finally sputtered. "He stole money from the foundation. No one framed him."

"Did you know Marie kept two sets of minutes from the board meetings?"

"That's ridiculous," he said, making a dismissive gesture with one hand.

"You know how exacting she was, how meticulous. She couldn't just throw away the original minutes or her notes. That's not who she was. No matter what you told her to do."

My heart began to pound in my chest so loudly I wasn't sure I'd heard Liz's last words correctly.

"I don't know what you're insinuating," Wilson said.

Liz adjusted the scarf at her neck. "I'm not insinuating anything. I'm just stating the facts. Marie was working under your instructions. You stole money from the foundation. You're the embezzler. You set up Rob Andrews but you got Marie to do your dirty work just in case. I know you were having an affair." Her tone was conversational, unemotional, as though she were discussing the weather or asking for a refill for her tea.

"You're getting old and senile, sister dear," he said.

"And you didn't cover your trail nearly as well as you think." She looked at him for a moment. "Mama should have made you wash a few dishes," she said. It was the first spark of anger I'd seen from her. She shifted in her seat. "Sarah would you open the door, please?"

I nodded, crossed the rug and opened the office door. Two police officers and the prosecuting attorney were waiting there. Michelle was standing off to one side in the hallway.

"The police have a lot of questions for you," Liz said. She got to her feet and walked out of the office. I followed. We stood next to Michelle as Wilson Emmerson was led away. Unshed tears shone in Michelle's eyes.

Liz turned to her. "I am profoundly sorry. I know it doesn't fix things, but I will use every resource at my disposal to make sure everyone knows that Rob Andrews was not a thief."

Michelle nodded. "Thank you," she said, her voice raspy with emotion. She hesitated and then threw her arms around Liz. I saw Liz swallow hard. Michelle gave my arm a squeeze and then she was gone.

I wrapped my own arms around Liz's shoulders. "How did you figure it out?" I asked.

"Do you remember that bracelet in the box?" she said, turning her head to look at me.

I nodded.

"Wilson bought the same bracelet for his wife, Mary Anne. When our mother was alive he would buy the same gift for her and Mary Anne because it was easier. He used Marie. He used the fact that she was in love with him."

"I'm sorry," I said. I couldn't imagine what it must have felt like to realize what her brother had done.

"When I went to see Michael yesterday he admitted he'd always suspected Wilson was having an affair with Marie based on the way they interacted at the office—small things, really: the way Marie would fix his tie or tell him he needed a haircut, how they seemed to have little inside jokes no one else got. It was the last piece of the puzzle. That and the money trail Channing's accountant uncovered."

She shook her head. "The irony is Michael was most likely in jail because he was willing to take the blame for something he hadn't done to protect someone he loved, while Wilson was willing to let someone else go to jail to protect the only person he loved—himself."

I linked my arm through hers and walked her back to her office. Jane was standing in the open doorway. Seeing the police lead Wilson out of the building had to be a shock but it didn't show in her face. "Do you want to send out a press release?" she asked. I remembered Liz saying once that when things were at their worst Jane was at her best.

Liz took a deep breath and let it out. "Yes, I do," she said.

"I'm going to need a few details," Jane said.

"You can have them all, my friend," Liz said. She turned to me. "Thank you for riding shotgun."

"Anytime," I said. "Call me if you need anything."

She nodded. "I will."

I started for the door. "Love you," I said.

This time I didn't get the usual answer. "Love you, too," she said.

I swallowed down the sudden lump in my throat and kept walking.

Chapter 22

After an early lunch, I collected Charlotte and we drove across town to pick up Mallory Pearson and her brothers. We were taking them to see their father. It had taken the efforts of both Liz and Judge Halloran to make the visit a reality. I had no idea what strings had been pulled or favors called in. And I didn't care.

At first glance the prison building reminded me a little of a generic office building. It was clean and white and an American flag snapped in the breeze on a manicured patch of grass. Then I caught sight of the high fence topped with barbed wire.

We were taken to the warden's office. It had been decided that it was the best place for the meeting. I realized best probably meant safest. The office was smaller than I expected, with off-white walls, dark wood furniture and a charcoal and cream carpet on the floor.

The warden, whose name was David Ramsey, was a tall man in a black suit with a blue shirt and striped tie. Ramsey had smooth, dark skin and keen eyes behind black-framed glasses. His was the kind of a strong handshake that told me he likely never had a problem opening jars.

"You're Nick Elliot's mother," he said to Charlotte, a statement, not a question.

"Yes, I am," she said.

"I worked with him years ago. I used to be a paramedic."

Charlotte's gaze narrowed. "You were at Maiden's Cliff."

Maiden's Cliff.

Nick had received an award for bravery several years ago for rescuing a six-year-old boy who had fallen down the rocky outcrop above Megunitcook Lake, as well as the off-duty paramedic who had sustained a badly broken leg trying to get to the child. It was a cold and wet late October day and both the boy and the paramedic had been suffering from hypothermia. Without Nick's efforts, things could have ended very differently for both of them.

"Nick saved my life," Ramsey said. "He's a good man."

"I believe the same can be said about you," Charlotte said with a smile.

The warden smiled back at her and it occurred to me that maybe Liz and Neill Halloran hadn't been the only ones calling in favors to make this visit happen.

A guard brought Michael Pearson to the warden's office. He was wiry with no excess body fat. His dark hair was cut close to his head. He moved slowly—not surprising since he still had broken ribs and was still dealing with the effects of the concussion he'd suffered when he was beaten. The right side of his face was bruised but the color was fading to mostly greens and yellows. There was a wariness in Mike's eyes as he stepped into the room as though he expected that somehow this hope, this happy ending might be snatched away from him. But it disappeared the moment he saw his children.

Austin flung himself at his father and it must have hurt with those broken ribs. But there was no sign of pain on Michael Pearson's face as he hugged his younger son and pulled his older boy to him with his free arm.

Had Mike been trying to protect Greg when he took that plea deal? Watching the two of them now I was certain he had.

Mallory hung back, eyes locked on her father, not moving. Charlotte put a hand on her shoulder. "Go hug your father," she urged.

"This is real, right?" Mallory asked, her voice shaking.

"Absolutely," Charlotte said. She gave the teen's shoulder a squeeze. "Go!"

Mike held out his hand then and the smile on his face, in his eyes was pure joy. Mallory bolted to her dad, laying her head on his chest and for the first time since this case began I saw her cry.

Charlotte put her arm around me. I laid my head on her shoulder for a moment and brushed away a few tears of my own.

Mike spoke to each of his children in turn, putting a hand on their faces, studying each one of them as though he were looking for what was the same and what was different. Finally he turned his attention to Charlotte. "Charlotte Elliot, it's so good to see you," he said.

"It's very good to see you, too," she said. Her eyes were suspiciously bright.

He looked at me then. "You must be Sarah Grayson."

I nodded. "I am, and I'm very happy to meet you at last."

Mike swallowed hard and momentarily seemed to be at a loss for words. "Thank you just seems way too inadequate," he finally said.

"It seems just right to me," Charlotte said.

Mike extended his left hand. Austin was gripping the right one like he was never going to let go. Charlotte caught it and gave it a squeeze.

"Thank you," he said.

Then he offered his hand to me. Like Charlotte, I took it and gave it a squeeze.

"Thank you," he said again.

"You are so, so welcome," I told him. I don't think I'd ever meant the words more.

Gram picked up Charlotte at the end of the day. They were taking dinner to Liz. Avery left with Rose and Mr. P. to meet Greg for the second night of the film festival at the library.

Jess had a date. Michelle was at the station. And Liam was taking Nick out, because, as he'd put it, "Nick's love life is lamer than yours."

"Looks like it's just you and me, furball," I said to Elvis as I locked the back door. "What do you want on your pizza?"

He seemed to consider my question for a moment then meowed loudly. "Pepperoni and mushrooms it is then," I said.

I changed into sweats and ordered the pizza as soon as I got home. Liam was right, I decided, padding out to the living room in bare feet. My love life was lame. It was Saturday night and I was spending it with my cat. The furball in question had already settled himself on one of the stools at the counter.

My phone rang. I looked at the screen. It was Mac.

"Hi," he said.

I smiled. "Hi back at you."

Elvis turned his head to look at the door. A moment later I heard a knock.

"That was fast."

"Excuse me?" Mac said.

"It's just my pizza. Hang on a sec."

I set the phone on the counter. "Talk to Mac," I told the cat.

I opened the door. And Mac was standing there holding a pizza box. "Special delivery," he said with a grin.

For a moment I just stared at him. Then I threw my arms around him in a hug.

He was here.

He was *home*.

Love Elvis the cat?
Then meet Hercules and Owen!
Read on for an excerpt from the first book in
the Magical Cat series.

CURIOSITY THRILLED THE CAT

by Sofie Kelly. Available now!

The body was smack in the middle of my freshly scrubbed kitchen floor. Fred the Funky Chicken, minus his head.

"Owen!" I said, sharply.

Nothing.

"Owen, you little furball, I know you did this. Where are you?"

There was a muffled "meow" from the back door. I leaned around the cupboards. Owen was sprawled on his back in front of the screen door, a neon yellow feather sticking out of his mouth. He rolled over onto his side and looked at me with the same goofy expression I used to get from stoned students coming into the BU library.

I crouched down next to the gray-and-white tabby. "Owen, you killed Fred," I said. "That's the third chicken this week."

The cat sat up slowly and stretched. He padded over to me and put one paw on my knee. Tipping his head to one side he looked up at me with his golden eyes. I sat back against the end of the cupboard. Owen climbed onto my lap and put his two front paws on my chest. The feather was still sticking out of his mouth.

I held out my right hand. "Give me Fred's head," I said. The cat looked at me unblinkingly. "C'mon, Owen. Spit it out."

He turned his head sideways and dropped what was left of Fred the Funky Chicken's head into my hand. It was a soggy lump of cotton with that lone yellow feather stuck on the end.

"You have a problem, Owen," I told the cat. "You have a monkey on your back." I dropped what was left of the toy's head onto the floor and wiped my hand on my gray yoga pants. "Or maybe I should say you have a chicken on your back."

The cat nuzzled my chin, then laid his head against my T-shirt, closed his eyes and started to purr.

I stroked the top of his head. "That's what they all say," I told him. "You're addicted, you little furball, and Rebecca is your dealer."

Owen just kept on purring and ignored me. Hercules came around the corner then. "Your brother is a catnip junkie," I said to the little tuxedo cat.

Hercules climbed over my legs and sniffed the remains of Fred the Funky Chicken's head. Then he looked at Owen, rumbling like a diesel engine as I scratched the side of his head. I swear there was disdain on Hercules' furry face. Stick catnip in, on or near anything and Owen squirmed with joy. Hercules, on the other hand, was indifferent.

The stocky black-and-white cat climbed onto my lap, too. He put one white paw on my shoulder and swatted at my hair.

"Behind the ear?" I asked.

"Meow," the cat said.

I took that as a yes, and tucked the strands back behind my ear. I was used to long hair, but I'd cut mine several months ago. I was still adjusting to the change in style. At least I hadn't given in to the impulse to dye my dark brown hair blond.

"Maybe I'll ask Rebecca if she has any ideas for my hair," I said. "She's supposed to be back tonight." At the sound of Rebecca's name Owen lifted his head. He'd taken to Rebecca from the first moment he'd seen her, about two weeks after I'd brought the cats home.

Both Owen and Hercules had been feral kittens. I'd found them, or more truthfully they'd found me, about a month after I'd arrived in town. I had no idea how old they were. They were affectionate with me, but wouldn't allow anyone else to come near them, let alone touch them. That hadn't stopped Rebecca, my backyard neighbor, from trying. She'd been buying both cats little catnip toys for weeks now, but all she'd done was turn Owen into a chicken-decapitating catnip junkie. She was on vacation right now, but Owen had clearly managed to unearth a chicken from a secret stash somewhere.

I stroked the top of his head again. "Go back to sleep," I said. "You're going cold turkey . . . or maybe I should say cold chicken. I'm telling Rebecca no more catnip toys for you. You're getting lazy."

Owen put his head down again, while Hercules used his to butt my free hand. "You want some attention, too?" I asked. I scratched the spot, almost at the top of his head, where the white fur around his mouth and up the bridge of his nose gave way to black. His green eyes narrowed to slits and he began to purr, as well. The rumbling was kind of like being in the service bay of a Volkswagen dealership.

I glanced up at the clock. "Okay, you two. Let me up. It's almost time for me to go and I have to take care of the dearly departed before I do."

I'd sold my car when I'd moved to Minnesota from Boston, and because I could walk everywhere in Mayville Heights, I still hadn't bought a new one. Since I had no car, I'd spent my first few weeks in town wandering around exploring, which is how I'd stumbled on Wisteria Hill, the abandoned Henderson estate. Everett Henderson had hired me at the library.

Owen and Hercules had peered out at me from a tumble of raspberry canes and then followed me around while I explored the overgrown English country garden behind the house. I'd seen several other full-grown cats, but they'd all disappeared as soon as I got anywhere close to them. When I left, Owen and Hercules followed me down the rutted gravel driveway. Twice I'd picked them up and carried them back to the empty house, but that didn't deter them. I looked everywhere, but I couldn't find their mother. They were so small and so determined to come with me that in the end I'd brought them home.

There were whispers around town about Wisteria Hill and the feral cats. But that didn't mean there was anything unusual about my cats. Oh no, nothing unusual at all. It didn't matter that I'd heard rumors about strange lights and ghosts. No one had lived at the estate for quite a while, but Everett refused to sell it or do anything with the property. I'd heard that he'd grown up at Wisteria Hill. Maybe that was why he didn't want to change anything.

Speaking of not wanting change, Hercules was not eager to relinquish his prime spot on my lap. But after some gentle prodding, he shook himself and got off. Owen yawned a couple of times, stretched and took twice as long to move.

I got the broom and dustpan from the porch and swept up the remains of Fred the Funky Chicken. Owen and Hercules sat in front of the refrigerator and watched. Owen made a move toward the dustpan, like he was toying with the idea of grabbing the body and making a run for it.

I glared at him. "Don't even think about it."

He sat back down, making low, grumbling meows in his throat.

I flipped open the lid of the garbage can and held the pan over the top. "Fred was a good chicken," I said solemnly. "He was a funky chicken and we'll miss him."

"Meow," Owen yowled.

I flipped what was left of the catnip toy into the garbage. "Rest in peace, Fred," I said as the lid closed.

I put the broom away, brushed the cat hair off my shirt and washed my hands. I looked in the bathroom mirror. Hercules was right. My hair did look better tucked behind my ear.

My messenger bag with a towel and canvas shoes for tai chi class was in the front closet. I set it by the door and went back through the house to make sure the cats had fresh water.

"I'm leaving," I said. But both cats had disappeared and I didn't get any answer.

I stopped to grab my keys and pick up my bag. Locking the door behind me, I headed out, down Mountain Road.

The sun was yellow-orange, low on the sky over Lake Pepin. It was a warm Minnesota evening, without the sticky humidity of Boston in late July. I shifted my bag from one shoulder to the other. I wasn't going to think about Boston. Minnesota was home now—at least for the next eighteen months or so.

The street curved in toward the center of town as I headed down the hill, and the roof of the library building came into view below. It sat on the midpoint of a curve of shoreline, protected from the water by a rock wall. The brick building had a stained-glass window that dominated one end and a copper-roofed cupola, complete with its original wrought-iron weather vane.

The Mayville Heights Free Public Library was a Carnegie library, built in 1912 with money donated by the industrialist and philanthropist Andrew Carnegie. Now it was being restored and updated to celebrate its centenary. That was why I had been in town for the last several months. And why I'd be here for the next year and a half. I was supervising the restoration—which was almost finished—as well as updating the collections, computerizing the card catalogue and setting up free Internet access for the library patrons. I was slowly learning the reading history of everyone in town. It made me feel like I knew the people a little, as well.

ABOUT THE AUTHOR

Sofie Ryan is a writer and mixed-media artist who loves to repurpose things in her life and her art. She is the author of *Telling Tails*, *A Whisker of Trouble*, *Buy a Whisker* and *The Whole Cat and Caboodle* in the *New York Times* bestselling Second Chance Cat Mysteries. She also writes the *New York Times* bestselling Magical Cats Mysteries under the name Sofie Kelly.

CONNECT ONLINE

sofieryan.com

NEW YORK TIMES BESTSELLING AUTHOR

Sofie Ryan

"A surefire winner."

—*New York Times* bestselling author
Miranda James

For a complete list of titles,
please visit prh.com/sofieryan